# THE
# EMPEROR'S
# CONSPIRACY

*a novel*

# MICHELLE DIENER

## GALLERY BOOKS

NEW YORK   LONDON   TORONTO   SYDNEY   NEW DELHI

Gallery Books
A Division of Simon & Schuster, Inc.
1230 Avenue of the Americas
New York, NY 10020

This book is a work of fiction. Names, characters, places, and incidents either are products of the author's imagination or are used fictitiously. Any resemblance to actual events or locales or persons, living or dead, is entirely coincidental.

First Gallery Books trade paperback edition November 2012

GALLERY BOOKS and colophon are trademarks of Simon & Schuster, Inc.

For information about special discounts for bulk purchases, please contact Simon & Schuster Special Sales at 1-866-506-1949 or business@simonandschuster.com.

The Simon & Schuster Speakers Bureau can bring authors to your live event. For more information or to book an event, contact the Simon & Schuster Speakers Bureau at 1-866-248-3049 or visit our website at www.simonspeakers.com.

Library of Congress Cataloging-in-Publication Data

Diener, Michelle.
   The emperor's conspiracy / Michelle Diener. — 1st Gallery Books paperback ed.
    p. cm.
   1. Great Britain—History—Regency, 1799–1811—Fiction. 2. Courts and courtiers—Fiction. I. Title. PR9619.4.D54K44 2012          2011028892
823'.92—dc23

Designed by Jaime Putorti

Manufactured in the United States of America

10  9  8  7  6  5  4  3  2  1

ISBN 978-1-4516-8443-8
ISBN 978-1-4516-8444-5 (ebook)

# Also by Michelle Diener

*Keeper of the King's Secrets*

*In a Treacherous Court*

Praise for Michelle Diener and her "imaginative"* Tudor
novels, *In a Treacherous Court* and *Keeper of the King's Secrets*

"Richly detailed historical setting and intrigue-filled plot."

—*Chicago Tribune*

"Taut suspense. Diener enlivens history."

—*RT Book Reviews*

"A masterfully spun tale!"

—*Fresh Fiction*

"Compelling . . . fast-paced."

—*Publishers Weekly*

"The characters are going to hook you first, and the intrigue will
keep you turning the pages. Diener's writing style is beautiful, to the
point, vivid, and exciting. This author is one to watch."

—*Reader's Entertainment*

"Packed with unexpected twists and turns, solid prose, always-
fascinating court intrigue, and a unique story."

—*Diary of a Book Addict*

"Dramatically original with imaginative scenes of suspense and one
mystery after another."

—*Single Titles**

"One fast-paced historical fiction novel! It reads like a thriller."

—*Girls Just Reading*

"The characters in this book are wonderful and believable. . . . An
interesting, emotional, and dramatic story."

—*Romance Reviews Today*

"An action-adventure-mystery-historical that grabs the reader on
page one and doesn't let go."

—Kate Emerson, author of *The King's Damsel*

"An enormous talent! I was absolutely enthralled and thoroughly
enjoyed every last page of this story!"

—*Affaire de Coeur*

*To Mom, for everything*

# ACKNOWLEDGMENTS

My thanks as always to my editor, Micki Nuding, her assistant, Parisa Zolfaghari, as well as Lisa Litwack and her staff for the amazing cover and layout of the book. Jean Anne Rose and Jillian Vandal make sure my work gets as much exposure as possible, and thank you to Simon & Schuster's sales team for all they do to get my books into readers' hands. My amazing agent, Marlene Stringer, is always the best advocate for my work, and I thank her for always being so supportive.

Liz Kreger and Edie Ramer, my trusty critique partners, help me make my work the best it can be. Thanks to Celeste Truran and my sister Jo for their help in giving the manuscript another pair of eyes, and to Bridget Ryan for answering all the medical questions I had.

And to my husband and children, you are the best.

# THE
# EMPEROR'S
# CONSPIRACY

# 1

"What seems to be the matter, Mr. Ashcroft?" Catherine, Lady Howe, watched as Ashcroft reversed out of the fireplace, where he'd built a little pile of kindling. The thin man's knees scrabbled a little on the soot-covered dust sheets.

"My sweep's stuck in your chimney, is wot, mi'lady," he said angrily. "Blighter's got too big."

"That's surely your fault for sending him up, not his for growing," she said crisply, the first sparks of anger licking up inside her.

Ashcroft huffed. "Well, got to come out, and the only way's to light a fire under the little beggar."

Catherine's mouth fell open. "Light a fire under him?"

"'Mazing what the 'uman body can do, when there's a fire under it. They lose a bit o' skin, but they's out, and that's the main thing."

"Mr. Ashcroft." Catherine spoke slowly. "Under no circumstance *at all* will a fire be lit under a little boy in this house while I am drawing breath in my body."

"Well," Ashcroft said, affronted, "'ow's youse expect to get 'im out? Starving's hardly better. And my Charlie's no little boy, anyways."

Catherine breathed deeply. "Starving is out of the question, too. There must be a more humane solution."

"None I know." Ashcroft started packing up his things. "I got work to do, and the blighter's no good to me anymore anyway. So pre'aps you can think on it, mi'lady."

Catherine's mouth dropped open. "You'd abandon a child who's worked for you for what, a year?"

"Eight, actually. Charlie's been wi' me since about four years old."

"He's worked in chimneys since he was four years old?" Catherine tried to keep hold of her composure. What a naive fool she was. Of course he had. "And his life means nothing to you?"

"It's a 'ard world, mi'lady. No one gave a toss about me at that age; why should I give a toss about anyone else?"

"Why indeed?" Catherine looked him straight in the eye.

Undaunted, he gave her a cheery wink. He walked to the fireplace and called up, "Mind 'ow you go, Charlie. Good luck."

A muffled cry came from within, panic-stricken.

"Good day to you, then, mi'lady." Ashcroft touched his cap and was off, leaving Catherine standing in the drawing room amid the dust sheets.

The muffled calling continued, and she pulled herself together. She rang the bell for Greenfelt, then leaned into the fireplace.

"Charlie, I'm Lady Howe. I wouldn't let Mr. Ashcroft light a fire under you, so he's left. But I'm going to get you out of there as soon as possible, I promise you."

The little voice fell silent.

"My lady?" The butler appeared at the door. "Is there something—"

"Greenfelt, call on Dr. Pennington without delay. Have the carriage brought round and bring him here yourself." At Greenfelt's blank look, Catherine stamped her foot. "Well, hurry! There isn't a moment to lose."

"My lady?"

"There's a small boy stuck in our chimney and he's scared witless, so stop dithering and go. We need Dr. Pennington's advice on how to get him out."

She was aware that she sounded . . . not herself. Wild, almost, much as a mother would, it suddenly occurred to her, if one of her children were in danger.

"Greenfelt." Her voice was sharp. "Close your mouth and get Dr. Pennington right away."

Greenfelt fled, and Catherine went back to the fireplace.

"How about I tell you a story until the doctor gets here, Charlie?" Catherine sat down, leaned against the hard, cold stone of the fireplace, and put her arms around her knees.

"Once upon a time . . ."

# 2

## 1811 . . . TWELVE YEARS LATER

Charlotte Raven recognized Lord Frethers the moment she laid eyes on him. It was very long ago, but she never forgot a face. Especially not the face of a person trying to do her harm.

She'd been introduced to him by Lady Holliday, and she'd wanted to gag when he took her hand. For the first time, she was grateful for the gloves she always wore, so that she wouldn't have to feel his skin on hers.

She'd smiled sweetly at him. *Now I know your name and your face, you bastard.*

She liked to think herself beyond fearing the past, but the sight of his face so close, his breath, smelling of cigars and liquor, took her back to the day when he'd beaten the living daylights out of her for not being a boy.

Since her first season three years ago, he was the third man she'd been introduced to whom she remembered in a dark light, and he was by far the worst. She'd toyed with the idea of revenge since she'd seen the first one, and seeing the sly gleam in Frethers's eyes it suddenly occurred to her, like an unexpected stinging slap across the cheek, that she had been remiss in letting things go.

How many victims had Frethers had in his grasp since she had escaped him? She felt sick to her stomach at her delay.

Her gaze returned to Frethers, now on the far side of the room. He was talking to Lady Holliday, their hostess, and a few other guests. All thrown together for diversion from the heat of London and the ennui of having too much.

She enjoyed watching the power plays and the flirtations, the deals struck and the liaisons begun or ended. But something darker was behind Frethers's eyes as he laughed with a man as rotund and bald as himself. Something that sent a spike of fear and rage down her spine.

He was up to something.

She started making her way across to the group and arrived just as Frethers turned to speak to Lady Holliday.

"Your husband says your boys are welcome to come back with me to Worthington," he said, his face pink with excitement. "Boys love a working farm, don't they?"

Charlotte saw Lady Holliday frown. "When did my husband say that?"

"Oh, just a moment ago, my dear lady. You don't mind, do you? Just a short little visit—be nice to have some young things about the place for a bit."

Caught in the trap of politeness, Lady Holliday demurred. "Well, no, it's just I had planned to take them—"

"Nonsense. Got to cut those apron strings some time, eh? Do them good, a bit of bracing country air."

Charlotte bit the inside of her cheek. So that was his game.

There was plenty of bracing country air right here, and Frethers sounded a little too jolly. She knew what he wanted with the Holliday boys. If she didn't stop him, she'd be an accomplice to the crime.

Charlotte laid a hand on her hostess's arm, the touch of her satin-gloved fingers on the fine silk sleeve of her hostess's dress the first step to possible ruin. She straightened her spine and tapped a little more firmly. "Lady Holliday, might I impose upon you for a moment?"

"Certainly, Miss Raven." Her hostess turned toward her.

Charlotte drew her away from Frethers and, tucking her arm through the other woman's, murmured in her ear.

"Could we go to my chamber? No one will interrupt us there."

"Can we not talk here, Miss Raven? I have so many guests . . ."

"Please, my lady. I think you will very much want to hear what I have to say, and want to keep it as private as possible."

Charlotte wondered what secrets Lady Holliday had that she blanched at her words and then gave a short, tight nod, allowing herself to be led upstairs to Charlotte's bedroom.

"I'm sorry to be so melodramatic." Charlotte walked to the window, leaving her hostess standing by the closed door of her small guest chamber. "Not many people know what I'm about to tell you, and believe me, I do not tell it lightly. However, I saw a look on Frethers's face when he spoke of having your sons to visit, and that look persuaded me I must share the full story, so that you are never tempted to leave them alone with him. Ever."

Lady Holliday gasped. "This is about Frethers? I thought—" She stopped abruptly and sat down on the armchair in a corner of the room. "You know something . . . bad about Lord Frethers?"

Charlotte nodded. "When I was four years old, my mother, who was a rookery whore, died."

Charlotte made sure she was looking at Lady Holliday as she said it, and she saw the surprise on her hostess's face. But the lady didn't bluster, and she didn't leave, so perhaps Charlotte's instincts were right. They often were.

"She was very ill, my mother, and I can only imagine what she died of. The thing was, she was barely cold in her bed when the other women in our tenement began talking about how much they could sell me for. There was apparently a demand for very small girls at brothels. For men with . . . peculiar tastes."

"Oh." Lady Holliday could not help her exclamation, sitting rigid in her chair, her back ramrod stiff.

"I wasn't too keen on being sold, as you can imagine." Charlotte realized she was gripping her hands, and forced them to relax. "I stole some boys' clothes off a washing line, dirtied my face, and found work as a chimney sweep's boy.

Charlie, I called myself." She smiled. Shrugged. "Not that I kept my gender a secret. My employer didn't mind, so long as his clients didn't know. Some didn't care, but others objected to girls working in their chimneys. I didn't grow as fast as the boys, which he liked, and while he called me a lad, and dressed and treated me like the others, he knew I was a girl."

"You were a sweep?" Lady Holliday's voice was incredulous, and Charlotte looked down at her sky blue silk dress, touched the pile of dark curls on her head, and nodded. "Hardly seems possible, doesn't it?"

She sat on the edge of her bed.

"When I was twelve, or thereabouts, I got stuck in a chimney at the home of Lady Howe. My master wanted to light a fire under me, to force me out, and Lady Howe wouldn't hear of it. So my master packed up and left me to her. I've been warm, safe, and cared for ever since."

"An amazing story, Miss Raven." Lady Holliday leaned back in her chair. There was no sign of scorn or disbelief on her face. "But what has this to do with Lord Frethers?"

"I needed to tell you my background, so you would believe the story I'm about to tell you of Frethers." Charlotte got up and began to pace, running her fingers along the pale yellow wallpaper.

"Once, when I was up a chimney, I popped out into a fireplace on the second floor of a mansion. The room I'd arrived in was Lord Frethers's bedroom, and he was sitting in an armchair . . . pleasuring himself."

Charlotte looked sidelong at Lady Holliday, hoping she

wasn't the kind of woman who affected horror at blunt talking, but she did nothing but incline her head for Charlotte to
continue.

"When he caught sight of me, he leaped to his feet, hands
still on his . . . er . . . nethers, and said something about my
being a gift from above."

Lady Holliday made a strangled sound.

"I know," Charlotte agreed. She sat on the bed.

"Anyway, I tried to back into the fireplace, and get into
the chimney, but it was a tight fit and he was able to get hold
of my foot and haul me out. He grabbed the top of my shorts
and jerked them down." Charlotte thought back to that
moment again, and managed to laugh. "It was the one and
only time being a girl was ever to my advantage. The look on
the old lecher's face when he saw I wasn't a boy."

She sobered up at Lady Holliday's expression. Decided
not to tell her about the beating she got from Frethers afterward.

"Don't let your boys within ten foot of the old goat, Lady
Holliday. Don't even let them in his sight."

---

"Geoffrey." Emma Holliday claimed her husband with a
sweet smile from the men he stood with, but she dug
her fingernails into his arm like claws as she dragged him off
into her private drawing room.

"What's the matter?" He shook off her hold, rubbing where
she'd gripped him. His quick frown and wary eyes told her

more than words how far things had slipped without her realizing.

"Lord Frethers says you told him he could take the boys with him after the weekend."

The uncomfortable way his eyes cut away from hers started a chill deep in her core.

"My God." There was a faint roaring in her ears, and she held out a hand to steady herself on her portmanteau. "You *know*."

"I have no idea what you're wittering on about, Em. Know what?"

He must be very sure she couldn't know, or he was a far better liar than she realized. She had a terrible feeling it was the latter.

"Know that Frethers is a predatory lech who molests little boys like James, Ned, and Harry whenever he can."

"Where did you hear that?" he asked, aghast.

"One of our house guests overheard Frethers telling me you'd said he could have the boys for a few days, and told me all about it."

"What, rumor and speculation?" Geoffrey scoffed.

"Oh no." Emma shook her head, her heart still trying to come to grips with the evidence before her. "This guest had a run-in with Frethers at the age of twelve. I was listening to a firsthand account, and I know every word was true."

"Who is the fellow? I'll tell you if he's sound or not."

"I don't need you to tell me who I can and can't trust," she said sharply. She drew in a shuddering breath. "Your own children, Geoffrey? We can't survive this."

"What do you mean?" His face was working, trying to find outraged innocence, and failing.

"What deal did you make with the devil?" Anger kept her upright and together. Her boys needed her and she would not fail them. "When I told you to put an end to that other business, I had no idea you'd go off and find some even worse way out of the debts you've managed to accumulate."

Again, he wouldn't look her in the eye.

"Oh heaven help us," she almost moaned. "You didn't end the other business, did you? You've gone ahead with it, *and* you've made a deal with Frethers."

"We're on our skids, dear girl," Geoffrey said sadly. "About to reach the end of the purse strings."

"What have you done? Why are we having this weekend if we have no money?"

"Already planned it, hadn't we? I'd hoped the investment I made a few months ago would pay off. I backed a merchant ship to the East, and the bloody ship went down off the Cape of Storms. I'd put everything into that ship, Em. Everything."

Emma drew herself even higher. "So what was Frethers going to do?"

"Clear our debts, loan me a little for a new investment. I didn't think he'd touch them, maybe just look at them in an improper way, but not touch them."

"You're so used to lying, you're lying to yourself." Emma moved past him, to the door.

"What are you going to do?" His voice was plaintive, almost childlike. It shocked her.

"Leave with my sons. Don't try to come near us, Geoffrey. Selling your own children to a child molester is not something I can forgive." She stared him up and down. "I've loved you for the last eight years. Through the gambling, and the poor investments. The way you ran through my dowry chasing this rainbow or that. But the moment you refused to look me in the eye when I mentioned Frethers, that love died. You killed it."

She spun on her heel and wondered where on earth she was going to go.

# 3

"I apologize for disturbing you, but I wanted to say goodbye and thank you for your hospitality, my lady." Charlotte stood in the withdrawing room, uncomfortably aware she'd called her hostess from her bedchamber, and that this was not a good time. Nevertheless, good manners demanded it.

"You're leaving?" Lady Holliday asked faintly, a very different woman from the vivacious beauty Charlotte had drawn aside only a few hours ago.

"I'm sorry. I find I cannot face a weekend in the company of Lord Frethers, pretending to be polite."

"Perhaps . . ." Lady Holliday's voice was uncertain, desperate. "Would it be a huge imposition to ask you to take me and my children with you to London, Miss Raven?" Lady Holliday twisted her hands. "I need to travel there as a matter of urgency. We'll be ready to go within the hour."

Charlotte stood very still. Her eyes widened, and she saw

the flush on Lady Holliday's face as the astute woman watched her come to the inevitable conclusion.

"Of course." Charlotte forced her voice to be even and strong. "You will be most welcome. I can take you wherever you like."

"Thank you. If you could take me to my brother's house in town, I will be in your debt." She paused for a moment. "That is, even more in your debt than I already am."

"It is the easiest of favors." Charlotte gave her a smile.

"My lady."

Charlotte looked up and saw the Hollidays' butler standing uncomfortably in the doorway.

"Yes, Irving?"

"I need a word, my lady."

Emma Holliday gave him a nod. "Well, I must complete my packing. Please excuse me. I won't keep you waiting long."

Charlotte inclined her head and walked out of the room. As she passed him, she saw the butler's relief that he could speak with his mistress alone.

Emma Holliday's abrupt departure from her own home would set tongues wagging and stir up all manner of speculation. She would know this, but she still chose to leave. Charlotte could only imagine she felt she had no choice.

This was most definitely not a happy home.

---

"We're going to stay with my uncle." Harry, the youngest of the three Holliday boys, had the dark hair and wide hazel eyes of his mother.

All three boys did. Only the eldest, James, had the look of his father in his face, but still he had his mother's hair and eyes.

"So I hear, Master Harold. Aren't you lucky?" Charlotte leaned forward to bring her face closer to his and rested her elbows on her knees.

"We don't know if we're lucky or not," Ned, the middle boy, muttered.

"You don't? Why not?"

From the corner of her eye, Charlotte saw Lady Holliday's face take on a rigor of horror at what her child might be about to say, but it was too late to stop him.

"Well, the only one of us who's ever seen him is James, and only when he was a baby. He doesn't remember him, or anything. Uncle Edward doesn't like my daddy, so we never visit him, and he won't visit us."

Lady Holliday put her hands over her face.

"Oh." Charlotte waited for her to compose herself. "My lady, should you require it, my and Lady Howe's home is always open to you. I know I can speak for my guardian when I say we would both be delighted to have your company, should you ever choose to take pity on two quiet spinsters."

The laugh Lady Holliday choked out was too high. "I know who is taking pity on whom in this situation, Miss Raven, and it's not me on you."

"Let's leave pity out of it, then," Charlotte said. "Let's rather call it a mutual delight. For I do not have many people I can talk with who know the true story of how I came to be

Lady Howe's ward, and I would very much enjoy the pleasure of your company and conversation. Whether you would like to take me up on my invitation to stay or not."

"Let's rather stay with Miss Raven, Mama," James said earnestly, his seven-year-old face serious and tight with worry. "If Uncle Edward doesn't like Daddy, I don't like him."

"Hush, angel." Lady Holliday reached across the carriage and rested her hands on his knees. "Uncle Edward loves you, and he loves me, and we will deal splendidly together. Daddy and Uncle Edward are grown men, and they can handle their differences without us having to worry about it."

"Are you sure he loves us?" Ned asked, a frown on his face. "And why do we have to stay with him, anyway?"

Charlotte could see Lady Holliday had reached the end of her rope on what must be the worst day of her life.

"Who could resist three lovely children like yourselves?" she asked them with a grin. She fished inside her reticule. "Now here in this little paper bag I have some peppermints. Who would like one?"

---

Lord Durnham's town house was in Mayfair, not far from Charlotte's own home, and as the coach pulled up to his door, Charlotte turned to Emma Holliday and pressed her card into her hand.

"I am most sincere, my lady, in my invitation, and I truly live less than five minutes from here. Should you wish to take up my offer, you need give me no warning. Come whenever you like."

Lady Holliday gave a quick nod. "Could I impose again . . . that is . . . would you mind if I meet with my brother alone for a few minutes, keep the boys in the carriage with you while I explain . . ."

Charlotte nodded. Lord Durnham was obviously no fool if he despised Lord Holliday, and no doubt the situation was awkward between him and his sister because of it, but surely he would not deny her refuge in her hour of need?

"One last peppermint before you meet Uncle Edward?" she offered the three worried faces before her as Lady Holliday was helped from the carriage. "And perhaps a story?"

---

E mma's shoulders relaxed slightly as she heard her boys debating which story Charlotte Raven should tell them. While her world may be crumbling around her, it would have been much worse without Miss Raven's generosity.

Night was falling in London, and the sky was burnished orange to the west. The lamplighters were out, lighting the streets, calling to each other in the balmy summer evening air.

She fought a deep inclination to run and instead pulled the bell, realizing Edward would most probably be getting ready to dine. There was no right time to break the kind of news she had, nor to throw herself on the mercy of a brother she had once shouted at to mind his own business.

She felt travel weary, bone tired, and heartsore. But for her boys she would get down on her knees and beg, if that's what Edward wanted.

"Good evening." The door was opened by a butler Emma did not recognize.

"Good evening. Please inform Lord Durnham that his sister, Lady Holliday, is here to see him on an urgent matter."

The butler stepped back quickly and motioned her in, his eyes going to the waiting coach. Like a discreet butler should, he asked no questions.

"This way, my lady. If you could wait in the withdrawing room, I will inform his lordship of your presence."

Emma nodded her thanks and stood just inside the beautifully proportioned room she remembered well from her childhood. It had been redecorated in fresh blue and white, and she wondered how often her brother used it. She would wager never, but she didn't gamble. Her husband did enough for the both of them.

"Em?"

She turned at the sound of his voice, and for a moment they stared at each other. He looked just the same, a few more lines around his eyes, perhaps. His hair was still wet from his bath, and he smelled of soap and home.

"Oh, Edward." She flung herself at him and he caught her in surprise, pulling her back from his chest, his eyes searching her face.

"What is it, Em, what's happened?"

But for the first time that day, Emma could not find the

strength within to calmly hold things together. She wrapped her arms tighter around her brother and sobbed.

---

"Why is Mama taking so long?" Harry asked, a decided whine to his voice.

"I'm not sure," Charlotte answered. She had just finished telling a third story, and she wondered what on earth could be keeping Emma Holliday. Was her brother such a cad that she was having to beg and plead with him to let them stay?

"I need to find a chamber pot, Miss Raven," Ned said, tugging at Charlotte's skirts.

"Well, let's go in search of one, shall we?" Charlotte knocked on the roof and Gary opened up for her.

"All right, miss?"

"I think we'll see what's taking so long."

She accepted his hand of help, and he gave her a wink as she jumped lightly down. She grinned back.

The boys crowded around her as she rang the bell, and she could feel their little hands anchored firmly on her skirts.

The butler who opened up took one look at the boys, and her fine traveling cloak, and motioned her inside.

While she stood waiting for Emma Holliday to be called, Charlotte took in a staircase that swept, elegant and glossy as a woman's coiffure, to the right. A beautiful crystal chandelier hung above it, throwing a warm light and tiny rainbows onto walls covered with seascapes.

The scent in the air was spicy—clean and sharp—as if

Emma's brother had come straight from his bath to talk to her. Charlotte breathed it in, her eyes on the passageway down which the butler had disappeared.

There was the sound of a door opening, and Emma Holliday hurried forward, her face strained and her eyes red from crying.

The boys crowded closer to Charlotte in alarm, held her skirts tighter. They had perhaps never seen their mother cry before.

"Did Uncle Edward make you cry?" James asked, his voice clear and loud in the hush of the hallway.

Emma Holliday's eyes flew up to Charlotte's in dismay. "No. No, it was me just so happy to see him after so long. They were happy tears." She smiled at her sons, an effort of will that made her lips tremble. Even a young child could see there was no happiness involved.

"Is this the boys' governess?" A deep voice spoke from behind Emma, and Charlotte started, amazed she had not heard him approach, or seen him before now. Lord Durnham would surely be difficult to miss. He loomed in the passageway, seeming to block it entirely.

Emma shook her head. "No, no. This is Miss Raven. She kindly gave the boys and me a lift here in her carriage. She has put herself to much trouble on our behalf." Emma stepped closer to her sons, and the boys went to her, Harry grabbing on, while Ned and James stood close by, furtively watching the uncle they had never met.

Charlotte raised her own eyes and met Lord Durnham's

gaze. His brows were straight and dark, his eyes the same warm hazel as his sister's and her children. The rest of his face was in shadow.

She had not been introduced. She knew his title and that his name was Edward, but she could not call him that. He stared at her, hostile and suspicious, and she could not help it. She gave him a cheeky grin, straight from the streets. "Good evening, Lord Durnham. It is a pleasure to meet you."

He blinked.

Dismissing him, enjoying that he was acting badly and would always now have the disadvantage with her, Charlotte turned to Emma. "Do you need to avail yourself of my invitation, or shall we have your trunks unloaded?"

"Of course, you will want to be off home. I know I have delayed you, and I am sorry for it." Emma's expression was stricken, her eyes overlarge on her face.

"It was no imposition, Lady Holliday, but I would like to be home if you no longer need me."

Her brother said nothing, glowering in his shadows like the prince-turned-beast of a fairy tale. The boys were too scared to look at him directly.

"I . . ." Emma Holliday looked from her brother's forbidding form to Charlotte, and Charlotte knew, standing in the light of the hallway in her soft blue cloak, she looked the more attractive option.

"Let us go with Miss Raven, Mother." James spoke with a tremble in his voice. "She says we would be most welcome."

"Am I to understand you are considering where to stay?"

Emma's brother stepped, at last, into the full light of his hall-way. His voice was incredulous.

It was Charlotte's turn to blink, but she was pleased to see his focus was entirely on his sister and missed her reaction. He had what would probably be called classical features. Straight nose, beautiful mouth, high cheekbones and forehead. And he was athletic. She felt the skin on her neck and chest heat.

Very athletic.

In the rookeries they'd call him *all the way there*. She'd never appreciated a slang phrase as much as she did at that moment.

Why she'd pictured him as gouty and corpulent she could no longer remember.

"I was unsure of my, our wel—" Emma cut herself off, her gaze going to her boys.

"For pity's sake." He cast a hard glare at Charlotte. "You will stay here."

His voice, sharp, commanding, seemed to snap something in his sister. She drew herself up, far more fierce and angry than Charlotte had seen her all day. "We will not." She took hold of Harry's hand. "We will be just around the corner from you, Edward. You can come and visit us, with Miss Raven's permission of course—" Emma looked at her for guidance, and Charlotte smiled sweetly, although her heart was thumping in her chest.

"But of course your brother would be most welcome, any time." She felt an urge to wet her lips, and pressed them to-gether instead. She always reacted like this in the face of an angry male. Ready to run. Only this time she was unsure of the direction she would head. Away . . . or toward?

"Then let us be off. It has been a long, tiring trip, and Lady Howe will no doubt be anxious about you."

Charlotte did not point out that Lady Howe did not expect her return for another two days. She merely murmured something indecipherable, and held out a hand for Ned to take.

"Em." Lord Durnham watched as his sister ushered her children out the door in front of her with disbelief. "I don't understand . . ."

He caught Charlotte's eye as she waited for Ned to go through first, and Charlotte stared straight back. "I'm sure you will, if you think about it enough," she murmured.

Then she closed Lord Durnham's front door in his face.

# 4

"I need a favor." Edward did not sit down, choosing to remain standing in the office. It was the only one occupied on the whole floor, the rest of the occupants long since gone home to dinner and bed, but he kept his voice low. Sound had a way of echoing in the empty building.

"I don't think you've ever asked me for a favor before. I'm intrigued." Dervish put the paper he had been reading aside and watched him with sharp eyes.

"You go to balls and such, don't you? Know a few people?"

"If you're asking if I'm halfway sociable, then yes. And you should attend a few yourself. It's amazing what you pick up at the things. Especially when it's possible our quarry is present at some of them."

Edward said nothing. The idea of prowling through the crowds eavesdropping had never appealed to him.

He preferred the direct approach.

"Would you like to tell me what this favor is?" Dervish leaned back in his chair.

"Have you heard of a Miss Raven?" Dervish was the only person he knew who he could ask this question of without being thought interested in the woman. Or rather, interested in a sense other than he was.

"Yes, I have. I know her, in fact."

"Oh?" Edward forced himself to relax.

"Charlotte Raven. Ward of Lady Howe. Quite a catch, actually, given Lady Howe has a sizable fortune and seems disinclined to remarry, and Charlotte Raven is her only family."

Edward thought about that. At least she was respectable, although he'd thought there was something about her—a cheekiness, a liveliness that reminded him of the streets. "Who are her parents?"

Dervish shook his head. "I don't know. I always assumed some distant relatives of Lady Howe. What is your interest in her, Durnham?"

Edward trusted Dervish, but he would not discuss his sister's problems until he learned more about them. "My sister is staying with her, and I wished to know about her without drawing attention to the fact."

"Your sister?" Dervish's gaze sharpened. "I thought she and her husband were having a house party this weekend."

"You know more than I do, then." Edward looked down at his hands, then up again. Throw caution to the winds. "My sister has run away from her husband, it seems. Not that I'm at all surprised. He's a bastard and my stepfather should never have accepted his suit."

"But why is she staying with Miss Raven and not you?"

Edward laughed. "Apparently I'll figure it out eventually."

Dervish gave him a strange look. "Told her you told her so, did you?"

Edward was about to give an indignant denial, and stopped, mouth half open like a fool. Was he really such a terrible old man? Good grief, he was only thirty years old.

"Spot on, I see." Dervish shook his head. "Any details you can share with me? On why she ran?"

Edward's reaction was to say no, but something made him stop. "She was crying when she told me, making no sense. Said Holliday had planned to sell their children to Lord Frethers." Edward was halfway into a confused shrug when he noted Dervish's face.

It had gone curiously blank, and it was white and slick, like he had a fever.

"You know what she meant, don't you?" He spoke slowly.

Dervish gave a shuddering sigh, and then forced himself to look disinterested. "I've heard Frethers likes little boys, yes."

"My God. You mean Frethers . . . ?" A deep, sinking horror pulled at him. He'd thought Holliday a cad, but this was beyond— He wiped a hand across his forehead. And there he'd been, wittering on to Em about how her wastrel husband had run through her money and tried to ask him for more.

That had to be the last thing she cared about.

He suddenly saw the scene with Miss Raven in a different

light. Her eyes had been knowing. Sharp. She understood the circumstances far better than he.

And there was a mystery on its own. What young society miss would have such information and be so cool and collected, so self-possessed?

"How old is Charlotte Raven," he asked.

"What?" Dervish frowned. "I don't know. Early twenties, I think. Not a schoolroom miss. She's had at least three seasons, and came late to her first season as it was."

But that still did not explain it. Even a young woman with a few seasons under her bonnet would not be so calm.

"I might hire someone to look into her." Edward realized he'd spoken aloud, and he caught Dervish's surprise.

"Why?"

"There is something off about her. Looking back on our meeting, she knew the true circumstances of Emma's troubles. It was in her eyes." She'd been pitying him, Edward realized. Pitying him, and dismissing him as not bright enough to have caught on. Despite himself, he let out a bark of laughter. He had a strong urge to show her just how bright he could be.

---

"Edward has sent a message to say he will be calling later today." Emma set the card Lady Howe's butler had handed her next to her breakfast plate and looked at her two hostesses.

Outside, through an open set of doors, the boys played with a ball on the fine lawns, their own breakfast long since eaten. The sound of their laughter and shouting soothed her. They were happy, for now, and safe. That had been all she had thought of when she'd left her home, and she had achieved it. Thanks to Charlotte Raven.

"I look forward to meeting Lord Durnham," Lady Howe said, her smile genuine in her strong, beautiful face. "He doesn't go about much in society, and I haven't ever been introduced."

Emma nodded, her chest clutched by the hard, sharp claws of guilt and sadness she always felt when conversation turned to her brother. "He hates Geoffrey so much, hates that I married him so strongly, that he does not go about in case he meets us. Which, of course, he most likely would."

"He had no say in your marriage?" Charlotte Raven lifted a cup of coffee to her lips, and Emma was struck by how lovely she was. She seemed more beautiful in this setting, as if she deliberately made herself less attractive when she went out. Emma suddenly wondered if it could be true.

"My stepfather accepted Geoffrey's suit. Edward was only twenty-two at the time. And I was under my majority. But it has always rankled with Edward. He and my stepfather disagreed over it so strongly. They openly hate one another now, and it's one more thing I destroyed in my determination to marry Geoffrey." She closed her eyes. "And of course, Edward was right. He was quite, quite right."

There was silence at the table for a moment, and when Emma opened her eyes, she saw both women looking at her with sympathy.

"What can I say?" She shrugged, trying to keep her voice steady. "I loved him. With all my heart."

"Then you were right to marry him." Lady Howe's words were soft. "Would you be better off if you had denied your love and married someone more suitable, and pined for him?"

Charlotte watched her as well. "And of course, there are the boys."

Emma glanced out the windows to catch a glimpse of James tossing the ball to Ned. "And look what nearly happened to them, because of their mother's poor choice in husbands."

"No." Charlotte leaned forward at the table, her eyes intense. "I learned long ago to refuse to take the blame for things I had nothing to do with. You gave your husband your love, and three beautiful boys, and if that was not enough for him, if he chose to despoil what he had, then the blame rests on him, not you. You took the action you needed to take to safeguard them, despite the risks to your reputation, and you have succeeded."

"The thing . . ." Emma cleared her throat. "The thing that worries me, though, is that I would not have even known the danger they were in, I would not have been able to run away, were it not for you, Miss Raven."

"Ah, but sometimes"—Charlotte Raven slid a tender look at Lady Howe—"sometimes, fate steps in and provides you with a guardian angel. I am happy to have been yours this time. Someday, no doubt, you will be someone else's." She stood, and Emma noticed for the first time she was in a riding habit. "I will be off now. I'm sure Kit is cursing my lateness."

After she left the room, Emma continued to stare after her, but a movement by Lady Howe finally ripped her gaze back to her hostess.

"She is magnetic, isn't she?" Lady Howe smiled the proud smile of a parent.

"She is the most interesting woman I have ever met."

Lady Howe nodded. "And if you were to say that to her, she would look at you as if you had lost your reason. But I warn you, she has never followed a conventional path. Since she came to live with me at the age of twelve, she has continued to keep her friends from the streets. She refused to allow her good fortune to ruin her ties with the people who had helped her and kept her safe as a child, and I could not forbid it, because without them, she would never have been alive to come to me."

"How does she manage that? Without a scandal?" Emma tried to think if she had ever heard any whispers about Charlotte Raven, but could not. Miss Raven kept to the corners at balls, never dancing, underplaying her looks. Trying to live safely in two worlds.

"For a start, a lot of her old friends work in my house, now, and at my country estate." Lady Howe stirred sugar into her tea. "You would have thought it would cause trouble. Her the lady, they the servants, but it hasn't. When she was younger, she felt it more keenly, but she never returned to the streets because she always knew she could be of more help to her friends as a lady than as a pauper."

"That is not entirely true," Emma said. "I saw the way she looks at you. She would not have wanted to leave you."

Lady Howe hesitated, then nodded. "You are right. But there were times . . . I thought I would lose her. One of her old sweeper friends in particular has made his fortune. Those of their comrades from the early days Charlotte has not employed, Luke Bracken has taken in. And ever since he was able, he's tried over and over to persuade her to leave me and go into his care."

"But she has not."

Lady Howe shook her head. "I've fought for her like a lioness fights for her cub. I've never met Luke Bracken, but we've battled a war against each other, he and I."

"And you were the winner." Emma leaned back and smiled.

"Who really wins a war?" Lady Howe shrugged. "I've kept Charlotte, but Luke Bracken continues to insinuate himself in her life. And I don't think I will ever be rid of him."

"And what is wrong with Luke Bracken?" Emma was beyond curious now.

Lady Howe gave a tired, tight smile. "Luke Bracken is a London crime boss."

Emma gaped.

"At least I don't fear for Charlotte's safety when she's out late at night." Lady Howe rubbed delicately at her temple. "No rogue in the whole of the West End would dare lay a finger on her."

# 5

"**D**o you take sugar in your tea, Lord Durnham?"

Catherine's gentle tone had the effect of forcing Lord Durnham to quit scowling at the very tasteful Turkish carpet and behave with some semblance of civility.

Charlotte, so used to the practiced, slick manners of the ton, which meant nothing and usually hid venom and ill will, was delighted by him. Of course, this was precisely the type of man she would never meet at balls. He would attend them only if forced.

Perhaps this was her sign to stop going about in polite society.

"Charlotte?" Catherine was looking at her, eyebrows raised, a cup of tea in her hands.

"Sorry." Charlotte smiled and took it. "Off elsewhere, I'm afraid."

"Did you enjoy your ride?" Lady Holliday asked her, trying to keep the conversation alive. Her brother certainly didn't feel compelled to do so.

"I did. We had a lovely run." She took a sip of tea, relishing the almost unbearably hot tang as she swallowed. "What about you, Lord Durnham? Do you ride?"

He looked at her, at last. A look that seemed vaguely threatening, as if he intended to find out everything about her, and use it against her. Charlotte raised an eyebrow and gave him a serene smile.

He hunted for a place to set his cup, the fine china ridiculously fragile in his hands, and gave a sharp nod. "I do."

"And you are involved in government?"

He started, and plunked the tea down too sharply on a small table. He turned that direct gaze on her again. "Why do you ask that?"

Charlotte shrugged, but she could see the fire in his eyes. She had touched something with her question, startled him. It intrigued her. "You do not go about in society, Lord Durnham, so I assumed you were involved in the government. In the war."

"Perhaps I'm just an unsocial hermit."

She laughed, and even to her own ears, it was breathless. Good grief! She'd better get a grip. She so seldom sparred with men who were not trying to flatter her, it was making her heady. She formed a rejoinder, then thought better of answering at all. She was not accomplished enough as a flirt, and she was usually too blunt.

He waited a moment or two for her reply, but when it was not forthcoming, he seemed to relax, as if he had dodged a bullet, and took up his teacup again.

Perhaps he was a spymaster. Or a diplomat. Charlotte could think of little else that would require such secrecy, unless she was mistaken in his reaction . . . She lifted her eyes to first Catherine and then Emma, and saw they were both regarding Lord Durnham with a good deal more interest than they had before.

"I must say, I never knew you worked for Whitehall," Lady Holliday said. "You are very sharp to have worked that out, Miss Raven. It's obviously a well-kept secret."

"I didn't say I worked for Whitehall." Edward frowned at his sister.

Charlotte could not help leaning forward. "Oh yes, Lord Durnham, you did."

"Stop baiting our guest, Charlotte. Lord Durnham obviously has no wish to talk about his duties for the Crown." Catherine lifted a plate of beautiful little cakes and held it out to him.

He gave Catherine a look of hunted frustration, and Charlotte could see him considering arguing with her that he had no duties to talk about. He looked down at the plate, let it go, and took two cakes.

---

Edward walked beside his sister while her three boys danced and ran ahead of them across the lawns. He was glad to be out of the house, and out from the knowing, laughing gaze of Charlotte Raven. The woman was confounding and annoying.

His work for the Crown was secret. No one knew what he did—the projects he undertook for the prime minister or the foreign secretary—but for a very small, select group. It was the only way he could be effective.

But Charlotte Raven had somehow guessed it, or found out.

"You should come home with me." He had thought to be firm about it, but surprised himself when he spoke softly.

Emma looked up at him. "I will. But not now. I'm enjoying the company I have, and they are far more sympathetic than you." She shaded her eyes with a hand to watch the boys.

"I'm sorry I was such a curmudgeon last night. It was not well done of me."

Emma shrugged. "You were right. But I did love him, and truly, for many years, he was a very good husband. Yes, he risked our money, but we were happy. It's only in the last three years that things have become bad. And I would never have thought he was capable of what he arranged with Frethers. Never."

"I didn't quite understand what you meant, when you told me that. I'm sorry. If I had, I would not have been half as stupid as I was."

Her mouth pulled into a reluctant smile. "I understand. I was hard-pressed to believe it, myself. If it weren't for Miss Raven—" She stopped, closing her mouth in a definite snap.

"What has Miss Raven to do with it?" He hadn't meant the intensity of his question to come through, but Emma stopped and turned to him, her head a little to one side.

"She was the one who warned me about Frethers. If she

hadn't, I'd never have confronted Geoffrey and discovered the truth."

"And how did she know? That's what puzzles me. How did a society miss like her know?"

His sister turned away, as if to watch his nephews at their game of catch, but he wasn't fooled. She did not want to discuss this with him. Eventually she spoke. "Miss Raven's secrets are her own. She revealed them at great personal risk to help me, and she has my steadfast loyalty for it."

How had he never heard of Charlotte Raven before, but now, all he wanted was to know as much about her as possible? He was fascinated. And disturbed.

"I'll warn you, Edward, as you once warned me." Emma had turned to watch him, her face serious and knowing. "Charlotte Raven is not a woman whose life you can poke at without consequence. I know she has at least one powerful friend you would not like to cross."

"What makes you think I'm the slightest bit interested in her?"

She laughed at him with genuine humor and walked away, shaking her head.

# 6

Charlotte saw, from the way Kit stood, that he wanted her attention. He was almost straining toward her, like a dog held back on a leash.

She sometimes wondered who held that leash. Her or Luke. Maybe it was both of them.

She crossed the yard and came over to him, but walked past, into the stables, leaning into her horse's stall and rubbing her flank. "You have a message?"

"Luke wants you to come to him later."

She turned her head. "When?"

Kit shrugged. "He just said later. Whenever you can, I 'spect."

She nodded, tried to make sure none of the disquiet she felt showed. "I don't have any engagements tonight. We can go after dinner."

Kit ducked his head and Charlotte thought she had probably hidden her unease better than he.

Luke was . . . not the same as he had been. Since she'd

ended his hopes of her returning, chosen to stay with Catherine, he'd become more and more difficult. More and more unpredictable. But even those early days, when he was still raw with disappointment, were nothing like now.

Whether it was the money, or the power, or the injury that afflicted him, it hurt to see him sucked slowly into a downward spiral.

She felt just like she had as a sweep, stuck in a chimney, with the slowly growing pain of a fire lit below her boots. Nowhere to go, trapped and helpless. Unless she went up, and then she'd lose skin.

Whichever the outcome, pain was assured.

But this was worse. She didn't want to scramble away to safety, leave him behind. He deserved so much more. And he wouldn't see—

"Who's the nob, then?"

She stepped back from the door of the stall and frowned. "Lord Durnham, you mean?"

"Pro'bly. The one with the good horses."

"Lady Holliday's brother. He's come to visit her."

Was it her imagination, or did Kit relax at that. "Ah, well. Just wondered."

"Kit, Luke hasn't asked you to report to him on who comes to call on me, has he?" She didn't need his answer; it was clear on his face as he ducked away, muttering about watering Durnham's horses.

Oh, why did Luke do this to himself? Why did he torture himself with it?

And why did she?

Charlotte rubbed a gloved hand across her eyes. She'd never encouraged a single suitor. Not once.

She'd told herself they didn't appeal. They were after Catherine's money. Her dowry. All manner of excuses. But she faced the truth suddenly, with a fierce relief.

She did not encourage them because when she looked into their eyes, she couldn't bear to think of them harmed or killed, even if they *were* just after her money.

And now that she was facing why she had shied away from the men of the ton like a marriage-shy rake, she also acknowledged to herself that Luke, the way he was now . . . Luke might just do it.

Might just kill them.

She dropped her hands to her side and skirted around Kit and Lord Durnham's tiger, watering the horses and talking good-naturedly about the quality of his lordship's horseflesh.

She'd thought to ask Luke to help her bring down Frethers, but had hesitated to do it. Now she understood her reluctance.

Frethers and his ilk required a fine hand, not a blunt instrument. And much though she lamented it, that is what Luke had become.

---

E dward wondered what he was doing.

He was standing in the narrow access lane that ran between the houses opposite Lady Howe's address, watching her house.

The lights were on downstairs, and Edward was not surprised they weren't out tonight. There was very little on in London at the moment.

The heat pressed down on him even now, and the sun had only just set half an hour before, even though it was after nine.

He had only meant to go for a short walk after dinner. But his feet had led him here, and he wondered whether he should go up to the door and knock, or do the sensible thing and head back home to his study and the troubles that lay on his desk, waiting for him to solve.

The pity of it was that those papers did not hold even close to the same interest for him at the moment as the woman behind that door.

The side entrance of Lady Howe's opened, the light from within the kitchen spilling out into a service alley just like the one he stood in, and two people stepped out.

Edward edged deeper into the shadows.

"I see you 'ave your sturdy stampers on," a man said softly, as they turned right, onto the pavement just in front of him.

"I'm not walking to Tothill Road in heels or slippers, that's for certain." The woman's tone was dry and amused.

Edward went still. He couldn't move for a moment, as if shock and surprise had encased him in amber. Then disbelief, and something else, something darker, snapped him out of it, and he strained to watch them as they passed under a streetlamp. He was hoping, hoping he was mistaken.

They came under the weak glow, and the woman stilled. Stopped and turned, as if sensing his fierce concentration.

"Someone walk over your grave?" The man with her was young, dressed like a footman or stablehand would when off duty. He was no one Edward recognized. He spoke familiarly, but not with disrespect.

"Yes." The woman shivered and took his arm. Let him move them along their way.

Edward was frozen to the spot, watching Charlotte Raven disappear into the night with one of her servants.

Then he looked around, to make certain there was no one else about, and began to follow.

# 7

Luke's headquarters in Tothill Road were in a gin house.
However, if any of his own men took too much of a liking to gin, they were gradually taken off duty. The loss of respect and power was not something many of them could contemplate, so Charlotte knew there to be a solid body of sober men keeping an eye on her when she came to this place.

But it was hard to keep that in mind sometimes, with the raucous shouting and shoving and shrieks.

She hated it.

It was poverty twisted into something even more desperate, more degrading, than it already was.

The front door opened, not, as one would expect, into a room, but onto a small landing with a staircase leading only downward, to the heaving, shouting mass of people below in what had once been a cellar, but was now a sort of open pit.

The smell of sweat, vomit, urine, and cheap alcohol rose off the crowd like steam.

As they stepped off the last stair into the seething mass, a woman slammed into her, and Kit swung her out of the way.

The woman was laughing, but desperately, as if this would be the only time she would laugh for a month, and she wanted to make sure she laughed long and loud.

She frightened Charlotte.

Someone tapped her on the shoulder and she saw Bill Jenkins. He said nothing, jerking his head to the back of the room.

Charlotte followed him, sensing Kit just behind her, and found the going easier. People moved out of the way for Bill Jenkins. Being built like a garden outhouse had its advantages.

Advantages Luke wasn't shy to use.

And there was Luke himself, sitting in his corner in an old armchair, surrounded by a few of the old lads, but mostly people she didn't know. There were more strangers hanging about him each time she came here. Another reminder that they were losing something. Losing the connection they once had.

He would say she was the one trying to sever it, but she knew it was not so. Not entirely.

When he saw her, a look passed across his face; pain, a need to hurt, and she went very still, wondering if they would play the same game they had last time. Humiliate Charlotte. It wasn't a game she cared to repeat, and she'd told Luke if he ever tried it again, her visits were over.

He seemed to remember that, at the last moment, or

maybe it was the look in her eye, because he pushed himself up and walked over to her.

His old injury hurt him this evening, she could see, and her whole body softened, her arms coming up before she was even aware, to embrace him.

"We're feeling lovey-dovey tonight, are we?" He spoke against her ear, his warm breath holding a hint of brandy—the fine stuff they drank over on her end of town.

"You know I will love you until the day I die." She shouldn't have to say this to him, but she suddenly felt the need to remind him that she truly never would be free of him. He was buried deep in her soul. It might be a different kind of love to the one he wanted, or thought he wanted, but it was stronger than that love, to her mind. The love of family. No matter what he did, no matter how it hurt her, she would always love him, even if she could no longer see him because of what he'd become.

He said nothing to that, but took her hand and led her past the curious eyes of his hangers-on and into the back room he used as his office.

He looked over her shoulder, and she turned her head slightly, saw Kit waiting to be told what to do. Luke gave a tiny shake of his head and closed the door, muting the roar to a manageable level.

They were alone in the beautiful room. It was polished, and gleaming, each piece as fine as any to be found in the best homes. A haven of absolute luxury. In one corner, a tight spiral staircase twirled upward, the only way to access the rooms on the floors above.

Charlotte sighed and sank into a plush French chair.

"You came home early from your weekend house party." He did not even try to hide that he knew this. Had made it his business to know.

"I saw someone from the old days. Someone I didn't want to see again." She stretched out her legs and tipped back her head, eyes closed, suddenly tired to her bones.

"Who?"

She shook her head. "I don't think you'd know him. You were already in the Hulks when I worked his place."

"What'd he do?"

Something in his voice warned her and she opened her eyes, saw his fists were clenched, and the tendons in his neck stood out in cords.

"Tried to rape me." She spoke calmly, her thoughts racing. Why was he so angry, so ready to explode? His fury seemed to come from nowhere.

"Want him dead?" He spoke as if offering her a cup of tea.

She hesitated. She wanted Frethers to pay. Wanted him to pay some compensation to those whose lives he'd ruined, if that was possible. "Maybe," she conceded. "Not right away, though."

"And before then?"

She shook her head. "I don't want you putting your nose in this, Luke. I'm going to take care of it. It's high time I did."

He looked at her, his eyes sharp and hard. The way they'd been since she'd nursed him back from death after his time in the Hulks. It ripped something deep inside her every time she looked into them.

"You might want to rethink playing games with your victim before going for the kill." His voice was as hard as his eyes.

She frowned. "What have you heard?"

"Someone's been asking questions about you. Straight after you came back. Trying to find out about you from the servants of those useless nobs you hang around with."

She sat up straight in the chair. "Well, we both know they don't know anything about me."

He conceded this with a wave of his hand. "The fact they was asking the wrong people don't mean it ain't concerning that someone is asking at all."

She nodded. "How do you know about it? You don't hang around with the servants of useless nobs."

"Got my sources. You know that."

Oh, yes she did. Some of those sources were to help him steal from those nobs; some were to make sure the nobs didn't lay a finger on her.

"Any clue who was doing the asking?" She couldn't believe Frethers had recognized her, but if he'd heard from Lady Holliday's husband that she was the one who'd given his wife and children a lift to London, that might account for it.

"Whoever it is, those that were fishin' said they didn't know. And I was most persuasive in the asking."

A quick, hot flash of fear ran through her at that, at the casual way he said it. The way his lips twisted.

"Luke, you didn't—"

"You think I'd tolerate a couple of noses going round my own patch, ferreting out information on you, Charlie? You really think that?"

Her heart stood still a moment, then came painfully back to life again so that she almost cried out. She shook her head, her hand curling into a fist just under her left breast. "No. You wouldn't tolerate that."

He said nothing, turning his back to her and running a finger along a shelf of burnished leather books. She had taught him to read after learning with Catherine, and it was the one secret pleasure he had that only she knew of.

He devoured those books at night, in private. The rest of the gang thought he only had them for show. To thumb his nose at the nobs and prove he could own a library of books as well as the next person.

"I'm setting someone to watch you, Charlie. For that type to not know who they were working for—well, it's rum. And if they did know, they'd 'ave said. It ain't worth it to keep quiet. But these prats . . . they wouldn't change their story. No matter what I had Billy do."

She was quiet, not able to speak at the thought of what Bill had done. At Luke's order. She watched his back—broad, muscled. It had carried her burdens, once, and she had eased the muscles in his shoulders, soothed him, and given him some comfort.

He tilted his head, looking up and snagging a volume high on the shelf. His face in profile was strong. Hard but so achingly familiar and beloved. "There is something dangerous here, and I'm keeping an eye, no matter what you say about it."

She stood. "You wouldn't have killed them a year ago."

He shook his head. "I would have killed them a year ago." He turned back to her with a shrug. "I just wouldn't have told you about it."

# 8

A gin house?
  Edward stared at the door Charlotte Raven disappeared into with her servant, and knew there was no way to follow without revealing himself.

These places were notorious for their cliques. Strangers were not tolerated.

He felt uneasy as it was, this deep into the Tothill Road rookery. Especially without a weapon.

He'd never ventured here, though he lived only a twenty-minute walk away. He'd never had the need.

If he were going to wait for her, he should wait closer to home, rather than the rancid alley he'd wedged himself into. She would pass him on the way back. But the thought of her, in there, amid the ruffians and thieves, made him almost nauseous. And his feet would not move.

What possible business could she have?

She was so far beyond what she seemed that if he had not

been standing in the stink and decay of Tothill Road, he wouldn't have believed it himself.

At last the door of the house was flung open and he heard the muted roar of the drinkers as Charlotte and her man stepped out into the night.

They turned and spoke with someone behind them, their voices too quiet to hear over the noise that swirled around them. A simple, rhythmic melody was fighting to be heard over shouting and boozy jocularity.

As they took the stairs down to the street, a man stepped into the doorway, dominating it with his size, and closed the door.

The noise was suddenly gone, and the night too dark to see, after the light from within was closed off.

The two said nothing to each other, turning back the way they had come, and walking at a brisk pace. The man whistled the same melody Edward had heard coming from the house, but Charlotte Raven made no sound, so deep in thought, she must truly trust the man beside her to keep an eye out for foot-pads and thieves.

They passed him, hidden in his narrow alley, without a second glance.

They did not seem to be lovers, which had been his first, hot thought. They did not touch as they walked, and Edward sensed no spark between them, other than a comfortable friendship.

He started after them, keeping well back and stepping carefully, so his boots made no noise on the cobbles.

And then, suddenly, he was no longer on the street. He was up against a wall in another narrow alleyway, with a man slashing a knife terribly, terribly close to his eye.

It felt like someone was using a blacksmith's vise on his shoulder, and Edward made a strangled cry of pain as he dipped his knees, twisting as he went down and kicking hard at the shin of the man clamping him.

He got loose of the iron grasp, but his kick bruised the out-side of his foot and he hopped out of reach, his hand massaging his shoulder.

His attacker lashed out and Edward was slammed up against the wall again, with a hand closed over his throat. The knife was just visible from the corner of his eye.

"Mind telling me why you're following the lady?"

Edward's eyes widened. "Miss Raven?" He croaked the words out, past the unyielding chokehold on his windpipe. This cutthroat wanted an account of his interest in Miss Raven, not his purse?

"Aye, so you know the lady then? And what is your business, following her about at night?"

Edward lifted his knee, fast, vicious, as if trying to hit the man in the balls, and as the man moved slightly away, clicking his tongue in sarcastic chastisement, Edward used the space he'd opened up to hit out with his fist, driving it straight into the footpad's stomach.

With a soft whoosh of air, he let go of Edward's throat, getting in a hard smack of his elbow just above Edward's eye.

Edward punched out, his fist connecting with the man's

jaw, and with a choking cry, the man went down, his knife clattering to the cobbles.

"What is *your* interest in Charlotte Raven?" Edward asked, crouching down beside him.

The man spat, just missing Edward's face, and rolled away into the pitch black of the alley.

Edward heard the pounding of feet and then nothing.

Nursing his hand, he picked up the knife and walked back out onto the street. Charlotte and her servant were gone, and he had nothing to show for his evening but a bruised left eye, grazed knuckles, and a lot more questions.

Who the hell was Charlotte Raven?

---

"I wasn't aware you were a pugilist, Lord Durnham." Charlotte regretted the words as soon as they were out of her mouth, wishing to scoop them up and throw them out of the drawing room window. They'd rushed from her, unbidden, at the sight of his beautiful face so bruised and swollen. And his hand. It looked half again its normal size.

Her eyes flicked to the door, willing Catherine and Emma to return at once from tending to Ned's scraped knee.

"What makes you say that?" The look he sent her was icy. Completely emotionless.

Charlotte relaxed. She felt a little skip of excitement in her chest. She had thought her remark would reveal her regard, but instead it had irritated him.

She smiled. A smile of pure delight.

Lord Durnham's eyes locked on her face. He blinked. Jerked his head back in shock at her reaction.

She tried desperately to compose herself. "I ask because you have obviously been involved in fisticuffs with someone, and you do not strike me as a man who would brawl over cards or dice, or even a woman, so the only conclusion left was that you had taken a turn in the boxing ring."

"I was set upon by a footpad." He spoke quietly, as if the information should mean something to her.

Which of course it did.

Her eyes went wide, and she lifted a hand to her mouth. "Where?" she whispered.

"Tothill Road." He leaned back in his chair and lifted the cup of tea Catherine had given him to his lips. Took a sip.

Clutching shaking hands together to still them, Charlotte closed her eyes for a moment. "What on earth were you doing in Tothill Road? That is an invitation to be set upon."

"One would think so. But judging by the calm way you stroll around there, it seems safe enough for you."

Charlotte raised her head in horror, forcing her eyes open, forcing her gaze on his face. "I am not just anyone."

"Oh, Miss Raven, never was a truer word spoken. And I would very much like to know who you are." There was no artifice in his voice, no give in his tone. He was deadly serious. Determined to have answers.

"Is the person who attacked you all right?"

It was the last thing he'd expected her to say, she could tell by the flare of his nostrils. "Better than me." He slipped a hand into his pocket, drew out a knife. "I have something of his."

Charlotte held out her hand and watched him as he continued to hold it, with no indication he would hand it over. "I'll see it is returned."

He laughed, really laughed, and slipped the knife back in his coat. "I don't think so, Miss Raven. Next time he might not be so careful with it around my eyes."

She closed her own eyes again. "What did he look like?" She massaged her temple.

"Medium height, black hair, well built."

"Sammy." She sighed. "You need to watch your back now, Lord Durnham." She lowered her hands. "I'd apologize, but you rather brought it on yourself, following me around at night."

He conceded the point, which surprised her, lifting a shoulder as if to acknowledge it. "You interest me, Miss Raven. And seeing you walk in country boots to a rookery turned that interest very keen indeed."

"There is nothing to it. You will be bored to learn the truth, I assure you. But the damage is done now. No one has followed me before. He'll think this is serious. Maybe he'll do something equally serious in return." Gripped by a sudden urgency, she rang on the bell.

Her maid, Betsy, came, flushed and pretty, to the door, and Charlotte did not even try to use doublespeak. It was no longer necessary in front of her guest. "Find Kit, tell him to go to Luke and tell him I have to see him tonight. And he's to tell Luke to do nothing until then. *Nothing*."

Betsy's eyes went to Lord Durnham, then back to her, wide with surprise.

"Hurry."

Betsy gave a nod and disappeared, and Charlotte looked after her, the sight of an empty doorway far more appealing than the questions on Lord Durnham's face.

"Who is Luke?" From the corner of her eye she saw him put down his cup, stretch his legs out as if he had all the time in the world.

She needed to let him know his time was running out.

"Luke Bracken is the man who sent that footpad last night." She lifted her head, made sure she had his full attention. "He is the man who is planning a way to kill you."

# 9

There was no mistaking that Charlotte Raven was serious.

"Kill me?" Edward raised an eyebrow. "That sounds overly dramatic."

"Were you asking questions of me a day or two ago? Or rather, did you pay others to?" She spoke, not with outrage, but some other more intense, more focused, emotion.

Edward frowned. So much for discreet inquiries. "I did."

"Your men are all dead." Seeming unable to keep still, she stood up and walked to the window. "So you might want to keep that slightly condescending tone from your voice, Lord Durnham. And start considering that I may be right."

His mouth fell open. He forced it closed again. "Dead? Don't be ridiculous."

"Have you heard from any of them?" The challenge in her voice was unmistakable. As was her conviction.

Edward did not doubt for a moment that she truly believed

they were dead. "No, I haven't. They are due to report to me tonight."

"Well, you'll be in for a long wait." Her voice trembled. "If you know of their families, I would appreciate it if you would give me their addresses. And then both you and I will be contributing a generous sum to their widows." She lifted her head, and glared at him as she spoke the last sentence, expecting him to protest.

"If a crime has been committed, and you know of it, why haven't you reported it?" He stood, too, suddenly, and she froze, almost shrinking away from him. It disturbed him.

"I know only that they are dead. I do not know where they died, or the hand that killed them." She did not look away as she spoke, and even though he knew she was lying, and she knew he knew, she did not so much as flinch.

"You would protect their killers?"

"I don't know what you are talking about." She turned away, looked out the window, her back stiff.

"If they are dead"—and he was suddenly beginning to believe they were—"they were agents of the Crown, and their deaths will be investigated."

"Agents of the Crown?" When she spun to face him, her face was white. "Why? Why did you do it? What could you possibly wish to know about me you could not just have asked?"

"Would you have answered?"

She bit her bottom lip. "No."

"But you told my sister."

She stiffened in surprise at that, her eyes going wide, and Edward shrugged. "She would not tell me, either. So do you blame me for trying to find out on my own?"

Charlotte crossed her arms over her breasts. "If those men weren't dead, if they could have made their meeting with you tonight, they would have told you nothing you could not easily have found out for yourself. What you probably already know. They were asking in all the wrong places, and if they had asked in the right ones, they'd still have ended up dead."

"How do you know this?" Edward had to force himself not to swear. "How could you possibly know where they asked their questions?"

"I have a little army around me, Lord Durnham." She smiled, but it was cold, and searingly alone. "No one comes near me or asks about me who isn't vetted, and checked, and either allowed to go on their way . . . or not."

Edward stared at her. "Who does this?"

"My old lover. The boy who sat watch over me while I slept as a child, who fought off anyone who tried to touch me, and who was sent to Old Bailey because he struck out at someone who did me harm. The person to whom I owe my life."

"Why are you not with him, then?" The question exploded from him, because he did not want some other man to have this claim on her. It was wrong that she appeared free, able to give her affections where she chose.

"He wants that very much. But I . . . I do not love him that way. I never did. To me, he has always been my family."

"But you called him your lover?" He knew this was the

most inappropriate conversation he had ever had, and yet, he had to have the answer.

She dipped her head. "I think I can be forgiven, Lord Durnham. I certainly have forgiven myself, if there is anything to forgive. I became Luke's lover because it was the only thing he wanted, and it seemed wrong to deny him when he had done so much. I was twelve years old."

---

She had shocked him, which made her anger at him even stronger. Did he live in such a cloistered little world, this ignoramus? She had thought him more real, more insightful, more grounded than the idiots who attended the balls and soirees of the ton.

If he spent just one hour in the rookeries, or half an hour talking to the boys imprisoned in the Bailey, or the Hulks, he would know boys took lovers, had girls who kept house in the small corner of a room they might have for themselves, girls who tried to keep their little place, pay the rent on it, while the boys were in prison.

When you had to earn your living like an adult, go to prison like one, too, then you behaved like one in all areas of your life. Even if you were only twelve or thirteen. That was how it worked. That was how reputation and pecking order were established.

"Would you please leave." She eventually turned from the window, away from the horses walking placidly by in the high summer heat, to face him.

He hadn't moved. Was still sprawled in his chair, his eyes closed, a frown etched deep in his forehead. But she'd seen the look on his face as she'd told him about Luke. There was shock there. And something else. Horror. Whether for her, or for Luke, or simply the situation, she didn't know.

Shouldn't care.

"Where are you from, that you are mixed up in this?" He didn't open his eyes.

"The rookeries, just like Luke. I'm no lady, Lord Durnham."

"You pretend to be."

"She does not pretend." Catherine stood in the doorway, and her eyes were hard when they looked at Durnham. He sat straight in his chair at the sound of her voice.

"My Charlotte is more lady than most of the overdressed, overstuffed women of the ton, Lord Durnham. And I will not have anyone in this house who says otherwise."

Durnham's lips thinned. "You are right. What I said is inexcusable. I should have more control over my temper and I apologize."

Catherine stared him down with cool, cool eyes. Walked past him and sat at her usual spot. "You sister is tending Ned in the nursery. Perhaps you'd like to go to her?"

He rose slowly. Reluctantly. He had been maneuvered out of the room, and did not like it one bit. He gave a half bow and left.

Charlotte let her shoulders slump, and heard Catherine rise behind her, felt the cool, soothing touch of her hands on her neck.

"Luke is going to kill him." She leaned forward and let her forehead rest against the sun-warmed glass of the window.

Catherine touched her cheek and leaned over her. Kissed the top of her head. "You will have to stop him. This is not the usual witless idiot. Lord Durnham strikes me as a man who is very dangerous. Maybe as dangerous as Luke. And he has powerful connections."

"The way Luke is now . . ." She shuddered. "I'm not sure that won't make him more eager. He seems to want to die."

"No." Catherine stepped back. "He thinks if he is rash enough, you will offer yourself up to stop him."

Charlotte flinched, and turned slowly. Was that what he was doing? He had certainly done it before, and she had been young enough to fall for it. To be manipulated. "I should leave," she said, and stood. "I should leave to go somewhere else. I would like to go to Italy, or France, but with the war, that's obviously impossible. Perhaps the Lake District, or Scotland?"

"You think that will stop him?" Catherine tapped a long, slender finger to her lip. "Would he leave Lord Durnham alone?"

Charlotte shook her head. "No. He would still kill him. If I could get a promise from him not to, though, maybe I should leave."

"You would trust his promise?"

Charlotte looked across to Catherine and nearly wept. "I would once have said yes. Now . . . I don't know." She wanted to run, or ride, there was so much boiling inside her. She hugged herself. "His injury is worse. He could barely walk to me last night without crying out. His lips were almost white with pain. I wonder how much of his rage is fueled by agony. Bitterness."

"You sure it isn't a play for sympathy?"

She shook her head. She knew why Catherine asked but she had seen Luke when he'd come back from the Hulks. She knew this was all too real. And one more thing that lay between them that he would not talk about.

There was a furtive knock at the door, and Charlotte turned. Saw Betsy standing, flushed and flustered, in the doorway. "Kit couldn't find Luke. He's not at Tothill Road. No one would say where he's gone."

"Did they refuse to say, or don't they know?" It would make a big difference, because there were some she could force to speak.

Betsy's eyes went wide. "Kit didn't say."

"Thank you." Charlotte watched her walk away, dread sinking deep, sharp claws into her chest; they curled inward, holding her close.

"What will you do?" Catherine sat still and afraid. Afraid for her.

"Keep Lord Durnham close to my side." She glanced out the door, the way he had gone. "Until we find Luke, until I can talk to him, it's the only way I can keep him alive."

# 10

"Where are you going, my lord?" Charlotte Raven stepped in his way, a slim green-and-white-clad obstacle to a quick escape. He could not get into his phaeton unless he moved her bodily.

His fingers twitched.

"Home." He took a step closer, to crowd her. "Not that it is any of your business."

She said nothing to his rudeness, simply stared at him for a moment and then turned her head to the stables. One of the stablehands was watching them from just within a stall.

Another, older man stepped out of a small room to one side, and he saw her shoulders relax a little. "Gary." She kept her eyes away from his. "Lord Durnham will be staying with us for a few days, to visit with his sister. Would you have his horses stabled and his carriage put away until they are needed?" At last she turned to look at him. "Or would you rather have Gary return them to your own stables, and we can take you home when your visit is over?"

He could not help that his mouth fell open. He closed it with a snap.

"Ah, your horses are most likely fussy." The smallest spark of humor lit her eyes and was gone. "Gary, rather arrange for his lordship's horses to go to their own stables."

"Right you are, my lady." The stablehand stepped up beside him and held out his hand for the reins although his eyes were on Charlotte. He exchanged a look with her that Edward could only describe as mischievous.

Charlotte grinned back, her face transformed for an instant from inhospitable desert to an English summer garden.

This was not the man who'd accompanied her to the gin house in Tothill Road, though. He knew the stable boy watching them from the stall was the one who'd gone with her. The wiry strength of him was unmistakable.

Edward handed the reins over with an easy movement.

Charlotte held out her arm. "Shall Gary take a note with him for your butler to send round some clothes, my lord? Seeing he'll be going anyway?"

"Before that, I'd like a word." Edward was not having an argument with her in her stable yard. Especially as it was clear the men listening were more than just servants.

"Of course." Her lips twitched as his hand closed over her arm, and he wondered if she had any idea how angry he was.

He led the way to the back garden.

"You can start snarling now," Charlotte whispered near his

ear, making him jerk away. "They can't see your face. Although I'm sure they're listening, so you'll have to keep your voice down."

He kept his gait smooth, but inside he stumbled. "Do you always live like this? Afraid of what they'll see?"

She put out a hand, let her gloved fingers brush over the thick velvet of pink rose petals that lined their path. It occurred to him that he had never seen her without gloves that came to above her elbows or long-sleeved gowns, no matter how hot the weather. "I forget, sometimes, how much of my life it controls." She pulled a handful of petals off an overblown rose and rubbed them between her fingers, releasing their scent. "Gary is loyal to me, but Kit—he's Luke's ears and eyes here. Some of the house servants, too."

"Even though you pay their salaries?" He looked behind him, before the path swung sharp right, toward the back of the house, and blocked the stable yard from view. Kit watched them, leaning on a broom.

Edward tightened his grip on her arm and swung her through an arch of climbing roses, into the cool shade of the hedge that surrounded the garden in a wall of green.

"Luke might give them extra." She shrugged. "Or it may be because I'm not really one of them anymore. Luke's probably got more money than me, but he's kept to the rookeries. He doesn't put on airs."

He looked at her and raised a brow, and she laughed softly.

"I can simper with the best of them, Lord Durnham. You wouldn't recognize me at one of the balls you never attend."

He shook his head. "I doubt that's true."

She lifted her hands as if in defeat. "Perhaps. I turn down as many invitations to dance as I accept. I can't help looking at the men who approach me and wondering if they would think my dowry is worth bringing themselves to Luke's attention."

"And does it?" He stopped completely. He had to force his hand not to shake.

She frowned, and he cleared his throat. "Does it bring them to his attention? And how so, if you don't tell him?"

She shivered in the deep shade of the hedge, and he led her out onto the lawn, into the sun again. "Oh, this end of London is Luke's patch. He's got servants on his payroll everywhere. How do you think he found out about your men asking questions?"

He was such a fool. He had not thought of criminals being so organized, but why not? "You make him sound like a lord of crime."

She raised her face to his, startled. "I thought you understood. That is what he is." She turned away and neither of them said anything for a moment. He could still smell the sweet perfume of the rose petals, crushed where her hand had become a fist, and looking down on her face, at the dark lashes against her cheek, some emotion rose up in his chest, so intense, so huge, he was stunned. He was still holding her arm and his hand trembled against the fabric of her sleeve. He let go of her and stepped back to put space between them.

He'd thought himself incapable of anything this strong.

"I will not hide behind your skirts, Miss Raven. And I will not let a thug rule my life as he seems to do yours." He spoke gently, and she lifted those dark blue eyes to his, then cut away to study the lush, green grass of the lawn.

"You really don't understand." She let the petals drop and gripped her hands together. "This is not about pride. This is about your life. In the last few months, things have been getting . . ." She paused and looked back toward the stables as if Kit could still see them. "Getting worse. I truly fear he is capable of murder."

"According to you, he's already murdered my men."

She lifted her shoulders. "Men asking questions in his patch, that's fair game, to him. Someone paying me too much mind? Until now, he's limited himself to filching them in the street."

She used the word *filch* instead of *rob* deliberately, he thought, broadened her accent on purpose. Trying to push him away, make him understand she was truly of another world. It was too little. And much too late.

He let it pass for now.

"You may owe this man something, that you let him rule you like a despot, but he doesn't rule me. And I am far from the youngbloods and dandies of the ballrooms." He took another step away.

"Are you?" Her words could have been a taunt but were not. She was serious. "Have you spent your life fighting hard just to stay alive? Been thrown in the equivalent of a pit with hardly any food and way too many people, most of them much bigger than you?" She straightened her spine and lifted her head. "Luke and his boys—I—have lived like that, Lord Durnham. I worked from dawn to dusk with barely a meal to sustain me and so little pay that there was literally no way for me to ever better my circumstances legally. I was a slave in all but name. Luke and the men in his gang, they have been thieving and yes, killing, since they were children. It was either that or die themselves, and where you might hesitate, or think something through, they will not. They will act, act hard, fast, and they will not think twice about your death. It will not weigh on their minds."

She was trying to protect him. Either scare him off or give him the best advice she could.

He thought of the hours he'd spent learning to fight, and the desperation he'd felt when he'd first begun, to never be helpless. But the edge was off him now. When he'd hired the footpad who'd once tried to accost him to teach him street fighting, he'd had the beatings his stepfather had given him in mind. But his stepfather was in his power these days, old and dependent on Edward's largesse.

He didn't have the same fire in his belly. And as Charlotte pointed out, these men faced life and death in every fight they threw themselves into. Had been tempered in a much hotter furnace than he'd ever faced.

He looked at her again and wondered if this feeling that thrummed inside him at just the thought of her was enough to give him an equal footing. "If your Luke thinks I will be easy pickings," he said at last, "he is very much mistaken."

# 11

With sinking dread Charlotte watched Lord Durnham ride away. Out on the street, an urchin leaped up from the gutter and threw a half brick at his horses' legs, narrowly missing the left one's fine fetlocks.

She moved fast, and with his attention still on the retreating phaeton, managed to grab the little bastard by the neck and arm. "Who are you?"

He gave her a disgusted look, taking in the fine-patterned green-and-white lawn of her dress, her expertly dressed hair, and tried to eel his way out of her grasp. But she knew all the tricks. Had used them countless times herself.

"I said, who are you?"

He looked like he was going to spit in her face, and she raised an eyebrow.

"No one." It was a feral snarl.

Her heart hurt, looking at him. What was Luke about? This wasn't how this child should be. He'd promised her.

Promised! Every child who worked for him would have a better life.

"Luke sending balmy brats to do his dirty work? I am disappointed." She kept her voice cool. Emotion would be just another weapon to use as far as this boy was concerned.

"Wha-?" He was still a child, beneath the grime and the hard-edged layer of fury. He couldn't help show his confusion.

"That horse ever do you harm?" She tightened her grip.

The lad shook his head, his eyes narrow.

"Funny, looked like you was trying to cripple it, 'n' all. Do it down and have it sent to the knackers." She gave her tongue full rein and felt a twinge of regret she couldn't speak like this more often. She forgot she could, sometimes. "Luke's policy's always been hurt those what needs hurtin' an' not a poor sod more."

She leaned back a little, took the measure of him. "An' if you were here as a nose, to watch the house, the jig's up cos o' that stunt."

He said nothing and turned his head away, looking down the street, to where Edward had already turned the corner, oblivious to the near miss of his prize horseflesh. "Sometimes I can't 'elp it." His words were calm. Way too mature and measured for his age. "I look up at a carriage like that, nags like those, and wouldn't the sale of all of tha' set me up for life, an' all? Just want to break it all, I do. Just smash it. Cos no matter what, I can't 'ave it, can I? Why should anyone else?"

"Look at me." She held him even tighter, until he winced, and she loosened her hold a little, waited for him to turn to her again. "If you're working for Luke, you should know there's a chance. And a better than average one, if you're with him."

He shook his head. "Don't know who you're talking about, Miss 'igh an' Mighty."

"Luke didn't send you?" She blinked, and loosened her hold just a fraction too much.

He was out of her grasp and running before she could so much as shout.

"Who did send you, then?" She called after him, and he stopped, far enough away he knew she wouldn't catch him, even if she tried. He cocked his head, rubbed finger and thumb together.

Charlotte dug into the reticule hanging from her wrist and withdrew a shilling. Far too much, but it was all she had. She threw it, and watched the way his eyes tracked it as it bounced and rolled toward him, veering left as it hit a cobblestone, and spinning until it stopped, halfway between them.

He darted forward, grabbed it up, and backed away.

She waited. He was either considering legging it, or he was teasing her that he would, but he eventually stopped at his old spot. "Rum ol' gaffer sent me. Gave me a farthing to watch for that carriage."

"And if you saw it? Where were you to go?"

He looked at her. Considering.

"That was all the money in my reticule," she said shortly.

"Tol' me ta go round back o' his club, report to 'is coachman." He danced a little farther back.

"What club? How would you know his coach? What is his

crest?" Charlotte tried to keep the desperation from her voice. He was going to run without talking. She forced herself to accept it.

"Same crest as the one I was 'sposed to watch for."

His words were nearly drowned out by the clatter of a carriage passing nearby, but she heard them. Frowned.

"Nothing like family spying on family, eh?" And with that he ran. He shouted one last thing, most likely the name of the club, but she didn't hear him over the traffic this time.

Charlotte stared after him, standing in the street, until Kit came out from the yard and shifted from side to side, unsure what to do.

"Does Luke pay you extra, Kit? For watching me?" She turned to him, and he flinched from her cool expression.

"No, I . . . no." He looked away.

"Well then stop doing it. I pay your wages; I took you and Betsy in, not him. Remember that when you run off with your stories. Or, if you can't stop tattling, at least squeeze a bit more ready out of him."

She turned on her heel and stalked back inside.

The world was crashing around her, and she *still* hadn't dealt with Frethers.

————

Emma knew something had happened between her brother and her hostesses even before Charlotte came into the room with a sharp rap to her step.

Catherine had been sitting by the window, looking out, and when Emma'd inquired about Edward and Charlotte, her hostess had struggled to keep a calm face. "Your brother has left. I saw him riding past in his phaeton not a minute ago." There was something cold in her voice.

"What has he done?" She heard the weariness in her voice, the same weariness she'd felt too long with Geoffrey. She tried to cover it up with a smile, but when Catherine turned her gaze toward her, she could see she had not been quick enough.

"I'm sorry. None of this is your doing." Catherine rose and came to sit next to her, taking her hand. "Your brother has learned Charlotte's secrets, and he was rude to her, in the shock of his discovery."

"Oh, what a blithering idiot he is." Despair rose up in her, threatened to make her weep. These were her friends. She had never had friends like them before. Geoffrey had made sure of it. She'd only known the superficial niceties of the ton. And now Edward had ruined it, damn him.

"Shhhh. Shhhh." Catherine pulled her close, and before she knew it, Emma's head was on her shoulder and she truly was weeping. "You are not your brother, and we will not give you the cut for his actions. Never."

They both heard Charlotte coming down the hall toward them, and Emma sat straight in her chair, brushing away her tears as she heard the fury in every tread.

"I think your husband is having the house watched," Charlotte said as she closed the door behind her, and her announcement was so unexpected, Emma simply stared at her, her heart thundering.

"I just caught a pickaninny—" Charlotte brought herself up short as she said the street word. She drew in a deep breath, pinched the bridge of her nose, and exhaled. "A boy—spying on us. He said a man paid him a farthing to watch the house and tell him if Lord Durnham came to call."

Emma watched, fascinated, as Charlotte brought herself under control, forced whatever emotions were surging in her beneath a calm, serene surface.

"This isn't your Luke's doing?" She felt stupid, the moment she spoke. Charlotte would not make the accusation it was Geoffrey lightly.

Charlotte read her face correctly, because she waved her hand, as if to let Emma off the hook. "I thought it was, myself, at first. But no. The boy was instructed to watch the house by a gentleman, and to report to the man's club if he saw the same crest visiting us as was on the carriage of the man who hired him."

Emma got to her feet and forced herself not to bite her fingernails. "Geoffrey's crest isn't the same as Edward's," she said. "But my stepfather's is. He uses Edward's rather than buy his own. Geoffrey's gone to the old man for help."

"Is your stepfather friendly with Geoffrey?" Charlotte couldn't keep the surprise from her voice, and Emma winced.

Nodded.

"He never gives Geoffrey any money—I don't think he has much of his own—but he's steered Geoffrey toward some investments that at least offered a return, from time to time. Given him entry into places he might have struggled to gain access to." She shook her head. "He was the only one who didn't stand against me when I wanted to marry Geoffrey."

"Will this boy tell Geoffrey or Emma's stepfather that we know they are watching?" Catherine asked, and Emma saw she was pouring them all a cup of tea.

"He might." Charlotte shrugged. "If it looks like they'll pay him for the information. But he knows I'll pay, too. And better than Geoffrey. So he may be back with something we can use."

"Playing both sides?" Emma frowned. "Then we can't trust him."

Charlotte gave her a strange look. "Except for Lady Howe, you can't trust anybody."

# 12

"You don't want to be here." Gary left the reins to Smithy, the driver, and swung into the coach beside Charlotte, closing the door behind him. "I don't want to be here."

Charlotte raised her eyebrows. Fortunately, they weren't anywhere fashionable—in fact, that was Gary's complaint—so no one in her social circle was likely to have witnessed her coachman climbing into her coach with her and shutting out the world.

There would be only one conclusion drawn, if that were the case.

"I agree. Neither of us wants to be here." She peered out into the night, into a street illuminated only by the weak candlelight leaking from the windows of the tight-packed tenements. "Kit says this is where his friend will meet us."

Gary sneered. "I don't know that Peter is a friend of Kit's, rightly. I'd have thought more an enemy."

She cocked her head at that. She waited for Gary to elaborate, but he was looking out the window again.

Someone howled from close by, as if to the moon, and a prickle of fear skittered down her back. She raised her gaze to Gary's and he met it, grim.

A hand rattled the door, and Gary opened cautiously, and for the first time, Charlotte noticed a knife in his hand.

"Peter." He said the word neutrally, and moved back, allowing the man into the coach with them.

He brought with him a strange mixture of smells. The earthy, salty smell of sex, the sweet, cloying scent of rum, and on top of that, the burnt-edged smell of tobacco.

He sat next to Gary, and in the weak light, she could see he was handsome, must once have been angelic. Blond hair, fine features, his eyes a pale blue. But there was a hardness to the set of his mouth, a seediness to the bags under his eyes.

He said nothing, had said nothing since he'd arrived, and Charlotte wondered if it had been him earlier, howling.

Trying to set them ill at ease.

The silence stretched out, and Peter fidgeted, an unconscious twitch, adjusting his too-tight trousers, and pulling at the overlarge jacket he was wearing.

"Thank you for coming." Charlotte leaned forward. "Kit said you may have some information for me." She spoke like a lady, when she'd thought she would talk to him like the street urchin she'd once been. It had been a while since she'd surprised herself so much.

"Depends." Peter relaxed back against the cushions, folded his arms across his chest.

"Depends on what?" Gary asked, his voice quiet, and Peter shifted, just slightly, away from him.

"Depends on what you'll give me for the information." He spoke with a drawl, trying too hard.

She saw herself, suddenly, as she could have been, without Catherine. Hopefully without the same capacity for cruelty she sensed in Peter, but hard and brittle as this. Smelling just the same, of sex and drink and hopelessness. Wearing the same ill-fitting castoffs. She cleared her throat. "I will pay a fair price for useful information on Lord Frethers."

"Kit mentioned the name, but I don't know it."

Gary made a sound beside him, and Peter slid him a look. "They none of 'em use their real names. They take all manner of poncy monikers."

Charlotte gripped her hands tight together. "Frethers is portly, hair thinning on top, florid cheeks from too much brandy." She thought back to when she'd seen him at the Hollidays' house party, amazed to think it had only been five days ago. "Wears a gold pocket watch and carries a cane with a silver tip shaped like a ram's head."

Peter closed his eyes for a moment, tipped his head back against the seat, as if in thought, but she saw his hands were tight-clenched fists. "That would be Cherub."

Cherub. She would laugh at the name Frethers took when catting about in the rookery whorehouses, but the tight, vicious look on Peter's face turned the impulse to ash. "You know where he goes? Which places, how often?"

Peter cocked his head. "What are the chances of him finding out who peached him?"

"He will certainly never hear it from me." She slid her gaze to her coachman. "Or Gary. As long as *you* don't say anything, there is no chance."

He watched her for a moment, then turned that same, piercing gaze on Gary. Eventually nodded. "And what are you offering?"

She had thought to offer money, and the bag of coins was beneath her cloak, but she could not look at Peter without thinking of all the years, two or three at least, that she'd had it within her power to do something about Frethers, and had not. Had allowed other things to take precedence. The look Peter had had on his face while he pretended to think who she could be describing had cut her deep, and she should bleed. She deserved it.

"I am going to give you a choice. I have money for you, and you could take it and never see me again." She sensed Gary tense, as if he knew what she was about to say, sensed him willing her not to say it, but she ignored him. "Or, I will give you the option of a different kind of payment. The kind where I work out a place for you in my household, either the country or here in town, and give you a permanent livelihood."

He laughed, a choked, shocked sound. He slid his gaze from her to Gary, and she saw him register Gary's fury at her offer. He laughed again, this time with an edge. "I'm tempted to accept." He smirked as Gary hissed out a breath. Waited a beat. "But I'll take the money, love. If it's all the same to you." He held out his hand.

She nodded. "First, I need to hear something useful."

The corner of his mouth kicked up in an annoying way. "Cherub. Likes the Moon-faced Pixie. Lots of babies to be had there. Mainly girls, but enough boys to keep him coming back. And the Red Rose Inn. The boys are a bit older there, but there's a more steady supply." He fiddled with the buttons on the velvet jacket that seemed to billow about him like a dark sail. "Usually Mondays and Thursdays. If he's well taken with a lad . . ." He cleared his throat, and Charlotte thought she might cry out. He looked across at her, and then hastily, angrily away, speaking the next words in a cool, disinterested tone. "If he's keen, he'll come back Friday, maybe even Saturday, for more."

"You ever hear of him trying his luck outside the rookeries, with the children of acquaintances?" She was thinking about the Hollidays, whether they were the first, because surely Frethers would not risk exposure without some collusion, as there had been between himself and the boys' father.

Peter hunched his shoulder. "May have heard 'im braggin'."

"Did you hear names?" She wondered if this line of questioning was even useful. No one would admit to any abuse of this sort, for any reason. Frethers knew it. He must have no self-control if he was not only fishing in the pond of the socially connected, but bragging about it, as well.

But Peter shook his head. "No names. He's not a complete bufflehead."

She felt around for her money bag and held it out to him, and he took it with a practiced hand. He dipped his fingers in and brought out a coin, tilted it to the window, to see it in the weak light. Gave a nod. "Nice doing business with ya." His eyes flicked around the interior of the coach. "I know how you must 'ave got this, and 'tis people like you give the rest of us hope." His words did not relay disrespect or even insinuation. He thought he was speaking one professional to another.

"It could have happened that way," she said. "But I did not come by my current situation by anything I had to do on my back." She did not look at Gary but could sense his disapproval at her openness. "I was saved from the street by kindness and have had to do nothing to keep it but be myself."

He looked at her, as if trying to detect some joke or a lie. And when he looked away, she had the feeling he was angry with her. "Then I take it back. You're a hope-killer. 'Cause at least if you'd done it on your back, that's something we c'n understand. Something we c'n do ourselves. But kindness? Luck like that—it's a million-to-one chance, and you already took the one chance going."

She did not dispute it. She agreed.

Gary opened the door and hopped out, and Charlotte saw him look to the right and gawp, his eyes wide.

She held out a hand to stop Peter clambering after him and he froze as she touched his shoulder.

A figure stepped into the doorway, crowding Gary, who had not moved away, but hadn't said a word, either.

It was Luke.

"Peter, me lad." He looked between them, and Charlotte felt Peter tense.

"What are you doing here?" She hadn't realized how angry she was until she spoke. Her hand trembled as she pulled it back. This was too many betrayals. Kit must have told him where they'd be, Smithy had let him come up on them without warning, and Gary . . . So far, Gary had been nothing but loyal, but the way Luke approached, it was clear he had no fear Gary would stop him.

Luke must have heard the deep hurt, because he stepped back. As he did, Peter leaped out, eel-quick, but just as fast Luke clamped a hand on his arm, jerked him close, so his mouth was right beside Peter's ear.

"Mum's the word, eh?" Luke's voice was pleasant enough, but Peter did not turn his head, or even nod in agreement. "The lady isn't looking for Cherub no more. You can take the money, but nothing'll come of it. And if I hear even a peep . . ." He didn't continue, let the silence stretch out, and finally released his hold. Peter jerked away and began to walk into the darkness, eyes down, hand clasping the money bag in his hand. He did not say goodbye.

"What was that?" Charlotte leaned out of the door, into Luke's face. "What are you doing, interfering in my business? And why do you keep asking my friends to betray me?"

"They ain't your friends no more, Charlie." Luke flicked a

look up at Smithy, across to Gary, and finally back to her. "They're your employees, and as such, subject to bribes and offers, just like any others."

"Fine." She felt frozen, the cold reaching its hoary hand deep into her core. "How would you like it if I approached *your* employees, got them to act against you or spy on you for money or for favors owed?"

He cocked his head, considering. Said nothing.

"You wouldn't stand for it. And even though I could do it, I have never stooped that low."

"Well, there you have the difference between us." Luke smiled. "When it comes to you, there are no depths to which I wouldn't stoop."

There was nothing to say to that. Nowhere to go from this conversation. She felt the rift between them rip a little more. Soon only a thread or two would remain.

She sank back into her seat, drained and tired. "And warning Peter off? Saying I'll do nothing against Frethers? What's that about?"

"I'm afraid I didn't realize it were Frethers you were talking about, t'other night. You can't go after him. 'Twould mess up my plans."

She frowned, and he swung into the carriage with her, and after a moment's hesitation, Gary closed the doors on them.

"What plans?" She curled tighter into her corner, away from him. Felt him reach out and take hold of her cloak. Tug it a little as he fingered the corner.

"I have a little deal going with Frethers and his lot. Anything you've got in mind, love, will have to be put aside."

Charlotte jerked her cloak from his grasp and glared at him in the darkness of the carriage as it began to rattle its way back home.

"I'm not one of your *employees*." She spoke quietly. "This has weighed on my conscience too long, and I'm not putting it aside for some chisel you have going." She watched him, but he said nothing, showed nothing on his face. She sighed. "I'm going ahead, Luke. And nothing is going to stop me."

# 13

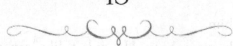

"Two of your men are dead?" Dervish dropped the papers in his hands, letting them flutter across his immaculate desk, and leaned back in his chair, his full attention on Edward's face.

"So I'm told. And they cannot be found, so I assume I've been told the truth."

Dervish tapped a finger to his mouth, absolutely silent, and eventually Edward decided to sit in the chair he had originally declined.

"Do you know who killed them?"

Edward hesitated. Thought of Charlotte, standing by the window, defiant in her refusal to point a finger. "I have an idea."

Dervish raised a brow, waiting.

Edward returned his stare. Dervish was someone he trusted, but he wasn't ready to trust him with anything that could harm Charlotte.

He realized, suddenly, that he was going to lie. Keep all mention of Charlotte's name out of this and let Dervish think his men were killed while conducting genuine government business.

It jolted him.

"A local crime boss. He didn't like my men on his patch."

Dervish frowned. "The rookery lords don't usually get mixed up with our lot. I always like to think they're loyal Englishmen, in their way."

Edward lifted his hands. "The smugglers on the coast should be loyal Englishmen, too, but clearly they are not."

"This is serious, Durnham." Dervish stood abruptly. "Very serious."

"Two men have died. I'm taking it very seriously, I assure you." Edward stood as well, and gripped the back of his chair.

"What area is this crime lord's patch?"

Edward considered lying again, but he saw no reason to shield Charlotte's Luke. "Tothill Road. Right next to the finest homes in all of London."

"Say again?" The way Dervish went still, the sudden fear in his voice, set a bell ringing in Edward's skull.

"The top dog in the Tothill Road rookery sees Mayfair as his personal patch. He took exception to my men's questions."

"I see." Dervish sat down abruptly, and his hands shook as he gathered his papers together.

Edward forced himself not to frown. "What is it?"

"Nothing. It's just terrible news to hear that two men are

dead." Dervish was sweating. Edward could see the glisten of moisture on his upper lip and on his forehead.

What would make him so afraid? The thought of men from his department asking questions around and about Mayfair and the West End? Usually, Dervish wouldn't care whose nose was out of joint in an investigation. Unless . . .

Bribery? Blackmail? Edward couldn't think of another reason for this reaction. If Dervish knew who was involved in the mess he'd dragged Edward into to sort out, wanted Edward to keep away from them . . . Edward tightened his hold on the chair, and saw his knuckles were white.

Dervish lifted his eyes from his desk. "You never told me you were taking the hunt to the homes of the ton." His voice was back under control, but the damage had been done.

"You were the one who inspired the idea." Edward tipped the chair forward, then back, watching Dervish carefully.

"I did?" Dervish tried to smile.

"Yes, your mention of attending balls the other night, because the men involved in this are right at the top of the social ladder. Of course, you were right. Now we have to decide whether my men were killed because they were asking questions someone didn't like, or because they were infringing on the territory of a rabid dog."

"They take respect very seriously in the rookeries. If your men showed disrespect or were too dismissive—that may have been enough."

Edward shrugged. "Perhaps. But as you say, some of the men involved in this plot must be noblemen. If they caught wind of my men's questions, they could well have paid this thug to get rid of them. That would have been a neat solution."

The lies tripped off his tongue, and he felt no regret now in speaking them. Luke had killed his men because of their interest in Charlotte, but Dervish would never discover that. Just how nervous would Dervish get if he thought Edward was getting too close?

Dervish closed his eyes for a moment, his face suddenly haggard.

Blackmail, Edward decided. If it were bribery, he'd look guilty, perhaps. As it was, he looked genuinely stricken.

"Customs caught another boat full of gold a few days ago. I just heard the news this morning. Twenty thousand guineas found on it. Twenty thousand! Hidden in the cabin ceiling, in hollowed-out pigs of iron ballast. The smack was too low on the water; that's how they caught them." Without opening his eyes, Dervish rubbed at his temples. "They think for every boat they find, at least ten are slipping past them. Ten." He lifted his head and snapped open his eyes, and they looked wild.

"So we really are hemorrhaging gold?"

Dervish nodded. "And I don't know why, dammit. Yes, they can get more for the gold in Europe than they can here, but it's a punishable crime taking guineas out the country as it is, so they risk jail, not to mention taking it through France while we're at war with that country, and the bribes they'd have to pay, the risk of having it confiscated or stolen . . ." He shook his head. "It doesn't make sense."

"It's worse than that." Edward thought of the facts and figures lying on his desk, of all the information he'd gathered already. "But I haven't worked it all out just yet." And he wouldn't be telling Dervish when he did.

Dervish pinched the bridge of his nose. "Edward, I . . ." He gave himself a shake. "Nothing. Just, be careful. Keep your focus on finding who in England's behind this gold smuggling. Don't take on this man from the rookeries."

Edward gave Dervish a nod of farewell. "I'm afraid it's too late for that. The Tothill Road man has already decided to take on me."

The look of horror on Dervish's face as he walked out gave him no satisfaction at all.

———

Someone was watching them. Charlotte sensed it. She'd spent too long in the rookeries not to trust the prick between her shoulder blades.

She turned, casually, as if to keep track of the Holliday boys running with their hoops and sticks across the lush grass of the park, lifting her hand to shield her eyes.

She saw nothing but the fine houses of their little square, and the trees and bushes that surrounded the small park in the center of it.

"What is it?" Emma asked, and as Charlotte swung back to her, she saw her face was tight with worry, her eyes never leaving the boys.

"I think we're being watched." She would not lie to her friend.

Emma jerked her gaze to Charlotte's face. "You saw someone?"

Charlotte shook her head. "Just a feeling. But my feelings are usually right."

"A touch of the gypsy?" Emma frowned.

"A touch of the rookeries. Brings out your senses." She spun again, slowly and carefully. "You don't learn to trust what your body tells you, you're dead."

"Yet you never gave it up." Emma lifted a hand to her own eyes.

"It wasn't so much I didn't give it up as I couldn't." Charlotte went still, her eye catching something, but she smoothly turned her head to Emma. "It clung to me." She gave a laugh. "Like the dust from the chimneys used to do."

The wind was coming up, and the boys' hoops raced ahead of them, Ned's flying out into the street.

The sky darkened, and Charlotte lifted her face to the sky as Emma called to Ned to stay out of the road. The clouds that tumbled and boiled over the sun were purple and bruised, and the air that gusted over her was a hot, blowsy tart with drunken mayhem on her mind.

Leaves and papers, and all three of the boys' caps went airborne, and Charlotte saw a flick of movement in the narrow alley between two houses on the other side of the square again.

Whoever crouched there, watching, was closer to the boys than either her or Em, and a sudden fear clutched her, that Frethers may still be determined to have them, or their father may still be determined to hand them over.

Why else watch them, otherwise?

She began to run, not the fleet-footed dash she'd been capable of in her childhood. Hampered by skirts tugged and twisted by the gusts, and shoes that were the height of fashion but ridiculous for anything but a slow walk, she called to the boys, and saw their attention was still on Ned's hoop, which had halted its mad dash for freedom, and had finally fallen over, to lie in the middle of the road.

A carriage came round the corner, and Charlotte sensed the moment Ned decided to retrieve the hoop before it was crushed.

"Stop!" Her shout was ripped away by the wind, lost in the tossing branches of the trees as they began to whistle and shake. Ned reached the paved edge of the square. She put two fingers to her lips and gave a piercing whistle that cut through the noise.

The boys turned to her, eyes wide, and in the street, the carriage rolled to a stop, and Edward jumped out of it.

He walked to where the hoop lay and picked it up, his eyes never leaving her.

She hadn't seen him since yesterday, and Charlotte did not understand the sensation that gripped her at the sight of him. As if she were a lightning rod, waiting for the storm above to strike. As if she had lost all control over her life and was thrown into chaos.

She ripped her gaze away from him, to where the watcher had been, but there was no telltale shadow anymore. Whoever had been there had slipped away.

When she turned her attention back to Edward, he had given Ned his hoop and was walking toward her.

The first heavy drop of rain hit her cheek, and she flinched.

Emma came up to her side, gesturing for the boys to come to them, and then stopped. "What is it?"

She was talking to Edward, and Charlotte raised her eyes at last to meet Edward's bleak gaze. The world dropped away from her and she swallowed.

The rain started to fall with a sudden sizzle of sound, drumming off the roofs and paved street. The boys whooped, running wild.

Edward flicked a look over his shoulder, to determine if the boys were occupied enough not to hear. "I'm sorry, Em."

Charlotte could hardly hear him over the hammering rain.

Emma frowned. "What is it? What?"

Edward took her hand. "Geoffrey's dead."

## 14

Emma sat on the couch in Catherine's sitting room, a blanket around her, pale and shaking as a victim of influenza. Her rain-plastered hair only added to the impression.

A drop of water ran down the side of Edward's forehead, over his cheek, and clung to the edge of his jaw. He shook it loose and rubbed the towel Catherine had given him through his hair.

Catherine poured Emma a cup of tea, loading it with sugar, and he nodded in approval as his sister took a sip.

Charlotte was with the boys, settling them into the nursery with some afternoon tea and cakes, and he missed her strong, unshakable calm. He did not know what to say to Emma. He was not only not sorry about his brother-in-law's death, he was glad.

Catherine knelt at Emma's feet, holding her hand. Edward knew they had only met since Charlotte offered Emma a place in this house, but looking at them, he wouldn't know it. They seemed old friends.

"How did he die?" Emma asked suddenly, her eyes searching his face, and Edward shifted uncomfortably.

"Shot. His body was found in the woods behind the house. It may have been a hunting accident." That is what the magistrate was calling it. Edward wondered whether it was suicide.

Emma went still. "He was deep in debt. He planned to clear it by selling the boys to Frethers, but I took them away. I took away his only way out. Perhaps he realized there was no getting out of it, this time. Could he have . . . ?"

There was silence in the room, and Edward watched as his sister curled in on herself. He wanted to shout that the worthless bastard did not deserve even one tear to be shed for him, but he kept his mouth clamped shut. As far as he was concerned, if Geoffrey had taken his own life, it was probably the most honorable thing he'd ever done.

"What is wrong with me?" Emma looked at him with an aching uncertainty. "I can't find it in me to grieve for him. I don't want to forgive him. All I can feel is rage at what he was going to do, and relief I will never have to see him again."

Edward let out a long-held breath. Catherine looked up at him and shook her head.

"He recently gave you no reason to feel otherwise. You may one day think back fondly on some of your moments, but that is in the future, if at all." She rose to her feet and smoothed a hand over Emma's head.

The way she spoke, with a deep sense of knowing, made Edward wonder for the first time the circumstances of Catherine's own marriage. Why she had never remarried, although she could not have been more than fourteen or fifteen years older than Charlotte herself.

"He may have killed himself, but Geoffrey was never one for discomfort. He would have had to have been lower than I've ever seen him before for the idea to hold any appeal. And I have seen him very low." Emma rocked in place, and Edward stared at her, trying to work out her meaning.

"You think he may have shot himself accidentally, or been shot by one of his friends?"

Emma shook her head. "No. I was thinking more along the lines of murder."

---

"**W**hat do you make of Emma's suspicions?" Edward would not sit. Instead he prowled and paced, turning the large, simply furnished sitting room into a zoo cage. His constant movement was getting on her nerves, but Charlotte held on to her irritation.

She could see Edward was simply unable to do anything else.

The rain had stopped, and late afternoon sunshine poured through the windows, bringing his tense, drawn face into sharp relief.

She recalled Emma's reaction when Charlotte had first asked to speak to her about Frethers, back at her country estate. How Emma had assumed Charlotte was there to speak to her of something else. Something she was afraid of. Perhaps that is what prompted her thoughts of murder. But that was not Charlotte's secret to tell.

When she raised her head, she saw Edward was finally still, but not the still of calm—rather, the still of the tiger before it pounces. "You know something."

She shrugged. "I know nothing. But I may have picked up a sense that something was wrong, that Geoffrey was involved in something that made Emma afraid, and I can only say you'll have to ask Emma. I may not be right."

The look he sent her should have burned her where she sat. He turned away, furious.

"I truly *don't* know. But I would not tell you if I did; you're quite right. It is for Emma to tell us both." She paused. "Did you know your stepfather sent a spy to watch this house the day before yesterday?"

Her swift change of subject was like a jolt of lightning in the room. He froze, then stared at her.

"The little bugger tossed a brick at your matched set. Nearly made the one on the left lame."

"How do you know it was my stepfather?" Edward crossed his arms over his chest.

"I caught the spy and bribed him." She shrugged. "He didn't know it was your stepfather but mentioned the carriage of the man who hired him had the same crest as yours. Emma says the only man with use of your carriages is your stepfather."

"She's right." Edward began to walk again. To the fireplace and back to the window. The atmosphere had gone from anger and hurt to genuine puzzlement, though, and Charlotte was glad for the change. "What could my stepfather want to know in secret that he could not ask me directly?"

Charlotte had wondered the same. "Emma says he was in touch with Geoffrey. Gave him investment advice and so forth. I thought he may have been spying on Emma and the boys for Geoffrey. I even wondered if Geoffrey might try to force her to hand the boys back to him, if Frethers was the only way out he could see. He would have had the law on his side, as the boys' legal guardian."

"Hmm." He considered what she said, the sound he made at the back of his throat vibrating through her, and she forced her knees and thighs together with an edge of desperation she would usually associate with fear. "My stepfather knows full well what I thought of my brother-in-law." He paused. "He knew I would never allow Geoffrey access to my sister and her children if I could help it, whether I knew what Geoffrey planned to do to his own sons or not."

"Would Geoffrey have told your stepfather what he planned?"

Edward shook his head. "I wouldn't have thought any man would admit to something like that. He is more likely to have claimed to want his family back."

"At least he can't have them anymore." Charlotte stood and walked to the far window. Looked out at the front street.

"No. Although I doubt my stepfather knows that yet. Perhaps I should go and tell him." His voice was level, but Charlotte looked across to him and his mouth was tight and his eyes narrowed.

She turned back to the window. "You could save yourself some time, and just walk out into the street."

"What do you mean?" Edward joined her, and his warm breath brushed the back of her neck.

She gripped the curtains with one hand, made herself stand perfectly still. "Your stepfather's spy is back in his place. Watching the house again."

# 15

His stepfather had interfered in his life from the moment his mother had married the bastard. The beatings, the cold disdain, that he could have borne. But the constant meddling, the way Gerald Hawthorne had snatched every enjoyable thing from him, and forced him in directions he did not want to go, had ignited a leaping, raging fire in him that had never abated.

He had thought it banked down now he was in control, rather than Hawthorne, but it had begun to consume him from within since Charlotte had told him about the spy.

Edward knew he was hanging on to civility by a thread, fighting back a rage so hot and black, he wanted to choke.

The boy who crouched on the pavement, near where he himself had stood only a few nights ago, watching the house, leaped to his feet and was out of grabbing distance before they were halfway across the street.

"What are you doing back here?" Charlotte called to him.

The child smirked. "Talking highbrow again, now there's a nob to 'ear you?"

Charlotte smiled. "I don't need to worry about it with him, so I'll go gutter, if you like?"

"Don't mind me." The boy lifted his chin and stood in a good imitation of a dandy preening, and the anger loosened its hold on Edward's chest a little. This boy was not responsible for Edward's stepfather's actions. He was a baby. No more than six or seven years old.

"Why are you back so soon?" Charlotte asked again, and the boy rubbed finger and thumb together.

Edward pulled a crown from his pocket and held it up. Waited. Saw the moment the child realized how much it was.

He strained forward, like a dog held back on a leash. "Just following 'is lordship." He jerked his head toward Edward and Edward realized he knew him, had seen him a few times already, and not just in the last few days.

"How long have you been following me?" Edward flicked the coin high in the air, caught it in his fist.

"Since day before yesterday, m'lord." The boy kept an earnest, honest face.

"And you report my activities to the coachman behind a gentlemen's club, Miss Raven tells me."

The boy slid a look at Charlotte, one Edward couldn't read. He nodded.

"Which club?"

"White's, sir."

Edward shook his head. "You're lying." He flicked the coin

again. "You've been following me for longer than just yesterday. I've seen you on and off since last week. And the only man who rides in a coach with my crest on it is not a member of White's."

The boy tried to look offended, then gave up and shrugged.

"Are you bamming us?" Charlotte asked, and she sounded colder. Harder. "Want some money for nothing?"

"No." The boy sounded so indignant that despite the situation, Edward had to swallow a laugh. "It's just . . . I weren't supposed to be seen." For the first time, the child looked uneasy.

"What's your name?" Edward was tired of thinking of him as "the boy," but he shook his head, his lips pressed tight together.

Edward sighed, held the crown between finger and thumb. "What *can* you tell me?"

The boy flicked his gaze between them and Edward realized they'd lost him. Whatever he'd been threatened with was strong enough to make him think twice about playing a double game.

He turned and ran.

"Wait." Edward found himself throwing the crown at him, sensed Charlotte's quick frown. The boy spun, darted forward, and scooped it up.

He stared at Edward, then down at the coin in his hand. "It's Twigs," he called, walking backward. He did a little jig, lifting his legs and kicking them out, then he turned and ran, disappearing around the corner.

"Twigs?" He turned to Charlotte as she came up beside him. "What does that mean?"

She was smiling. "It's his name. Because of his legs. They're like twigs."

"He was afraid."

She nodded. "But unless he's part of a gang, and the contract to spy on you is through the gang leader, he'll be all right now."

"How?" Edward watched her face, at the satisfaction on it.

"You gave him a crown." The eyes she lifted to his were shining. "That's more than he'll ever have seen at one time. He can go to ground good and proper with that." There was a vicarious satisfaction in her voice, as if she were putting herself in Twigs's place and chuckling to herself at her good fortune.

Her hair shone like a raven's wing in the sunlight, and he wanted to touch it. "Do you take your surname from your hair? Because it is like a raven?"

She smiled, full of amusement, but her cheeks flushed pink, as well. "I never knew my surname, only my first name. The lads decided to choose one for me. I was only clean enough that they could tell what color my hair was a couple of times, but yes, it reminded them of a raven's wing." She shrugged. "We saw enough dead ones in the chimneys, anyway. We felt a connection to them. A camaraderie. You'd look at a dead raven, lying curled up in the soot, and think it could be you. Might be you, one day."

He lifted a hand, forcing it not to shake, and brushed her cheek. "I missed seeing you these last two days."

She blinked, and he wondered why he had said that.

Cursed himself for it. Then slid his fingers up until they were buried in her hair.

"I was worried about you," she said. "Worried that Luke would do something."

"As far as he knows, there is nothing between us." He buried his fingers even deeper, and she turned her head so her cheek rested in his palm and let him take the weight of her head for a moment. Then she lifted her own hand and curled her fingers around his, pulled his hand away, and glanced at it, eyebrows raised, head cocked to the side.

And suddenly he recalled they were in the street, and that he had touched her as intimately as a lover. That they stood with hands entwined.

He wondered if he'd lost his mind.

"He knows now, at any rate," she said. She did not release his hand. "And he is coming for you. It isn't a matter of if, only a matter of when."

As he looked down at her, he understood her old lover for the first time. Because now, like Luke, if anyone stood in his way with her, he would bring them down.

———————

Harry was asleep, lying in abandon with his arms thrown above his head. Too small to understand that his father was dead.

Ned was sleeping, too, but he was curled up on himself, deep under the covers, the position so protective, Emma's throat ached at the sight of him.

James lay stretched out, under the blankets but with eyes wide open. They were fixed on her, glittering with tears he would not let fall. "If we'd been at home, Daddy would still be alive."

Emma shook her head, forcing herself under control so she could answer. "Daddy went hunting whether we were there or not. It would have made no difference."

"Why did we leave? Perhaps Daddy was missing us, and that's why the accident happened. He was thinking of us, and didn't see—"

"No." Emma was firm. "The man who shot the gun was the one not thinking about what he was doing, not Daddy. And it was because of Daddy that we were here in London." She would never let him think they were to blame by their absence. And if Geoffrey had committed suicide, there would be time enough, after the wounds were less raw, to explain to him later.

"I wish . . ." James's voice broke on a sob that ripped her heart out, threw it down, and stamped on it. "I wish we could have been there to see him a few more times. I didn't even say goodbye properly."

Emma crouched down beside him and gently stroked the hair back from his forehead, silent tears tracking down her cheeks. "I love you, James. And Daddy loved you, too. And I know he knows that you miss him." She sat until the muscles in her legs burned, her hand cupping his cheek, until at last he fell asleep.

She rose, taking a step toward the bed she'd had made up

in the nursery. She did not want her children to sleep alone for the next few nights. She needed them near her.

But the idea of sleep was almost repugnant.

She was as wrung out as a wet bedsheet. The news had drained her—of energy, of the anger she had been nursing toward Geoffrey since she'd left their estate. She felt nothing. Did not want the dreams and thoughts and worries that she knew would crowd her head when she closed her eyes.

A soft knock came at the door, and she opened it with relief.

Charlotte stood outside, a small tray with a steaming cup of tea in her hands. Emma stepped out and closed the door.

"Can you sit with me while I drink?"

Charlotte nodded and turned, walking down the passage to the snug red and brown sitting room at the top of the stairs. She set down the tray and took a seat, and Emma forced herself to do the same.

"James is so confused. He thinks we should have been there. He feels if we had been, Geoffrey wouldn't have died." She tried to lift the cup to her lips but it shook too much and she set it down again.

"If you had stayed, James, Ned, and Harry would not have been there anyway. They'd have been with Frethers, being raped. And their father would have been the one who sent them there." Charlotte's voice was neither angry nor annoyed. She spoke in a matter-of-fact manner that forced Emma's head up.

She couldn't hold Charlotte's gaze, and stared down at

the low table. "I know that." At last, she was able to lift the cup and take a sip. "I know that. But I cannot explain it to James."

Charlotte pressed her lips together. "No."

Emma wondered what she was thinking. Perhaps that at James's age, she had been working for years as a sweep, had been beaten, starved, and perhaps raped herself.

Then Charlotte smiled, and Emma realized she was wrong. Charlotte did not begrudge her children their innocence. "They have a mother who loves them, and an uncle who will protect them. They will come through this, Emma, and they will thrive."

Because she was overcome, and knew that if she tried to respond the tears that had fallen silently until now would come out in a wailing, keening mess, Emma forced herself to lift the cup again with shaking fingers and take a deep sip.

"Excuse me, my lady." Betsy stood at the door, wringing her hands, and Emma saw Charlotte go pale.

"What is it?"

"Kit 'as something to tell you." The maid would not look in Emma's direction.

"Can't it wait?" Charlotte murmured, and Betsy shifted uncertainly.

"It's sort of a confession." She grabbed her apron and twisted it in her hands. "Will you come?"

Charlotte rose and touched a gentle hand to Emma's shoulder. "Shall I come back after?"

She shook her head. Their conversation had made clear

what her guilt and sadness had muddied. Geoffrey had betrayed them, and while she had never wished him dead, she had no cause for regrets.

She watched Charlotte follow Betsy down the stairs, her tread weary, and wondered if Charlotte was able to work her magic on herself as easily as she seemed to do in others.

# 16

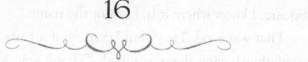

"That boy you spoke with today." Kit launched straight into speech as Charlotte stepped out of the back door with Betsy.

He had been leaning against the wall but he pushed himself upright and walked a little way from the house. Charlotte followed, happy to have this conversation out of the hearing of the other servants.

"What about him?" Charlotte tried to see his face, but the night sky was still overcast from the storm of the afternoon, and his features were in shadow.

"You spoke with him the other day, as well."

"Yes."

"I had one of the lads Luke pays to hang around the back of the house follow him the first time you spoke to him. Just wanted to know what he was up to." Kit spoke stiffly, and she knew it was because he was telling her something Luke wouldn't like.

She hadn't known he paid boys to hang around the house to follow people if needed. But she wasn't surprised. "And?"

"He went back to a small private club near St. James's Square. I know where it is, but not the name."

That was good. They could confirm if it truly was Edward's stepfather having them watched. "Thank you, Kit. That will help."

"Help with what?" His tone was sharp. Far too sharp for a stablehand to his mistress, and he spun from her with a curse. "Sorry."

"It's all right. I don't know what I am at the moment, your mistress or your friend, but I can take a sharp word or two without too much harm done. The boy says he was sent to watch Lord Durnham, and knowing the club will help narrow down who is behind it."

"He wasn't watching Lord Durnham." Kit turned back to face her. "At least, not since you spoke to him. He came back to the house; he didn't go anywhere near the nob. Luke's lad brought in some extra watchers, and they set themselves up in a net around the house as far as two streets away."

"Why?" As she uttered the question, she knew the answer.

"Luke wanted to see who was having you watched."

"It may not be me being watched. Lady Holliday was here to escape her husband. He made a deal with Frethers over his three boys—"

Kit swore viciously, cutting her off. "I didn't know that."

"No," she said wryly. Kit had no foundation to assume she would tell him her secrets. "I think her husband enlisted the help of her stepfather to watch her, maybe watch Lord Durnham, as well, and see if there was a chance to take the boys back."

"'Twas his right to have them. Why didn't he just make her?"

"Two reasons. He felt guilty about it. Before his wife knew and confronted him, he could fool himself into believing Frethers would look and not touch. But also because he knows Lord Durnham would fight him every inch of the way, and Durnham has more standing and considerably more funds than he does. Snatching them would have been far easier."

"You're talking about this like it's not a problem no more." Kit cocked his head to the side.

"Lady Holliday's husband died yesterday. Edward brought the news this afternoon. Unless Frethers is completely mad, he'll not touch the boys now, without the father complicit."

Kit spun a full circle, deep in thought. "Then why's there new watchers?" He was talking to himself, and Charlotte grabbed his shoulders to stop him.

"What do you mean, new watchers?"

"The boy's gone. But there are men watching now. Mostly wounded ex-soldiers."

"The stepfather probably doesn't know Lady Holliday's husband is dead. Edward plans to tell him this evening."

Kit gave a nod. But there was something in his face. A panic, which sent a thin, cruel hand of fear groping for her heart.

"What is it?"

"It's Luke." He looked away. "He thought—" Kit scrubbed

his hands over his face. "He thought it was the nob, Lady Hol-liday's brother, watching you. And wiv 'im following us the other night . . ." His words trailed off to nothing, sucked into the humid, damp hum of London on a high summer night.

"What is Luke going to do?" She spoke each word as if they were ripped from her, as if she did not have the air.

"I'm sorry." When Kit turned back to her, his eyes were stark with fear. "He's plannin' to take care of 'im tonight."

---

Gerald lived in a very carefully chosen house. Edward knew his stepfather had always been one to carefully weigh the odds, and Summer House was the perfect balance. Elegant and with a very good address, to make it eminently acceptable to polite society, but small and sophisticated, rather than large and domineering, with a much smaller price tag as a result.

He'd made it easy enough for Edward to pay for this little jewel, tucked neatly between two larger town houses.

Perhaps the only thing that had stuck in his stepfather's craw was that Edward had bought the house in his own name. Gerald had been barely able to grit out his thanks when he worked out that the house was not his, free and clear.

Edward liked the not-so-subtle reminder to his stepfather that if he was pushed too far, he could push back.

Push the old man onto the streets, if he so chose.

There was no way the bastard was getting a house out of him.

Gerald's greatest misstep was his treatment of Edward in

his youth. Perhaps his financial situation hadn't been so dire in those days, and he hadn't foreseen a time when he would need to rely on Edward for his upkeep. Or perhaps he thought he could cow Edward permanently with his treatment. Forever hold him under his thumb.

Most likely, he simply couldn't help himself. He was cruel and manipulative by nature.

He was no doubt unable to understand how things had gone so wrong for him.

Finally, reluctantly, Edward climbed the stairs and rang the bell, waited for the quick, efficient footsteps of Clavers, his stepfather's butler.

Clavers knew all too well who paid his salary, and welcomed Edward with what for him was an effusive greeting. "Good evening, my lord. His lordship is in the library. I will announce you at once."

Edward was forced to look around the hallway as he waited for Clavers to return. The paintings on the walls were familiar. Gerald had brought them with him into Edward's family home when he'd married Edward's mother. He'd been forced to cram them all into the room he'd taken for his study in those days.

Edward recalled the times he'd stood, gazing at the dour-faced men and women, the children in stiff and silly poses—a host of Gerald's disapproving dead relatives—while his stepfather had dressed him down or given him a beating.

He turned away from them. They should not have the power to bring back the worst years of his life with such clarity.

He faced the front entrance, and while he stared, cold and sick with himself, he saw an envelope pushed under the doorway. Heard the fumble of someone just outside, and then nothing.

With a quick look in the direction of the library, he walked forward and picked the letter up, turning it in his hands. There was no address on the front, just the words "Lord Hawthorne" scribbled in poor handwriting.

His stepfather had been paying someone to watch him, and Edward wondered if this was some kind of report. As he heard the light tip-tap of Clavers returning, he hesitated a moment, then slipped the letter into the inner pocket of his jacket.

Whatever he'd thought to do, and he hadn't been sure, he was unable to hand the letter over now. The question was whether he'd find some way to leave it behind, or slip it under the door as he left. Or keep it.

He wanted to keep it. To read it. To find out what was truly behind this new twist on his relationship with Gerald. And then again, it was no more than Gerald had done, so many times in his childhood.

He put the dilemma aside as he followed Clavers down the passage. He had time to decide what to do.

Clavers opened the door to the library and stood back for him, and Edward murmured his thanks as he stepped through. Clavers shut it behind him.

In his youth this moment, when he was alone with his stepfather, the door shutting behind him with an ominous click, had left him both sick with dread and shaking with fury. He had hated Gerald with all the passion he could muster but was all too aware of the power Gerald held over him.

The chains of the past were long broken, but Edward couldn't help the spike of intense dislike and anger that surged through him with that final snick of the door handle.

"Edward, not like you to arrive unplanned like this. What is it?" Gerald sat in a plush armchair, gouty foot raised on a footstool, with the doors out to the back garden open to let in what little breeze there was. The cool the rain had brought with it this afternoon was lush and calming as it mingled with the scent of roses and jasmine, and it stretched green, fresh tendrils into the room.

"Bad news." Edward stood back from Gerald and did not greet him otherwise. He had long ago made peace with his inability to speak meaningless inanities. He stayed away from balls for the same reason.

Gerald raised his brows and waited.

"Geoffrey is dead. The magistrate sent word to me today."

Gerald half rose, then sank back into his chair. "How terrible. Is Emma all right?"

Edward stared at him, trying to work out why his senses, always on full alert with Gerald, were screaming at him. "She is holding up, being strong for the boys."

"Will she come to London?" Gerald said after a moment.

"She's already in London. Has been for more than a week." Edward crossed his arms over his chest. "Didn't Geoffrey tell you?"

Gerald froze, only for the briefest of moments, but Edward caught it. "Why would he do that?"

"Emma says you were in touch with him often, and helped advise him on investments from time to time. I would have thought he would have let you know—if he were to tell anyone—that his wife had left him."

Gerald said nothing. Then, finally, coldly: "You were never able to master the art of social discretion. It will do neither Emma, nor Geoffrey's memory, any good to go around saying things like that."

"So you did know?"

"No. I didn't. I had no idea Emma was here in London."

"Interesting." Edward dropped his hands to his sides, quiet satisfaction at the way he'd worked Gerald up coursing through him. This shouldn't be so pleasant, but by God, it was. And he knew, unequivocally, that his stepfather was lying. "Aren't you going to ask how Geoffrey died?" That is what had first set the bell ringing in his head. Gerald had not asked how a young man in his prime, who was not ill, had died.

As if realizing his blunder, Gerald feigned tiredness. Closing his eyes and leaning back into his armchair. "Of course. I'm not myself. How did he die?"

"He was shot."

That provoked a response from the gargoyle. His eyes flew open, and he looked at Edward with those cold, muddy brown eyes. "Shot?"

"While hunting."

"The fellow responsible must feel terrible."

Edward shifted, aware that his stepfather had not offered him a seat. He perched on the arm of a burgundy- and cream-striped sofa, stretching his legs out in front of him, and noted Gerald's mouth tighten. "Not terrible enough to come forward. There is talk of foul play." Edward was not certain why he was taking this line with Gerald. He knew the magistrate would be only too happy to call this an accident. But then Gerald spoke, and he knew exactly why he'd taken this tack.

"Foul play?" The quizzical tone was overdone. Perhaps someone else would have missed it, but Edward had dedicated a good deal of time to understanding every nuance of Gerald's face. It had prepared him for, if not saved him from, many an unpleasant situation.

Edward shrugged. "Early days, of course."

"Of course." Gerald eyed him with dislike. Now that Gerald's ill will couldn't harm him, Edward found himself trying to earn it at every turn.

He stood, trying to shake off the ghosts of the past and look at Gerald through as unbiased an eye as he was capable.

Gerald had aged badly. He'd been handsome when he'd married Edward's mother, and the strong bones and high forehead were still there, the hair perhaps not as thick, but not bad. It was his eyes and mouth that Edward thought of as his giveaways. They were hard, cruel.

And he sat looking like a rat in its hole, eyes glinting, vibrating with the need for action.

Edward shook his head. So much for lack of bias.

Not that he was wrong. But he would never be able to see Gerald without feeling something. Perhaps the pure rage and fear had worn away, but a patina of both remained, staining him.

"Well, good evening. I thought you would like to know of Geoffrey's death before it makes its way to the papers."

Gerald's lips creased into a thin, pursed line. "I would hope you would have wanted me to know, anyway."

Edward didn't reply. He turned for the door.

"Ask Emma to come and visit me." Gerald spoke to his back. "She's staying with you?"

"No. She's staying with a friend. And I will not ask her. I don't want her boys anywhere near you." He had never said this to Gerald before, and was surprised to hear himself say it now. But he had long thought it.

"What?" Gerald's surprise was evident, and Edward schooled his face as he turned to face him.

"You are a sadist and a bully. I don't want you near my nephews. I don't trust you with them."

Gerald's eyes widened. "That's preposterous. Have you gone mad?"

He didn't answer.

After a moment, Gerald leaned back and looked at him with open dislike. "It's not up to you."

"As Emma's brother, it is. I'm the children's legal guardian now. And you will not see them. If Emma wants to see you on her own, that's her business."

They both knew Emma would come, out of guilt, if nothing else.

Edward turned away again and walked out, aware of Gerald's eyes on his back.

If Gerald hadn't needed Edward's money, if he could have gotten away with it, he would bet his stepfather would have pulled out a pistol and shot him between the shoulder blades.

Edward stepped out into the cool night air. He'd sent his coachman home when he was dropped off. He knew how this meeting would go, all too well. Knew he would need to walk and think afterward.

He closed his eyes briefly against the soothing breeze that seemed by some miracle to carry only the scent of rain and roses tonight, rather than the usual London odors.

A coach rumbled past, a little bedraggled and out of place to be in this end of town. It rolled to a stop a little way ahead of him.

The coachman jumped down and opened the door, and Edward wondered why they were getting out on a corner, rather than in front of a house, although if this was a lightskirt come to sneak in to see a lover, or a man coming back from the brothels, that would be explanation enough.

He walked past without looking within. He didn't see the sack coming over his head until it was too late.

# 17

The gin house at Tothill Road was silent. No wild shouting and singing tonight. It was as unkempt as any building in the street—unremarkable, as it was supposed to be.

Beside her, Kit shuffled in place, nervous.

He'd had to make a choice. Accompanying her tonight meant he was hers. Irrevocably.

He would have to break the hold Luke had over him. Stop the reports and the spying.

She finally walked to the door, pushed it open, Kit a step behind her.

The stale stink of old sweat and sour booze was choking. A single light burned below, a lamp hooked to the wall of Luke's office. The rest of the deep, wide pit was shadowed.

Charlotte lifted her face to the ceiling, listening for any sign of occupation in the upper floors. She heard nothing, but she would have to check.

She put a hand on the bannister. Looked down into the ill-lit gloom, and thought of hell.

She often wondered if Luke had created this place deliberately. A strange, mocking hark back to his time in the Hulks. She could barely imagine the horror, although nursing him, listening to him whimper and call out in his fever when she'd gotten him out, had given her a glimmer.

The Hulks had broken him, and forged him into something new. Something she had never truly understood, although she had tried as hard as she could.

She realized she had never come here alone of her own accord. It was always by invitation, always when it was wild and packed with desperation.

"Charlie?" Kit asked, confused at her hesitation, and below, someone made a small sound in the shadows.

She expected one of Luke's men would be lurking below. Luke would never leave his office unguarded. She only hoped it was someone she knew. Someone from the old days.

She moved at last, taking the stairs lightly, quickly, as if they led down to a private garden, rather than the strange purgatory Luke had fashioned.

Kit followed at a slower pace, and Charlotte knew he'd heard the sound as well.

She did not hesitate at the bottom. She walked straight through the darkness toward the light over the door of Luke's office, and made it almost all the way before a figure stepped in front of her. He blocked the light, silhouetted by it, so at first she could not see who it was.

Her eyes adjusted. "Sammy." She relaxed a little.

"What ya doin' here, Charlie?" His body couldn't seem to keep still, as if he were a greyhound about to race.

"I need to see Luke."

He turned to the office at her mention of Luke's name, then swung back to her. "He's busy."

She did not respond to that. Simply looked at him for a long moment.

His gaze slid off her face, looked beyond her, and focused on Kit. "You need to get her out o' 'ere. Things need doing and she can't be party."

Kit gestured to him, as if to have a discussion about it, and Sammy stepped around her, opening up the way.

Charlotte took advantage, ran to the door, and slipped through, slamming it behind her.

She turned the key in the lock, then gasped as Sammy threw himself against the sturdy wood.

The room, like the pit, was only lit by a single lamp, and there was no one in it. But now she thought she could hear the murmur of voices above, and she took the tight, cast iron spiral staircase upward.

It opened out in a sitting room of sorts, ill-furnished with things Luke's henchmen or their wives had found over the years, a mismatch of sofas and armchairs, wooden stools and tables.

Three men turned their heads to her as she ascended the last few stairs. Luke, standing closest to her, and Bill Jenkins, his right-hand man, kneeling beside Edward, tied to one of the wooden chairs.

Her eyes went straight to Edward, blood dripping from his nose but otherwise unmarked, save the bruise Sammy had left on his face a few days ago.

"Kit," Luke breathed.

"Not nice to find your friends choosing a different side, is it?" She made her words as icy as she could, her attention swinging to him.

He acknowledged the barb, lifted out hands in surrender. "I won't use him again."

If he was looking for a thank-you, he was mistaken. "No, you won't." She flicked her gaze to Bill, not daring to look directly at Edward again. "Untie him."

Bill looked across to Luke, who gave a tight nod.

But she wasn't fooled. Luke knew he and Bill could have Edward back in that chair in under a minute if he wanted to. This was far from over.

She saw a few things were laid out on the small table next to Edward. An envelope, a watch, and a small pile of coins.

She knelt next to the chair and started untying the ropes at Edward's hands, while Bill worked on the ones on his feet.

Edward had said nothing at all, but he watched her, his eyes glittering in the light. Close up she saw that his lip was slightly swollen.

"Tell me about the men watching my house." She lifted her head, looking at Luke as she spoke.

"Ask him." He jerked his head at Edward, his face stone.

"He knows less than I do. The person who sent those

watchers is either his stepfather or his brother-in-law. Or some people his brother-in-law was involved with."

For the first time, some emotion played on Luke's face. "You're so sure?"

"Yes. I spoke to one of the watchers myself."

Luke crossed arms over his chest, turned his gaze to Edward. "Who is your stepfather?"

Edward hesitated a moment, but Charlotte couldn't see a reason for him to hide the information. Luke could find out easily enough later. "Lord Hawthorne." His voice was hoarse, as if he'd taken a blow to the throat, or been throttled, and she gave Bill a sharp look.

Luke was still, letting the seconds tick by, and then leaned over and picked the envelope off the table. "You have a letter addressed to him. Playing delivery boy?"

Charlotte, still crouched at Edward's feet, looked up at him. "Is it from Emma, letting him know about Geoffrey?" That made sense.

Edward shook his head. She could see in his face the anger at being helpless to prevent Luke from reading it. He spoke with a tight jaw. "Someone pushed it under the door while I was waiting for my stepfather to see me. I thought it might be from the watchers—a report—so I took it."

She was surprised he would take something not addressed to himself. She didn't think less of him for it. She'd have done the same, but it was the first indication she had that he wasn't a stickler for the rules.

Luke slit it open with a knife from his pocket and drew out

a single piece of paper. As he read it, she was surprised to see his eyes go wide and then become shuttered. She held out her hand from her position crouched beside Edward, and he shook his head. "Think I'll 'ang on to this."

He folded it and tucked it into a top breast pocket of his tattered coat. He could afford a hundred new velvet ones, but he only ever wore clothing that looked slightly worse for wear.

"Let me read it at least. We need to know what's going on—more than you do. And how did you think this"—she gestured at Edward on his wooden chair, her voice climbing higher—"would help? What is it supposed to achieve?" She was poking a lion with a very sharp stick. She knew it, but she was suddenly angry enough not to care.

He shook his head slowly at her. "Charlie, when it's you, all bets are off."

She tugged the last knot free and let the ropes fall to the ground, then rose and stepped back from Edward, giving him room to stand. She watched him anxiously. "I'm sorry."

Edward didn't get up. He sat back more comfortably in the chair and turned an unreadable face to her. "You're not the one who snatched me off the street." He looked around the room. "Is this where the two Crown agents I sent out asking questions were murdered?"

Bill hissed in a breath, his head jerking in Luke's direction. Charlotte saw Luke give a tiny shake of his head, then point down the stairs.

Bill moved quietly and fast for a man of his size. He took the stairs without saying a word. They were all silent until they heard the door she'd locked behind her in the study below open and then close.

"If you sent the first lot, what's to say you didn't send the second?" Luke propped himself up against the center wooden support of the room.

"I didn't need to. I've had a chat to Miss Raven since my men's . . . disappearance, and she told me what I wanted to know."

Luke looked across at her then, and she stared back.

His eyes narrowed. "So, you work for the Crown. And you send your agents to make personal inquiries for you?"

"It was a private arrangement, paid for with my own funds, on their time off, but that doesn't make their murder any less serious. They were agents of the Crown, and there will be an inquiry."

Luke sneered. "I'm not worried about that."

"No," Edward said. "I don't imagine you are."

Charlotte heaved a deep sigh, and both men looked at her, challenge and dislike for each other still reflected in their eyes. "I'm tired. Luke, until you give back that letter, it's pointless to talk, unless you two like snarling at each other. Time to go." She looked pointedly at Edward.

Luke's head jerked at that. "What do you mean? You're not leaving with this nob."

His voice was imperious. Incredulous. As if Charlotte was contemplating something beyond the pale. He couldn't have sounded more like a disapproving denizen of the ton if he'd tried.

Charlotte snapped. She almost heard the sound inside her as her patience finally gave. She had Luke by the front of his shirt before she even understood what she was about to do. She jerked him down, so he towered over her less, and she was so angry, not even the almost comical confusion and disbelief on his face could slow her down.

"I have had *enough*. Enough of being spied on, enough of worrying that any man I look so much as sideways at will find himself robbed and beaten before morning. I have given a lot to you, Luke, and while I'm the first to admit you have given a lot back, this has gone too far. I can't do this anymore." Her voice broke on the last sentence, and she realized she was weeping. Weeping like she had done over Luke's broken body when she'd gotten him back from the Hulks. It was as if that same terrible sorrow and pain was back, sitting on her chest like a stone. She let go of his shirt, pushing him away, and he stumbled back, his face white—for once the mask he always wore pulled away by the force of her grief.

"No matter what you've done to me since I left," she whispered, "never once have I wished you anything but free. Anything but happy. Why can't you wish the same for me?"

She groped blindly for the stairs, tears still streaming down her cheeks.

"Charlie." He called her name once, but she shook her head and kept moving.

There was nothing more to say.

# 18

"I want to kill you." Luke Bracken stared at him from the dark corner where Charlotte had shoved him. From the way he stood, breathing hard, fists clenched, he looked ready to take Edward apart with his bare hands.

Edward stood at last, sorry now that he hadn't done so earlier. He was stiff from lack of movement, and from the beating he'd taken. His reflexes would not be as quick as they would need to be. He rolled his shoulders.

"Stay away from her." Luke's voice had lost its cool. It was thick and shaking.

"I won't." Edward stepped away from the chair. "I wouldn't, anyway, but she's caught up in my sister's troubles, and I intend to help them both."

"You planning to marry a grubby street urchin, my lord?" There was challenge in Luke's eyes as he took the first step forward. Challenge and a simmering, righteous anger at what he thought Edward would say to that.

Edward hesitated. He hadn't thought of marriage. He hadn't thought of anything, except that he did not want to leave her alone. "I intend to find out if I do or not. I only met her just over a week ago."

"I've known her since she was four years old. A tiny, thin little thing, eyes too big in her face, the smallest little nose you ever saw." Luke relaxed his hands.

"She's not four anymore." Edward got his fists ready.

"I protected her then, and I'll keep doing it." Luke took a swing at him, the move so sudden he was caught by surprise, his head snapping back under the force of the blow.

Pain danced over his jaw, and he shook his head to clear it as he moved back. "You're not protecting her, you're manipulating her. Imprisoning her." Edward lunged forward with a jab and grazed the side of Luke's face as he dodged. "You're worse than any nob at trying to control her." He panted the words out, stalking Luke around the room, jabbing at him. Sidestepping as he jabbed back. "At least I'm not forcing her to do as I say."

It was as if Luke went berserk. With a cry, he launched himself at Edward, wild, deadly, fists and elbows and knees aimed without accuracy, but with such speed and strength, Edward had no choice but to lift his arms protectively.

As suddenly as it began, Luke stopped, crumpled to the floor, skin ashen, with sweat beaded on his brow and upper lip.

Edward knew that look. He'd seen it on his mother's face enough times before she died. "Where are you hurt?" He hadn't thought Luke had bashed into anything, and he hadn't connected hard enough or often enough to have caused this.

The eyes Luke lifted to his were so poisoned with hatred, his mouth went dry and his heart beat faster.

Luke clenched his teeth, shifted his body as if to find some relief. "You want to know where I hurt? My hips were smashed when I was sixteen, when I was thrown down four flights of stairs on the Hulks, and a barrel of water was thrown down after me, landing on me at the bottom." Luke sucked in a long, whistling breath of air. "I came by my hatred of nobs the honest way. Didn't like 'em much when they threw me in Old Bailey for hitting out at a nob who backhanded Charlie for smearing coal dust on his Turkish carpet. But when they sentenced me to transportation for stealing some bread a couple years later, and threw me in the Hulks to wait for a ship to take me, well, that's when I got my hate on good and proper." He shifted again, and the pain seemed to ease back a little. "Ever been in one of the Hulks, Lord Nob? Ever even been near one?" Luke laughed, hoarse and weary. "It is how I will always imagine hell. Dark, cold, damp; men crying, rocking, or giggling mad. It is starvation, and depravity, and pain come alive and floating on the Thames in the shape of ships."

Edward stared at him. "How did you get out?"

Luke got his legs under him and pulled himself up, using a table and his massive arms and shoulders to do it. "Charlie got me out. First thing she did when Lady La Di Da took her in was get the money to bribe the watch."

"Were you—?"

"I was almost dead. They probably thought I'd be dead any day. That it didn't matter turning me loose, because I wouldn't live to enjoy it." Luke cautiously moved first one leg, then the other, shaking them out.

"But you lived."

"Thanks to Charlie."

"And Lady La Di Da's money." God knew he wasn't exactly Catherine Howe's favorite person at the moment, but Luke seemed very able to forget who had contributed to his release.

Luke's lips twisted. He finally stood, but Edward saw the pinched look on his face. His pain was very real.

"Your men out there going to stop me leaving?" Edward looked down the stairs.

Luke shook his head. "I'll call down. You can go." He walked to the top of the stairs, and Edward felt a reluctant admiration for him. He refused to limp, but his lips were white with the agony the few steps cost him.

"Boys, let the man through." His voice trembled a little, but Edward heard two *ayes*.

He started down the first step.

"Wait."

He stopped, looked back over his shoulder, and stared at the white envelope thrust in his direction.

"Take it." Luke shoved it at him.

As Edward's fingers closed over it, Luke stepped away, his whole body hunched over itself. His eyes showed nothing but fury, though.

A fury stronger, more powerful than the pain.

In a wave of understanding that ripped any sense of superiority from Edward with the drama and flare of a toreador before a raging bull, he saw that fury had fueled Luke's rise to power; it fueled everything he did.

This was no lightweight opponent.

Edward descended the stairs slowly, aware of Luke's steady gaze on his back.

Luke already knew what the letter said, so giving it up was purely a way back into Charlotte's good graces. Handing it over was less a concession and more the throwing down of a gauntlet.

———

Her heels rang out on the cobbles of Tothill Road like castanets, the staccato sound as fast as the thoughts racing in her head.

She had cried. Shouted.

She didn't do that anymore, her temper and her responses muted through the years. Young ladies did not exhibit strong emotion of any kind, except devotion to their families.

She had certainly not played the lady tonight. She'd always winced at the sound of a raging fishwife, or the corner whore, shrieking abuse. But there was a certain catharsis in saying how you truly felt.

It would make no difference. Luke would still do as he pleased, would not take her into account.

Perhaps, when he'd first come back from the Hulks, when

he'd been more grateful to her, and brooded less over the system that put him there he would have. But not anymore.

He was a different person. It would be astonishing if he weren't.

She realized she was halfway down the street, and Edward was still not out of the gin house.

She slowed, stopped, and turned.

Kit was walking toward her, a limp in his step, and she frowned at the thought of Sammy turning on him for helping her.

They had fought. Chosen sides.

She had put friend against friend. Or Luke had. Or both of them. She rubbed her forehead.

This would have been her world, this street, if she'd stayed with Luke, as he'd begged her. She'd have been watched and guarded so that she would be safe. She would have had to listen to the sounds of despair below in the pit as the poor of Tothill Road made their pitiful kind of merry.

She started back. As fast as she had left.

Luke would say it was no different, her life with Catherine. She was required to walk about with a maid or groom, was chaperoned to every function. Forced to listen to the superficial social lies of the upper class as they made *their* kind of merry.

And he was right.

She smiled at the idea of being a captive princess in the rookeries, or a restrained mouse in the glitter of the ton.

But Catherine's love and generosity had never come with a single string attached. That was what had won her the battle.

She reached Kit, lifted a hand to his cheek, but he shook his head, straightening his jacket and standing tall to show her nothing was wrong. She took a step past him to the gin house, and he made a sound in the back of his throat, as if forcing himself not to speak. Not to advise her against it.

But she hadn't even got her foot on the first step when the door opened and Edward stepped out.

He looked even worse than he had before. There was the shadow of a new bruise on his jaw. And in his hand, he held the envelope.

# 19

"What does it say?" Charlotte sat close to the fire. Ridiculous to have a fire going in midsummer, but she was chilled, and basked in the warmth of it. Little luxuries like these always struck her full force at odd moments. Who would have guessed she'd be able to have a fire in midsummer if she wanted one? "Who is it from?"

Edward swirled the brandy Greenfelt had poured for him, the letter in his other hand.

He seemed to be weighing what to say to her, and she tried to suppress her irritation.

"It's unsigned." He took a sip. Held the letter out. "Read for yourself."

She took it, studied it. Lifted her head, frowning. "'His death is not my fault, whatever they're whispering. I didn't do a damn thing.' And then a little picture of an arrow."

He lifted a shoulder, and she could see, even though he tried not to show it, that the movement was painful.

"It meant something to Luke. I could see it did." Charlotte studied the scrawled note again. The paper was thick and expensive, the hand that wrote it careless, but with a carelessness that could not disguise a good education.

"There is only one death close to my stepfather at the moment that I know of, and that's Geoffrey's. I knew he was lying when he told me he didn't know Emma was here in London, but I didn't think he knew about Geoffrey's death."

"Perhaps he didn't. He didn't receive this note, after all."

Edward conceded the point with a nod that she thought held a hint of embarrassment. "But the writer of this note assumes he does. Declares his innocence. Which begs the question, what is my stepfather involved in that he would know of Geoffrey's death before me?"

"If they're talking about Geoffrey at all," Charlotte reminded him. "We don't know that they are."

"If the death is Geoffrey's, what connection has Luke got to all this? How did this mean something to him? That he's involved with my stepfather and my brother-in-law beggars belief."

Charlotte lifted her head in shock as a thought occurred to her, caught Edward's gaze. "Frethers." She looked into the fire. Thought it through. "It's Frethers."

When she turned back, Edward was watching her with complete attention.

"Luke has a deal with Frethers. He's involved in some scheme with him."

"I agree that's a start. Geoffrey at least knew Frethers, and you say Luke knows him, too?"

She nodded. Twisted her fingers together. "This arrow." She unclasped her hands, held up the letter. "Frethers calls himself Cherub, when he goes out to the brothels. It would fit that he signs his letters with an arrow."

Edward set his glass down with a sharp crack. "How do you know about Frethers? About what he calls himself?"

She looked up at him, surprised. He sounded angry. "I went deep into the stews the other night, met one of the boys he uses. Bribed him for information. I planned to stop Frethers's little habit. By blackmail, if I had to. Luke interrupted the meeting, told me my plans to bring Frethers down couldn't happen." She pushed a tendril of hair behind her ear. "I've tried for the last two days to get more information, but Luke has shut everyone down. I've gotten nowhere."

Edward said nothing. He strode toward the doors out to the garden, then swung back. "Why are you trying to bring Frethers down? I'm not saying he shouldn't be stopped, but why you?"

She realized he didn't know. That Emma had not told him. She wondered if this secret would be the one that finally did him in. Pushed him away. "Frethers tried to rape me when I was twelve. Thought I was a boy. I was dressed like one, and filthy black from cleaning his chimneys. When he realized I was a girl, he beat me in frustration, cracked a rib or two. He would have broken more, if Mr. Ashcroft hadn't heard the ruckus and come in to get me."

Edward had stopped his pacing; he stared at her. "You told Emma about it when you heard Geoffrey had made a plan to send the boys to him for a weekend?"

She nodded.

"Risky, wasn't it? Emma might have been a gossip." His voice was not quite steady.

She raised her eyebrows. "Gossip is one thing; seeing three boys sent off to Frethers without trying to do anything about it is another. I took a chance, because I couldn't do anything else."

"Do you know what business Frethers and Luke are doing together?" His voice was carefully neutral.

She looked at him curiously, then shook her head. "I wouldn't have known they had a deal at all if Luke hadn't tried to put a stop to my plans."

"So we can link Frethers to Geoffrey, to my stepfather and to Luke." He tipped back the last of the brandy and placed the glass on the table. "And somehow, Frethers is afraid someone will think he had a hand in Geoffrey's death."

"It isn't that far from the truth." Charlotte leaned back a little from the fire. "He set in motion the events that caused Geoffrey to lose his wife and sons. Forced him to confront what he had almost allowed to happen to his own children. Even if Geoffrey pulled the trigger himself, one might say Frethers was culpable."

---

Edward climbed the stairs to the main reading room of his club, but for once the quiet murmur of male voices and the click of glasses on high-polished wood did not soothe him.

He had left Charlotte only because Catherine Howe had

joined them, ending their frank discussion. He'd been forced to leave by the rules of propriety, and he had never felt so restricted by them until today.

He had decided that if he couldn't be in Charlotte Raven's company, he would poke at the new problem that was Dervish.

"Durnham." Dervish looked up in surprise as Edward approached him in his quiet corner. He nodded toward the empty leather chair facing him in invitation.

Edward sat, glad they were a little away from the other members. It was long after midnight, but the place was no emptier than usual.

He waved the waiter away before the man had taken two steps in his direction.

"What on earth happened to you?" Dervish's gaze was on the bruises on his face, his eyes wide.

"I had a little meeting with the crime lord I was told killed my men. Neither of us came away looking very good."

Dervish took a sip from his drink, and Edward noticed his hand shook. He looked even worse today than he had when he'd learned Edward's men had been killed while asking questions around Mayfair. There were dark circles under his eyes and his clothes had been thrown on either in haste or without care.

"Did you make any progress, at least?" Dervish asked.

Edward shook his head, watching the way Dervish pretended calm while his foot tapped beneath the table and his fingers drummed on the arm of his chair.

The morning after he'd worked out that Dervish was some-how complicit in the gold smuggling, Edward had hired four men to watch Dervish in teams of two. One man to stay with him at all times, the other to follow anyone Dervish might meet. The other team took over at night.

He hoped he'd offered them enough to ensure their loyalty. There'd certainly been nothing out of the ordinary in Der-vish's movements yet, though. With any luck, the next report would be waiting for him when he got home.

"I learned today that my brother-in-law was shot dead." He had not thought for a moment this would mean much to Der-vish, other than in a general way, but Dervish sat forward so suddenly, he knocked his glass to the floor.

"Shot?"

A cold hand brushed across the back of Edward's neck. Der-vish didn't look shocked, or even surprised. He looked terrified.

"Yes." He leaned back in his chair, watching.

"Do they know by whom?" With a shaking hand, and com-pletely unconsciously, Dervish bent down and picked up the glass. It was the action of a man who liked to clean up his own messes, and it pulled Edward to his side, a little.

"They don't. There is a possibility it was suicide."

Dervish stared at him. "Is that likely?"

"My sister thinks not. There is a chance it was, but she sus-pects murdered."

"My God." Dervish fumbled about in his pockets and came up with a pristine white handkerchief. "She all right?"

Edward nodded.

Dervish nearly wiped his forehead with the handkerchief, then at the last minute leaned down and patted the rug where he'd spilled his whisky.

When he rose up, his face was vulnerable, softer than it had been, and he opened his mouth as if he were about to confess to something.

Edward held himself still, but the eagerness must have shown on his face, because Dervish leaned back against his chair sharply.

They stared at each other.

"You know, don't you?" Dervish kept his voice even. "My reaction to your men's death gave me away."

"Yes." Edward tapped his fingertips together. "I thought I hid my response well, on that occasion. I didn't think you realized I was suspicious."

"I didn't." Dervish gave a short laugh. "I hire people to watch and see if anyone tries to watch me." His lips quirked at his paranoia. "You sent some people to watch me. Gave me a bad moment, before I discovered they were from you. Just got the report twenty minutes ago that they were followed to your house."

"There seems to be a lot of watching going on, right now."

There was a long stretch of silence, during which a waiter came past and replaced Dervish's empty glass with a new one with two fingers of whisky in it.

Dervish looked at it longingly but did not reach for it.

"What do they have over you?" Edward asked. "And who are they?"

Dervish gave a short, humorless bark of a laugh. "I thought at first you knew that better than I. But like everything else with this affair, that was only what they wanted me to think."

Edward frowned. "What do you mean?"

Dervish sighed. "This doesn't paint me in a good light, but I swear they made me believe you were already theirs." He reached for the glass of whisky, fingered the rim, then pushed it away.

"Before I asked you for your help with this gold smuggling puzzle, I was stumped. I was sending out agents to ask questions, getting the customs men to report their findings, but I was nowhere. But it seems even that was too close." He pushed the glass again, so it was out of his reach. "I got a note, telling me certain things about me would be made public if I didn't stop looking into it." He shrugged. "I didn't believe there was anything they could tell. I thought they were fishing, and the only thing I didn't want known . . ." He shuddered. "I thought only two people knew about that. Me and one other. And that person would never say anything for fear of incriminating himself."

"So you ignored it?"

Dervish gave a nod. "I felt encouraged, truth be told. I thought I must be close to something, to force their hand like that. And it also gave me a clue that men in the nobility were not only involved, but actively aiding the smugglers in this affair. My reports were only discussed in the highest circles of government. The chances of someone untitled having access to my progress was minuscule. So I had that, at least. That it wasn't just a number of independent smugglers, who all happened to have the same cargo, it was an organized operation."

"What happened?"

"When they realized their threat had no effect, I got a face-to-face meeting one night on a dark street." He reached again for the glass, and almost lifted out of his seat to get hold of it. Then sank back, empty-handed. "He was not a gentleman, but he worked for a gentleman, would be my guess. A big, muscular man in good clothes, putting on a roughness of speech that he may have been comfortable with but no longer spoke. I couldn't see his face in the dark, and he had me face-first up against a brick wall quick enough anyway. He told me . . . told me what they knew, and it was the secret I thought they could not know." He shuddered. "The way he held me down, the suggestions he made . . ." Dervish buried his face in his hands, and Edward felt the squirming discomfort of wishing himself far away.

Dervish let his hands drop and lifted his head, then continued in a steady voice. "I told him the truth of it. The matter had gone too far. That I was being ordered to place someone on the problem full-time. It was out of my hands. I had to choose someone by the following week, or Whitehall would choose someone for me."

At last he looked up. "The man left me, but another letter was under my door the next morning. Telling me to keep quiet, and . . ."

Edward leaned in close, excitement a hot, sweet rush inside him. "And?"

"They told me to choose you."

# 20

"**M**e?" Edward realized he'd all but shouted, and leaned back in his chair, his fingers stiff and spread out on his thighs, while he waited for the shocked silence in the room to give way and the usual murmurings and conversations to start up again.

Dervish lifted a brow. For the first time since their meeting he was more at ease. Less guilty. "Naturally I assumed they had you already. That you were a plant."

"What changed your mind?"

"You genuinely seemed to be looking into the matter. And I heard from the foreign minister how loath you were to come across to me and leave the work you were doing for him. He told me you said no twice, before he pulled rank on you."

Edward blew out a breath. "I could have been lying. Pretending."

Dervish shook his head. "I've been double-checking your facts."

"You think they have something on me? That one day soon I'll get a letter like you?"

Dervish nodded. "My only question is, why have they waited so long?"

"Because they don't have anything." Edward said. "The only way they could get to me would be through someone else—" He stopped. "Geoffrey."

Dervish stared at him.

"Why did you look fit to faint when I told you Geoffrey had been shot?" Edward asked the question slowly, his eyes on Dervish's face.

Dervish looked at his drink. "That second letter said they had decided that rather than reveal my secret, they would shoot me if I didn't comply. When you said Geoffrey had been shot, the first thing that jumped into my head was that he had been in the same situation as me, and had fallen foul of the men behind this."

"Geoffrey didn't have any influence in London. If he was involved it would be on their side, not ours. Or they set him up for ruin. They may have thought I would pay to save Emma's reputation. It is possible that he was already dealing with them when they sent you that first warning, which is why they gave you my name. They thought they could dangle Geoffrey's misdeeds over me. But if this does involve him, it has to involve one other man that I know of. Frethers."

Dervish gaped at him, his eyes wide with horror. He tried to speak, but nothing came, and suddenly Edward recalled the evening he had come to Dervish and told him what Emma had said about Frethers. How Dervish had reacted on that occasion.

"Frethers is what they have over you, isn't it?"

Dervish looked away, completely stiff.

"You said the only way they could know your secret was if the other person involved had spoken, and to do so would incriminate himself. But if Frethers is one of them, that would explain it."

The silence ticked by in the noisy movement of the common room grandfather clock and the murmur of voices as men discussed business and pleasure in their quiet nooks.

"How old were you?" Edward asked quietly.

Dervish shook his head, his mouth a thin, taut line. He shifted away, almost facing the wall, and did not speak for more than a minute. Finally he turned back, and he was devoid of any emotion. "If Geoffrey is dead, that leaves them with nothing over you. I wonder what they will do now?"

Edward heard the fear in his voice that they would come at him again. While they had thought they could manipulate Edward, they had left him alone, but if Geoffrey had been involved, and was now no longer of use, the focus swung back to Dervish.

"If Geoffrey was their man, this only lends weight to the idea that he took his own life. They wouldn't murder him if his death ends any plan they had to blackmail me. I may have hated the man, but there is no doubt he truly cared for Em. If he realized they were planning to use him to hurt her and get to me, perhaps he did the honorable thing, for once."

"It would be wise to find out for certain. One of us should go up to Holliday's place and ask some questions."

Edward nodded. "I'll speak to the magistrate. Emma and I will be going up tomorrow anyway, to deal with the house and the servants. She doesn't know the extent of Geoffrey's debts, but the estate is entailed, so that's safe. Above that, she thinks there's nothing left. Nothing left of her dowry, either."

"What will you do?" Dervish threaded his hands together.

"I'll pay any debts he has outstanding, and put some money into the estate so James has something to inherit other than a crumbling pile of rock."

"And if the magistrate thinks it was murder?"

"Then we have a puzzle. Unless Geoffrey was being as bloody-minded with them as he was with everyone else. It would have been just like him to tempt one of them to murder, even if it went against their plans."

Dervish began shaking his head, then stopped.

"What?" Edward watched him, watched the play of thoughts across his face.

"I was going to say that it was unlikely. These men have shown themselves to be cold and calculating. And with nerves of steel. To siphon England's gold right out from under their own countrymen's noses—it almost defies belief. But then I remembered they had your brother-in-law as a cohort, most likely, and Frethers." He said Frethers's name on an exhale. "Neither of those two men is rational, and I would characterize Frethers as an egotistical, sadistic hedonist, rather than a cold-blooded traitor. So they are like groups everywhere.

Some are no doubt steady and nerveless. Others are in it for the thrill. And it will be the latter men who give the others away."

Neither of them said anything for a while, thinking through the implications.

"Frethers is the weak link," Edward said at last. He was content, he realized with a start. He'd walked into the club angry, dismayed, and suspicious. But Dervish had told him the truth, and knowing he could trust him again made all the difference.

Dervish nodded, but his face was pinched. Just the mention of Frethers's name could do that to him. "He seems to get away with whatever he does, though."

"Not this time." Edward thought of Charlotte. Of his nephews. And of Dervish, sitting white and stiff where he'd been relaxed a moment ago. "We'll find a way to get to him."

Dervish gave a snort. "How? He obviously has someone in Whitehall in his pocket. And he's one of the richest peers in England."

Edward shrugged, admitting the truth of what Dervish said. "There'll be a way."

Dervish looked at him more closely. "Do I want to know about this?"

Edward shook his head. "I haven't even got a plan, yet." He stood and put out his hand as Dervish rose with him. Shook it, as though they were meeting for the first time.

As he turned away to take his leave, he only just heard Dervish's final words.

"I was fourteen."

# 21

Charlotte stirred her morning tea, sitting alone in the garden in the shade of an apple tree, the summer apples hanging heavy from its branches. The house felt empty without Emma and the boys.

She could have gone with them, if she'd wanted.

Edward had come yesterday to take them back to the Holliday country estate in Kent, and it had been a strangely awkward meeting. Her eyes had gone to the bruise on his jaw, the battered appearance of his face, and she hadn't wanted to look him in the eye.

She was a bad penny in his life. She wished she could take back the flirting she had done with him when they'd first met. Her delight with his complete lack of social veneer had made her lose her head. She recalled the way he'd touched her in the street, and in this very garden, no more than a few days ago, and knew she had stirred something to life that would have been better left alone.

But despite her attempts to avoid him, he had neatly maneuvered her away from his family during the mayhem caused by three small boys and a mountain of luggage, crowding her into the small drawing room just off the hall.

"Come with us."

She'd stared at him in amazement. This was not something to be said five minutes before leaving. This was something he could have broached with her the day before.

He must have sensed her astonishment.

"I don't want to leave you alone." His face was intent. Intense. He seemed to crowd the space around her, and she took a step back. "I know it's late notice, but as I was riding here, I realized I couldn't leave you behind."

She didn't understand. "I have no business there, and I can see Emma would like time to herself. I could help her with the children, but the staff there are familiar to them, more so than I am, and I would only be a burden. A guest Emma will feel obliged to entertain. If I thought I could be of help, I would go."

"I don't ask you to go to help Emma, I ask you to go so that I know you are safe. Under my care."

She had the sense of stepping into a strange new reality. "Under your care?" She choked a little on the words. "You did not understand anything from the other day? That I have a crime lord as my protector? That his men, some of the most vicious criminals in London, watch me constantly?"

He'd swept that aside with a chop of his hand. "There is something going on, and it involves Luke. Either because they were watching Emma and me, or watching Luke, these men know of you now. I don't know if Luke would stop them if they wanted to ask you what you know, or use you in some way."

She did not hesitate. "He would."

He frowned at that, instantly angry. "You have a lot of faith in him."

There was nothing to say to that. She did, and she didn't. But on the issue of her physical well-being, she had not a single doubt. Luke would let no one harm her. "How could they use me, anyway? Use me for what? I don't even know what this 'matter' is."

"Please. Just come with me." He spoke quietly and was in that moment suddenly open to her, so honest, set on his course of action. He took hold of one of her hands.

She drew a sharp breath and saw his eyes go to her neckline as her breasts pushed against the tight bodice of her fashionable sage morning gown.

It was a look of searing sexual hunger, and her cheeks burned at the feelings it stirred in her. She looked away. She could not be in proximity to this man and not want things it would be impossible to have.

"No. I will be perfectly safe here."

He gripped her hand a little tighter, and she thought she saw a ruefulness in his expression, as if he were only too aware that the intensity of what lay between them had played a part in her decision to stay.

"Then be careful while I'm away." He'd lifted a hand to her jaw, his strong fingers holding her so she was forced to look into his eyes. The touch was intimate, scandalous, and yet he did it anyway, with her guardian and his sister just a wall away. A man could be forced to marry a woman for doing something like this, in the world he'd been born to.

In the world she'd come from, it was the most minor of touches.

"What is all this about?" Her face flushed again as she spoke to him in a calm, even voice, because with his hand cradling her head, she'd felt anything but calm. Her heart thundered below her cool silk bodice.

"I'll be back in two days, and I promise I'll explain everything. Just keep aware. Use Kit as a bodyguard. Don't trust anyone."

She'd looked at him with her head to one side, recalling Emma had once said something similar to her. What a different life they had led to her.

He mistook her cocked head for either pique or stubbornness. He dropped his hands to her shoulders. "Promise me."

She raised her eyebrows. "I don't trust easily, and I certainly will watch my back if you say it needs more watching than usual."

He blinked at her cool tone and released her. His eyes never left her face. "You are the center of it, somehow. Without you, I wouldn't have known of Frethers and Luke. Because you have a foot in each world, you've shed light on something the Crown has been chasing for months. If the men behind this find out your role, it may be enough to make them want you silenced."

She stared at him as she turned over his words in her head. "If my only act was to link two men you would otherwise not have linked, then my role is surely over."

"We don't know that yet. There is so much I don't understand, including the why of this. I beg you to take this seriously."

She opened her mouth to answer, but just then Emma called out her name, and Charlotte turned. She stepped back into the hall and through to the front steps, where the little group waited to say their goodbyes.

"You will take care?"

He'd come up silently behind her, was walking just beside her before she realized he was there.

"Yes. It's a lesson I learned very early in life, Lord Durnham. If I don't look after myself, no one is going to do it for me."

He'd said nothing to that, and stepped back as she'd said her farewells and kissed the boys, telling them to hurry back.

He'd closed the coach door on Emma and the boys, swung himself up into his saddle, and waved to her and Catherine. She'd felt his eyes on her like a hot caress, and despite the warmth of the morning, she'd shivered as she turned back into the house.

And now a whole day had passed and she hadn't even been out. A listlessness had overcome her, and she had gone to bed early, and slept late. Her ride this morning with Kit had been short and left her with a pounding head, and now she'd retreated into the soothing shade and light breeze of the garden.

This was a tangled mess.

She could not understand Luke's involvement. It was one thing for Geoffrey and Edward's stepfather to be involved. They were related by family ties, and it was all too believable that they had gone into something together. Frethers, too, she could understand. He was part of Geoffrey Holliday's set, and a man with no moral qualms.

It may have been he who drew Geoffrey into the affair, and Geoffrey took Emma's stepfather along with him. But Luke?

He had nothing to do with the upper classes. Ever.

He hated them, and would do nothing with them that would allow them to profit, no matter how much he could gain by the deal.

There was something off here, and she would have to ask Luke to tell her.

She had no expectation that he would, though.

She took a deep gulp of tea, and it was almost painful as it quenched the dryness in her throat with its sharp heat. She took a more dainty sip and set the cup down, glad that Catherine was with a friend, shopping, this morning, so she could sit quietly with no demands on her at all.

Greenfelt came out of the house, his step as spry as it had been the day she'd met him, so many years ago, and he set down the paper, a fresh pot of tea and some ginger cake still warm from the oven.

The scent of it lifted her spirits immediately. She murmured her thanks and poured the tea, breathing the fragrance of ginger deep into her lungs. She barely glanced at the paper, but a single name caught her attention.

Heart suddenly tight and painful in her chest, she flipped the folded sheet open. Stared at it until the breeze rattled the paper in her hands, tugging at it.

Sometime yesterday, Frethers had been found dead.

There was a subtle sense of relief at Fairlands, Geoffrey's country seat in Kent. Edward felt it in the light steps of the staff, the extra effort of the cooks, and the quick service of the butler.

The estate manager had been almost manic in his delight at Edward's proposed injection of cash, and his threadbare clothing and gaunt look told Edward more than words how close to the bone Geoffrey had been running things.

Now he stood in the magistrate's rooms in Manston and noticed the lack of any real regret in Sir Humphrey's eyes over Geoffrey's death.

"Could have been his own hand," the magistrate said, voice gruff with discomfort. "It could go either way. The angle of the shot could be accounted for if he turned his head as he pulled the trigger, or someone stood close to his right shoulder, just behind him, and shot him."

"It would have had to be someone he knew, unless they crept up on him." Edward saw that the pile of clothing, the gun, and other small items found on Geoffrey's body were lying on the magistrate's desk.

"Couldn't say, one way or t'other." The magistrate pushed the release documents forward for Edward to sign. "No one has come forward. He was found by one of his laborers. The house was empty of guests. Butler said they'd all left earlier that morning."

Edward signed, and waited for a clerk to wrap the items up in brown paper for him to take away.

"There's one thing." The magistrate waited for the clerk to leave and close the door before speaking. He hesitated a moment. "We're not known as a smugglers' haven for nothing here; it's a way o' life. Damn Crown men don't understand how to deal with it, but never mind that. Lord Holliday was—" He fiddled with the quill on his desk. "There's rumors he were dabbling in owling himself. Them owlers aren't people to cross, nor to go in with lightly. If he did either . . ." The magistrate shrugged.

Edward could see he had no sympathy for Geoffrey if he'd been killed because he'd got into bed with smugglers. And he was also prepared to put it down to being the most likely scenario in which Geoffrey had gotten a bullet in his head.

He gave a nod, careful not to show his shock. "How long has the rumor been around? About Geoffrey being in with the smugglers?"

The magistrate gave him a considering look. "At least a year. I didn't do anything 'bout it—no proof, just whispers, y'know. But he had money troubles, that was clear from the way he ran the estate. Many a lord's been seduced by the danger and the profits o' owling, I'm sure."

"I'll warrant you're right." Edward collected everything and took his leave.

He walked out into the small town, savoring the fresh breeze off the sea. He'd never thought about the location of Fairlands in relation to his investigations. Had only connected Geoffrey to the gold smuggling since yesterday. But of course, his brother-in-law's local connections, the location of his estate, would have been a boon for whoever was financing the smuggling of gold guineas from England.

He'd worried over what Geoffrey had to offer, other than a connection to Edward himself, that could have drawn the men in this to his brother-in-law, but this explained it.

Explained a great deal.

Up ahead he saw Emma, stepping from the vicar's large house, her body drawn tight with tension. He raised a hand and she stopped short, waited for him in the road.

"What is it?" he asked when he reached her and held out an arm.

She latched on to it like a limpet. "It's the way they look at me, as if I'm lacking for not sobbing and wailing and gnashing my teeth because Geoffrey's dead." She drew in a long, shaky breath.

"Hush." He drew her down the narrow lane, toward the carriage, parked in the yard of the inn. "That's all in your head. They see you're distressed, and unhappy, and burdened. They think you're grieving him. And they're right. You are."

She was quiet as they entered the yard. He waited for the coachman to open the doors and then helped her in.

"I am grieving. And I'm not. It's all mixed up inside." She fell back into her seat and closed her eyes.

Edward followed her in. He waited for the carriage to start moving, for the noise of the horses' hooves and the rumble of the wheels over the cobbles to create enough noise that they could not be overheard. "Did you know Geoffrey was involved in smuggling?"

She looked up at him sharply. So sharply, there really was no doubt as to her answer. She gave a tight nod. "When I found out, I made him promise to stop it. He said it would save us from ruin, but he wouldn't tell me any more than that. I made him swear he would stop."

"He lied." Edward suddenly wished the words unspoken, but Emma was nodding, her lips twisted in a bitter smile.

"So I discovered. When Charlotte came to tell me about Frethers, asked to speak to me in private, at first I thought she'd heard something about the smuggling." She shook her head. "Instead, she saved my sons, and when I confronted Geoffrey, he told me he hadn't stopped the smuggling, and he'd got into some trouble with a ship as well, something about it sinking with all his money invested in the cargo." She rubbed her brow. "He'd sworn by all that was holy he would stop, but he hadn't, and he had sold our sons to a lech." She brushed a tear from her cheek. "How could he, Edward? How could he do those things? I never knew him at all."

She put her face in her hands, her body shaking with her effort to keep control.

Edward shifted, rested a hand on her upper back and held it there, not sure there was anything he could say to her that would help.

As they entered the long drive down to Fairlands, he could hear the boys whooping and laughing in the distance, and the sound of it seemed to center her. Slowly, the racks of her body lessened and she raised her face from her hands, dug into her reticule, and wiped the tears from her face.

"You never wanted me to marry him. What did you see in him that I didn't?" Emma turned to him, her eyes red-rimmed.

Edward shook his head. "Let's leave it now. It doesn't matter anymore."

She paused and shook her head. "I need to know. I never want to make that mistake again."

Edward shrugged. "I saw an ugliness in him, a sense of entitlement, which I didn't like. I knew his reputation as a gambler, and a risk taker, far beyond his means, and I didn't think marriage to you would change that. I didn't think he deserved you."

She looked at him, her face solemn and serious. "Well, you'll get no objection from me with *your* choice, not that I have any say in it."

He lifted an eyebrow. "What on earth are you talking about, Em?"

"Charlotte Raven." The coach slowed, and she concentrated on collecting her things. "If anything, you don't deserve *her*."

# 22

Charlotte refused to meet Luke back at the gin house. She would not. It was time, for once, that he come to her. He agreed to a meeting in the garden—he wouldn't come into the house.

But when he walked from the direction of the stables, he did so with familiarity and confidence in the dim moonlight. She had a strange, certain feeling that he had done this before. Come here before under cover of night.

She looked up from where she was standing and saw her bedroom, lit up with a warm glow from within, and Betsy's shadow as she made the room ready for Charlotte to sleep in. It was hard to breathe, suddenly. Her chest was tight and her hands shook.

She should've guessed he would keep an eye on her personally. Why hadn't she?

She turned her gaze back to him, and found he had stopped, and was watching her, watching her make the connections. But he said nothing.

He'd been limping when he'd come round from the stables, but he made an effort to walk without one as he took the last few strides to her.

Her fingers trembled, wanting to stroke him, ease the pain. She had been there when it was at its worst and she had never been able to shake the bone-deep empathy she had with him over this.

Falling from a height, lying helpless and in pain with no one to help, had been a fear, a daily, all-too-real fear, for so much of her childhood. He had suffered exactly that, except the irony was it was not in the chimneys he had long before gotten too big to climb, but the narrow, foul stairs of the Hulks.

His gaze met hers, and she could not read him at all. He was so closed, she shivered.

"Frethers," she said.

His eyes narrowed, and he pursed his lips. "I told you to stay out of that, Charlie."

"And I told you I wasn't yours to command. Was it you who killed him?"

The question surprised him, and he slid onto the garden bench beside her. He did not sigh with relief, or show the slightest sign of his pain, and her heart broke a little more. He was ripping her up from the inside out, and offering nothing in return—no kindness, no gentleness.

All for pride. Or it had been, at the start. Now she wasn't sure he hadn't truly become what he pretended to be.

"I planned to kill him, but later. It's inconvenient he's

dead, truth to tell. And I wouldn't have done it like that, anyway." He gave a contemptuous snort. "Shot dead in his library, in an armchair?" Luke shook his head. "I'd have slit his throat in a brothel and taken all his clothes. Maybe tied him up, put on a little rouge or powder." He snorted again. "Or like as not, he'd have been like that already. And I'd have nothing to do but the cutwork."

She hesitated a moment, the image he created tightening her throat, and then she slid next to him, stared up at the stars and the half-moon.

She believed him. He hadn't killed Frethers. "What business were you doing with him? What was enough to make you break your rule and get involved with the nobs?"

He was silent a long time. "They came to me. And I took them up on it 'cause I finally caught wind of something that would make the people hate 'em."

"Hate who?" She turned.

"The upper classes. Like the French. A revolution, Charlie. I saw a chance to maybe move this feeling of resentment that's all round us up another notch. And like the French did, we'll get some real change."

"How?"

"I'm digging a hole for 'em. Sure, I'm making money, but I put every cent o' it back into the rookery. An' all the while, I've kept a record of meetings, and I've written down names, and kept lists of transactions. The newspapers will 'ave a fine story with what I've collected."

"Who else is in this?"

Luke paused. "That's a problem. They've kept it small. Just the person who approached me to start, and Frethers. All the others are just lackeys. I don't know who came up with the scheme. I'll 'ave to wait and see if they send anyone else to me, now Frethers is dead. Just a matter o' time—my initial contact's too old to do the legwork. They need me. And I'd like to bring at least one more down, if I can. One dead peer doesn't make a conspiracy. But two or three live ones? That's convincing."

"How do you know Frethers wasn't the leader?"

He laughed. A genuine laugh, the like of which she hadn't heard since she was much too young. "Frethers was an idiot. There's no way he was behind this. He was the front man." He shook his head, still smiling. "I've 'ad someone on him from day one. Other than me and the trips to the brothels, he only met with nobs. They're in this, up to their starched white collars."

"And what *is* this?" Edward hadn't told her, and Luke wouldn't, either, the other day. She waited while he sat silent beside her.

"It's dangerous to know, Charlie." He shrugged, as if that were the end of that, and she stared at him.

She wondered if it was worth fighting him over it. Edward had promised to tell her when he got back. But how much would he actually tell?

She shook her head. "I'll have to do my own research then." She leaned back on the bench. Closed her eyes in the silence that had been thrown up like a barrier at her words.

"Why?" His voice was quiet. "Why would you even want to look into it?"

"Because I'm involved." She fiddled with the ribbons on her skirt.

"That's not a good enough reason."

She looked across at him, but Luke's eyes were closed like hers had been, his head tilted up to the sky.

"I've been told to watch my back. That I've come to these people's attention because of my visits to you, or because Emma Holliday was staying with me. But either way, I'd rather know what this is about than go around with a vague sense of fear for everyone and everything."

Luke straightened. "Who told you that? Your nob?"

"Yes, Edward told me." She looked him in the eyes. "Those men watching the house, he says it's them—sent by Frethers's associates."

He touched his jacket, and she noticed for the first time that he was dressed like a delivery boy. He never dressed as well as he could afford to, but he never pretended to be something he wasn't.

He caught her stare and shrugged. "Didn't want the watchers to suspect me. So I delivered some vegetables to the kitchen. They'll think I've stopped for a cuppa and a chat."

"So there are still watchers." Something didn't jibe here. Why was Luke tolerating them?

He must have sensed her surprise, because he finally looked at her. "This is a deep game, Charlie. Just stay the hell out of it. Trust me. I won't let the blighters watching you touch you. For every one of them, I've got a couple of watchers of me own."

She hesitated, not sure whether what she was about to say was a secret or not. But no matter what, she couldn't not warn him. "Edward is investigating this thing you're involved in for the Crown."

Luke went very still. "He's investigating it for the Crown." He repeated the words slowly. "And you're only just telling me now?" He threw himself back against the bench in disgust.

"I only found out yesterday morning."

He swore, low and vicious. "You've known a whole day and didn't let me know? He could ruin this, Charlie. I've been working on it for *months*."

She looked back at him without a shred of regret. "Well, I'm afraid I can't read your mind, and your people don't confide in me the way mine do to you."

He swore again and turned from her, looking farther into the garden, down to where the apple tree and oaks spread their branches and threw deep shadows over the lawn. His hands were fists resting on his thighs.

She reached out and covered one with her hand and he flinched. Pulled away.

"I asked you this before, and you said no, but I'm asking you again. Do you not come to me because of what I can't do—can't be—anymore?" His voice was hoarse.

She wanted to weep. She faced, in that moment, the truth that while the harm Luke might do to them was one reason she held back from any would-be suitors of the ton, another was this. This guilt and sorrow, all mixed up, because of how Luke's accident had left him.

"I don't come to you because I'm afraid you will swallow me up." She hesitated. Thought back to the first time she'd answered this, and realized she understood so much more now. Could say it better. "And I have always loved you, but not the way you want, or think I should. Even when we were lovers—could be lovers—I did that for you, not for me. Because it was what you wanted and I wanted to please you." She had been so young, and yet, so, so very old.

He was silent for a long time. "And this nob? What do you feel about him?"

She sucked in a breath. "I don't know." She hunched over.

"You're lying, Charlie. You do know." He spoke so softly, she almost didn't hear him. She closed her eyes and lifted up her feet, hugging her knees to her body.

When she looked at him at last, she found he had gone.

# 23

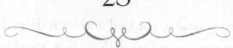

Charlotte approached Edward's house with tense, nervous steps. It was just after ten in the morning, and she was without a chaperone. There was no excuse for this. It was completely forbidden by the rules of etiquette.

That she was breaking with convention disturbed her. In the true way of the converted, she was far more a stickler for society's rules than most of those born and bred to it. She knew each one. Had forced herself to memorize them, so that she would never let Catherine down.

Her lips twisted. And all the while she was learning which knife went where, and the proper calling times, she had also been visiting the stews and bribing guards on the Hulks.

She had to wonder how Catherine put up with her and her strange inconsistencies. She didn't even make sense to herself. She must drive those who knew her to distraction.

She reached the glossy black double doors with gleaming brass handles, taking the stairs carefully so as not to make a sound. She had to make the choice whether to knock or to walk away and pretend this was merely part of an early morning walk that had brought her by chance past his house.

She raised a hand to the bell and let it drop. Turned slowly, and stood for a moment facing the street, thinking.

This was not a good idea.

Not least because she was not quite sure why she was here. To get news of Emma, yes, but that could wait. The thought of him being back, just five minutes' walk from her, had burned like a new penny in her pocket. She had had to see him. And she could not untangle why.

She took the first step down toward the short path to the street, and felt the gentle flutter of air behind her as the door opened.

She stopped. Turned back.

Edward stood in the doorway, and she knew her mouth gaped.

"You answer your own door?" It was the first thing that leaped onto her tongue.

"I wasn't answering my door. You didn't knock." He frowned. "You thought better of your visit?"

She forced herself to remain serene and unruffled. "It is too early to call but I was eager for news. I decided in the end not to disturb you until later." She looked past him, into the hallway, for his butler. "How did you come to open the door at that moment?"

"I saw you approach. From the breakfast window." He

cocked his head to the side. "You seemed very agitated and deep in thought."

She said nothing to that. He could not know the cause of her agitation or her thoughts, and so she was safe. As safe as it was possible to be in his company.

"Well, come in. If you are still eager for news?"

She nodded and he stepped back to give her room to enter, and then led her off the hall into a small, pleasant room in pale yellow and dark blue.

She refused any food, so he poured her a cup of coffee and she sat and watched him butter some toast.

"Frethers was murdered."

"I know." Edward touched the paper in front of him. "I would be interested to know who did it."

"Well, it wasn't Luke. Perhaps Frethers's associates worked out the side game Frethers was playing. Trying to gain access to your nephews by manipulating Geoffrey into a corner. If they worked out Geoffrey killed himself over it, before his usefulness was up, they may have decided Frethers was too much of a free agent for safety."

He stared at her. "How you do you know it wasn't Luke?"

"I asked him. Luke had . . . plans for Frethers. They weren't in place yet, and he's irritated Frethers is dead, if anything."

"What plans?"

But Charlotte was tired of giving information and never getting any back. She shook her head—let him interpret that any way he wanted. "Did Geoffrey kill himself?"

Edward paused in his spooning of lime marmalade over his

bread, eyebrows raised at her change of topic. "Not conclusive, either way."

He seemed to hum with energy, though. He had discovered something on his trip that had him excited. She wondered if he would tell her what it was.

"How is Emma doing?"

He lay his toast on his plate. "She feels guilty she didn't love him at the end. But I hope that passes. She should be back in London in a week's time. I don't think she can stand to stay there longer."

"I am glad she'll be back soon, for my own sake. I miss her. And the boys."

"I think they'll come back here, to this house. I know Emma would love to remain with you, but she doesn't want to outstay her welcome, and she does belong here."

Charlotte lifted her coffee cup to her lips. Took a sip. "You think it's dangerous for me and Catherine if she stays with us, don't you?"

He looked like he would deny it, but then he shrugged. "I can't watch them there as well as I can from here, and yes, I think their staying with you will attract the men who are trying to make sure I don't find out anything that would damage their plans. You and Catherine have nothing to do with it, and if Emma stays here, that will be clear enough."

"You didn't say I had nothing to do with it before. You said I was the center of it. The linchpin."

"You helped me by telling me about Luke and his role with

them. I would never have had that information otherwise, but you don't know anything about it."

"You're right," she said shortly. "I don't."

He finished his last bite of toast and leaned back in his chair, his gaze on her. "What are you planning?"

She shrugged and said nothing. If neither he nor Luke would tell her anything, she would have to find out some other way. Not go looking for trouble—she'd had enough of that in her life already—but she thought she could perhaps get some of Luke's people to give her enough to work it out.

"Charlotte, what are you planning?"

The doorbell rang and Edward rose in his chair. He gave her a look of frustration as his butler answered the door, but he did not go out.

She realized he was waiting to be informed of who was there. He would not invite them into the breakfast room with her there unchaperoned, unless it was someone he trusted. Her reputation would be tarnished.

The butler tapped on the door and opened it. "Lord Hawthorne for you, sir." He reeled back at the sight of Charlotte sitting at the table, and she remembered he hadn't known she was in the house—Edward had opened the door to her himself. "I'm dreadfully sorry, my lord, I didn't know . . ." He trailed off, stricken.

"Morning, Edward." The man who must be Lord Hawthorne, Edward's stepfather, shouldered the butler aside with his crutch and stepped into the room, and Charlotte caught a brief glimpse of Edward's face.

Fear touched the back of her neck with fluttering fingers. She'd never seen someone go so rigidly blank before; his face was a death mask.

"My lord," Edward said, inclining his head, his voice stiff and clipped. "As you see, I have a visitor. Perhaps if you return later, or I can come to you, if you need to speak to me?"

But Lord Hawthorne wasn't looking at his stepson; he was looking at her. He recoiled from her as if she were a venomous snake, clutching his crutch to him as if for protection. "You!"

She felt a drenching wave of terror at the raw hatred on his face. Something was dreadfully wrong. She had never seen him in her life before, but there was no doubt he thought he knew her. Hated her.

Edward stepped between them, his eyes narrowed, the gesture protective and angry. He blocked her fully from his stepfather's gaze. "I didn't realize you knew Miss Raven, my lord."

She craned her neck around him and saw Lord Hawthorne blink rapidly a few times, like a man coming out of a dream. "No. No, I . . ." He swallowed. "I was mistaken. She reminds me of someone, is all. I apologize for my outburst." He was already backing out of the room, awkwardly dragging his gouty foot. "I merely wanted news of Emma and to hear if you found anything more about Geoffrey's death. You can inform me later, at your convenience." He left, his walk stiff and jerky, and Edward watched him exit the room and then followed him out with cool speculation in his eyes.

Charlotte stood, more disturbed by the encounter than she

cared for. She was shaken to her core, her heart beating too fast, her chest tight.

She heard a low murmur at the door, and then it opened and closed again, and without knowing why, she stood from the chair and shrank back so that Lord Hawthorne could not see her from the path as he left.

She pretended interest in a painting near the door, well out of sight.

"I'm sorry about that."

Edward appeared so quietly and suddenly in the doorway, she jumped. It was all she could do not to put a hand to her heart.

She said nothing. She didn't trust herself to speak.

"You're afraid." He said it slowly, watching her from just a few steps away, and she tried to draw a sense of proportion and normalcy around her, like a comforting cloak.

"Just surprised." Her voice came out less sure than she'd intended, and she tried again. "He seemed so angry, so shocked. I wondered who the person is I reminded him of."

"You're sure about that?" Edward's words were sharp, and she could hear suspicion in his tone. "You've never met him or seen him before."

She gasped.

There'd been a time when nothing could have forced a reaction from her she didn't want others to see. For driving her to lose that, as much as for the insinuation he was making, vague and sordid, she pulled herself taller and walked past him.

"Good day to you, Lord Durnham. I can see myself out."

As she passed him, head high, deliberately not looking

at him, he grasped her by the arm and swung her around to face him.

For a long moment she looked straight at him, and realized, over the high-pitched whine that had started in her head, he was breathing as if he'd been running.

He pulled her closer and kissed her, his mouth coming down on hers, his hand cupping her head, tilting it at an angle.

It seemed to last a second, and a lifetime at once, and in that time, something stamped on the fingertips she was using to hold on to her perspective and her heart, and she fell.

As she did, she wrenched herself away from him and backed away, as if he were a dangerous animal. And as soon as she was out of the room, she turned and fled.

## 24

L ady Crowder hosted a good ball.

Charlotte eyed the swirling couples on the dance floor, a whirl of color and energy.

Even if she and Catherine hadn't already accepted this invitation some weeks before, and even if Lady Crowder weren't one of Catherine's few close friends, Charlotte would have enjoyed the outing.

She found her lack of focus, the way she'd spent the day floating with no clear purpose, disturbing and inexplicable.

However hard she'd tried to behave as though things were normal, she knew Catherine was worried about her.

At least Edward would not be here. She knew he never attended balls, and yet she had twice caught herself watching the entrance to the ballroom.

Could she both want to see him, and wish she never saw him again, at the same time?

That sounded like the thoughts of a madwoman.

She idly tapped her fan against a satin-gloved hand and watched the play of courtship and avoidance in the dancers before her.

A girl, fresh from her family estate, youth and self-consciousness clinging to her as close as her white silk gown, leaned away from the baron holding her in too tight a grip and looking too often at the scoop of her neckline.

Another couple twirled past—stars in her eyes, nothing in his. Charlotte wondered if he felt nothing, or refused to show it, if he did.

"Not dancing, Miss Raven?" Lord Tavenam slid beside her, crowding her against the wall.

Charlotte frowned, lifting her fan and opening it before her, as a sort of barrier. She would have laughed at the pathetic gesture, but the action felt all too real. The fan was better than nothing.

She lifted her shoulders, because, clearly, she wasn't dancing. She stared at his face, trying to read him. They had been introduced, and she had seen him at these affairs for the few years she had been about in society.

He had never sought her out before and she knew he was married. She waited for him to explain his approach.

"Not very talkative, either, I see." He made no attempt to prevaricate or speak politely, and she raised an eyebrow.

"I hear you were acquainted with Lord Holliday," he said after another pause.

"I'm a friend of his wife. I didn't know Lord Holliday at all."

He cleared his throat, and she couldn't tell if he had expected this answer or not. "You're a friend of Lady Holliday's brother, too, way I hear it. Lord Durnham?"

She inclined her head, still scrambling to work out where this was going.

He gave a sly grin. "More than a friend, actually. A very *close* friend."

She blinked. Her mouth fell open in astonishment. "I beg your pardon?"

He reared back a little, confused at her surprise. It was as if he'd expected another reaction altogether. "Holding each other in the street, Miss Raven? I think that suggests a different level of acquaintance than merely friends, don't you?"

Charlotte thought back to the day when they had bribed Twigs to tell them who was having them followed, and the way Edward had slid his hands into her hair, held her close to him in the road outside her house. She felt her cheeks heat at the thought.

Anyone could have seen them, it was true, but most likely if a gossipmonger of the ton had, she'd have heard about it already. She took a risk. "Your watchers reported that, did they?"

He narrowed his eyes. "We know all about you, Miss Raven. And if you don't do as we say, I'm afraid Lord Durnham will know about you, too. Everything."

She stared at him blankly. They were blackmailing her? How unfortunate for them it was with secrets she had already told.

And finally, she realized, she was face-to-face with one of the mysterious men Luke and Edward were so concerned about. No matter what, now she would have to find out what this was about. They had forced her to it.

"And we won't stop with Lord Durnham." He watched her, searching for a sign of dismay. "The rest of the ton will learn it, too. You will be a social pariah."

That threat held some power, she conceded. Not for herself. She felt an inexplicable relief at the thought of being beyond the pale in society. But Catherine would feel it. Would be made unhappy by it, and she did not want that. "What is it you know?" Charlotte wondered if his answer would give her some clue as to who had blown on her.

She had never asked any of her friends from her days in the rookery to keep quiet about her past. It was an unwritten rule from where she came from that no matter what, no matter the crime, you didn't blow the gaff on one of your own.

It jolted her to realize some may no longer consider her one of their own.

"Your mother," he hissed, seemingly goaded by her lack of reaction. "The bastard daughter of a whore. Lady Howe must have been mad to take you in, and how she came to, I can't imagine."

Charlotte's mind raced. His words shocked her, jolted her more than he must realize. She had thought he would bring up her work as a sweep, her association with Luke, but her mother? Yes, her parentage was just as damning, but it had been so long since she'd thought of her mother. Of all the things to make a scandal with, her mother seemed the least of it. There were far bigger fish to fry, when it came to her, but Tavenam had not mentioned them.

This did not smack of a rookery betrayal. It held a very upper-class taint.

"What do you want from me, in exchange for your silence?" she asked.

Her cool tone seemed to infuriate him. His face turned a dark puce, and he puffed like a pair of bellows. "You're a cold little number, aren't you? We want to hear whatever Lord Durnham has discovered regarding a certain matter he's investigating. We want his notes on it copied, we want his thoughts on it conveyed. Everything that he tells you, we want to know."

At last Tavenam got a strong reaction from her. She took a step back and bumped against the pale gold silk-covered wall. Anger pricked her, sharp and hot. Again, it was not what he was expecting.

"I cannot give you that which I have no access to." She spoke clearly. "I have only been to his house twice, once with his sister, and this morning, to hear news of his sister, and both times, I was never left alone, and certainly didn't have access to his notes. He does not discuss any matters of his business with me; in fact he refuses even to admit that he works for the Crown." She lifted her hands before her. "How can I be of any help to you?"

Tavenam sucked in a breath through his teeth. This was not what he wanted to hear. "Find a way. Use what charms you have, allow him to take you to bed, I don't care. If you want to keep this life, Miss Raven, you will have to work for it, whatever that work entails."

"Charlotte?" Catherine's voice cut through Tavenam's low-pitched diatribe, startling him. "Lord Tavenam, you seem most worked up about something. Whatever can it be that you disagree with my ward so strongly about?"

Tavenam stepped away from her, sent Catherine a violent look, and stalked away without responding.

Charlotte watched him go, watched him carefully reconstruct his habitual air of bonhomie as he made his way to a group of men standing beside the card room.

Were they part of this, too? Or merely his acquaintances? She made a note of those whom she knew or had been introduced to.

"What is it?" Catherine pitched her voice low. "He looked ready to kill you. I'm sorry I left you alone so long. I was too busy chatting with Lady Crowder to notice what was going on."

This always surprised her, Catherine's willful habit of seeing her as a well-brought-up lady of the ton. A woman who would have fainted dead away after a conversation such as she'd just had with Tavenam. A woman who needed a chaperone. Despite herself, she smiled.

"Stop that." Catherine drew her farther away from the dance floor.

"Stop what?"

"That pitying way you have of looking at me, when you think I'm being foolish in protecting you. You deserve the same respect and protection as every other woman here. Never forget that."

Charlotte lifted a hand and touched Catherine's face, sorry that she was wearing gloves and could not do it skin to skin. "I love you, Catherine."

Catherine made a little hiccup of sound and fumbled in her reticule, then brought up a handkerchief. "You always surprise me, Charlotte. You have given me more than I have ever given you, and you must never forget that. *Never.*"

There was a stir at the entrance to the ballroom, and Charlotte glanced over Catherine's shoulder to see what it was about.

Catherine gave a tiny sniff and dabbed at her nose. "Now what did that horrid little man say to you?"

"I'd rather not worry you with it," Charlotte said, frowning at the knot of people that had formed by the door. "I can sort it out without your having to . . ." She trailed off.

Breaking free of the crowd, shaking them off like a dog shaking off water, was Edward.

And as he walked straight toward her, she suddenly wondered, who in the ton had been talking about her past?

She had only told three people of good society—Catherine, who would never say anything; Emma; and Edward himself.

How had Lord Tavenam gotten his information?

# 25

Edward shrugged off the crowd and saw Charlotte standing to one side of the dance floor with Lady Howe. She was watching him with that cool look of hers.

She was in a pale blue gown with white satin gloves, her hair piled high on her head in a complicated style. His very own Ice Queen, in this, the hottest summer in London he could remember. The reserve and detachment on her face was certainly a bucket of cold water.

He almost stumbled, and wondered if the floor could be uneven.

The way she stood, the look in her eye, made him want to grab her again and kiss her until nothing was left but supple, warm compliance.

It had not gone that way this morning, but that had been on the heels of the angry insult he had thrown at her, and he hoped—prayed—that she had wrenched herself away and ran out of anger, not revulsion or disgust.

He had a chance with anger.

She and Lady Howe waited for him, and the look on Lady Howe's face was so set, he almost stumbled again. The lady looked like a tiger with a threatened cub, and as dangerous.

"Ladies." He bowed.

"Lord Durnham." Lady Howe eyed him with displeasure, and Edward could tell she was thinking about the last conversation they had had together, where he had insulted Charlotte and Lady Howe had come to her defense. "I will speak plainly. Charlotte has been inveighed against once this evening, and I will not have it again."

He narrowed his eyes. "By whom?"

Charlotte grinned at him, her haughtiness momentarily gone. "Only you can insult me, and no one else?"

"No, not even me."

The music started up, a quick polka, and he indicated to the dance floor. "Would you dance with me?"

Charlotte hesitated, and then shook her head. "I have not had much practice, I'm afraid." But it wasn't that. He could see she was lying.

He stared at her.

"Lady Crowder is beckoning me," Catherine said with exasperation, and Edward turned. His hostess was indeed trying to attract Lady Howe's attention. "I'll be back in a moment." With a dark look at him, Lady Howe moved away, and Edward realized Lady Crowder would be wanting details of why Edward had decided to come to her ball after he had refused every other invitation for the last five years.

"Why don't you want to dance with me?" he asked Charlotte, seizing with both hands the precious seconds Lady Crowder's curiosity had given him.

His question forced a surprised laugh from her. Then she narrowed her eyes, the Ice Queen again. "You would dare ask me that? After what you suggested this morning?"

He took her hands in a movement so fast she did not have time to draw away, and drew her close. "I'm sorry."

She tugged her hands free and fiddled with her fan, but did not flick it out.

"Apology accepted. Your stepfather did seem very shocked and afraid. Even I was racking my brain to remember if I knew him."

He was glad she hadn't implied his apology should also be for the kiss. He would never apologize for that.

"The question is, who did he think you were?"

She said nothing for a time, turning to watch the couples on the dance floor. When she turned back to him it was with steady, serious eyes.

"Have you been talking about me? To your friends, perhaps?"

He frowned. "No."

She watched his face, as if to discern the truth from it. "Do you know if Emma has?"

He shook his head. "Not while I was with her." The music

came to a stop and they remained silent until it started again. "Why do you ask?"

She flicked her eyes briefly in the direction of a small group of men. One of them was staring at them, then turned away, pretending disinterest. "That's Lord Tavenam." She spoke in a quiet murmur, and he bent his head to hear her better. "He just tried to blackmail me, with the threat of exposing the circumstances of my birth to you specifically and the ton in general. I have only told three people in these circles the truth of that—Catherine, Emma, and yourself."

Much as he wanted to look in Tavenam's direction, he forced himself to turn his back, to face Charlotte fully. "What did he want for his silence?"

She looked down at her fan, flicked it open and shut. "He wanted me to report on everything you know about the affair you are investigating. He told me to copy your notes, relate every word you spoke about it to me."

He almost turned then, but managed to keep his gaze on her. "How were you to get it?"

"I asked him the same." She smiled up at him, a hint of a blush on her cheeks. "He told me to let you take me to bed, if that would do it."

He could not hide his shock, and the fierce, hot anger that washed over him. And beneath it all, an intense interest in doing just that. Taking her to bed. He should be ashamed of himself, but he found that shame was the last thing he felt.

Her eyes widened a little, and her blush deepened. "So what will it be, Lord Durnham? Will it taking sleeping with you to finally discover what this is all about?"

---

C harlotte watched Edward's fists curl, and she could feel the control he exerted on himself not to turn back to Tavenam. There was violence in his eyes.

She had also seen a brief, heart-stopping flash of lust when she'd asked her question, and however angry he was at Tavenam's suggestion, he clearly would not turn her away from his bed if she wanted to go to it.

She had never wanted a man before. Not even when she'd become Luke's lover. She'd never enjoyed it, had tolerated it only because it was what he wanted from her, and seemed so little to give for all he had done for her.

Since he'd been taken to the Hulks, she'd never been with another man, had never considered it, until now.

She swallowed hard at the thought.

"You suspect either Emma or myself of betraying you? Why not one of Luke's people, or your servants?"

"It could be them, but the way he spoke, only of my mother, and mentioned nothing about my time as a sweep, or Luke's lover . . ." She shrugged. "It seemed a very upper-class outrage, to me. If I'd been snitched on from the rookeries, it would have been more detailed."

He looked at her thoughtfully.

She cleared her throat. "I don't think you told him yourself; he wouldn't have threatened to expose me to you if he already knew that you know my secrets. That is where his whole plan fell down from the start. But if you or Emma had told a close friend, and they had passed the information along without mentioning you—that occurred to me as a possibility."

"I haven't told anyone. Neither has Em. She owes her children's well-being to you, and she would never betray you." He checked himself in an unconscious move to look at Tavenam again. There was something primitive in the way he held himself.

"What will I tell him?" She didn't need to say who. "He threatened to tell everyone, not just you. I wouldn't care, but Catherine would, and I don't want her hurt."

"What I can't understand is why I was part of the threat in the first place."

She twined her fingers together. "Their watchers saw you holding me in the street the other day. They think we are lovers, or that I am interested in being your wife or your mistress. They made a guess I would not want you to know my past." She shrugged. "But they are obviously not sure enough, because they threatened me with the ton in general, as well."

Edward indicated the open doors to the terrace, which let in the sweet scents of jasmine and rose to the hot room. "Let's talk." He edged her toward the doors as he spoke. "I hadn't wanted to involve you, but it's too late now."

She looked up at him, refusing to move.

"Hurry. Lady Howe will look this way any moment, and we will have no time alone if she has any say in it." His smile was rueful.

She tried to find Catherine in the crowd. "If my guardian wouldn't approve, we should stay here."

His eyes widened in surprise, then his lips quirked in reluctant humor as she gave him a small, cheeky smile and placed her hand in his, and allowed him to take her out onto the terrace.

As she stepped over the threshold, she turned slightly and caught Tavenam's eye. He gave a satisfied smirk, and it was as if a slug had crawled over her skin.

Edward tugged her into the shadows, and his touch centered her again. "You almost had a second apology from me. I thought you were serious about pleasing your guardian."

She hesitated. "You make me think we should return, because I *am* serious about pleasing her. Always. I would be a whore or a beggar but for her, Lord Durnham. She saved me and Luke both, and I cannot forget that, even though she begs me to. But at the same time, I find myself doing things, like now, standing out on this terrace with you when I know she'd prefer me to stay within, or I walk down to the rookeries late at night and keep company with criminals." She shrugged, suddenly sadder than she'd been for a long time, weighed down. "I'm a worry to her, and I can't help myself. I am too old for my years, and have been too long my own person."

He did not say anything to that, no platitudes or trite words, and she felt the same sensation she had this morning, that her hold on something, herself, perhaps, had been dislodged and she was falling.

She leaned against the balustrade to stop the vertigo, and

looked out onto the garden, lit with lamps down some of the paths, and with lights hanging in the branches of some trees.

It was magical.

"Do you think Tavenam's cronies are in this, too?" Edward leaned next to her, so close she could feel his heat and the material of his jacket brushing her satin gloves. A woody green scent of soap came off him. She remembered that scent from the first time she'd been in his house, waiting for him and Emma with the boys in the hallway. She'd wondered then if he had come straight from his bath, because it was so strong.

She inhaled it deeply and tried to recall the question. "No. Or if they are, they have more control than I'd give them credit for."

"What do you mean?"

"He'd just suggested I prostitute myself to you to get the information he wants. But none of the men he joined afterward so much as looked back at me, let alone leered. And it is my experience, when men think you can be had for a price, they look you over to establish if they could pay it themselves, and if they'd want to if they could."

"My God, you think little of us."

She did not respond, but she did look at him sidelong, and he leaned farther over the balustrade and hunched his shoulders. "So, most likely it was only him." He conceded her point grudgingly.

"Am I finally going to find out what this is about?"

"Yes." He sounded angry. "And you won't have to prostitute yourself to me to do it."

Oh, she had hit a sore spot with that comment. Drawn blood, even. She gave a mental shrug. She had only spoken the truth. And it made her head clearer to think he was angry with her; better that than how he'd been a little earlier. Apologizing and holding her hands.

She felt the prick of goose bumps in the warm night air. "Can we start with what you do for the Crown?"

"I work on projects or help develop policies. And my involvement is secret. While no one realizes my role, I can ask questions, sound people out, and come and go from various offices without raising suspicion. Not one of my friends and none of my family know, and that is the way it needs to stay."

"So no teasing you about your role over tea and cakes?" There was a touch of laughter in her voice.

"I'd appreciate it." He shifted toward her, keeping his voice very low. "People are smuggling gold guineas out of England. Not just a few, but sometimes as much as twenty thousand at a time."

She turned slightly as well, leaning on her elbow, so they faced each other like two turtle doves. "That doesn't sound good for England."

"It's not. We don't know the exact effect it will have on the economy, but with gold at a premium, and the current recession, the law prohibiting guineas leaving the country has never been more important. The gold in the guineas themselves is worth more than the guineas. Give a Continental banker a guinea, he'll give you more than a guinea back, the current gold price being what it is. It sounds like a lucrative and almost risk-free way to make money. Except that it's illegal, and we're at war, and so nothing is risk-free. We can't understand where these guineas are going. If the French catch the smugglers, they'll lose everything. There's obviously something about this plan we don't understand."

"And it's the work of one group? Tavenam's group?"

"My colleague and I have found overwhelming evidence of a single group directing most of it. There may be a few rogue operators, but the overwhelming number are too consistently lucky, and too well spaced, to be anything but organized." He looked back at the ballroom. "Tavenam made a mistake tonight. He wasn't even close to being in our sights until now."

Charlotte followed his gaze. "Tavenam would never believe I would come to you with the truth, and out him. It would be beyond his comprehension. Of course, when they don't need me anymore, I will have to be silenced like Frethers and Geoffrey, most likely. A loose end to be tied up." She heard him take a sharp breath. And then she could not help the devil inside her that said: "He thinks I'm out here getting to work on you like a good little girl. Worming my way into your bed."

He made a choking sound. "I doubt that."

His words drew her up in surprise. "Why do you doubt it?"

"Tavenam knows I never attend balls, but not only have I attended this one, I have spent my time here with no one but you. I think he's quite aware, as is everyone here, that you don't need to worm your way into my bed, Miss Raven." He stepped away from her. "You need only crook your finger and I would be ripping your clothes off your body."

There was movement at the doors, and she turned. Saw Catherine frowning at them.

Edward bowed formally to her. "We will have to speak later. May I call on you tomorrow?"

She must have murmured a yes, because he was suddenly gone, and she turned slowly back to face the garden.

She sensed Catherine beside her. "What did he say to you?"

She shook her head. "We talked about things that concern Emma's husband."

"That's not all you talked about." Catherine sighed.

"No." Charlotte tugged a little at the shoulder of her suddenly constrictive dress. "That is not all we talked about."

She lifted her face to the cooling breeze, and marveled at the sweet, painful burn of desire.

# 26

Edward approached Dervish, who was sitting in his usual corner at their club but rose from his seat.

"When I told you you should be attending more balls, I didn't mean for you to create such a scene you are more or less considered leg-shackled to Charlotte Raven." Dervish spoke very low as Edward stepped up to him. "My guess is you only left Lady Crowder's two hours ago, and already the gossip is everywhere."

Edward recalled, with great clarity, why he never attended balls. He should have had more self-control. Chased Charlotte down somewhere less public.

"Come, let's take a stroll outside. The interest in you is too strong for us to have an uninterrupted talk here." Dervish set down his almost full glass.

Edward nodded. He liked the idea. The thought of a walk was far more pleasing than sitting under the curious, avid eyes of his fellow club members. "There's a bet about it already?" he asked as Dervish retrieved a small leather case from beside his chair.

Dervish snorted. "What do you think?"

"What is the bet?"

"Whether you'll propose, or simply make her your mistress."

Edward stood dead still while shock took a smithy's hammer to his heart. "Why would anyone think she'd agree to be my mistress?" He spoke quietly, but Dervish wasn't fooled and checked his progress toward the door.

The look he sent Edward was sharp. "There is nothing to suggest she would. You're right, it's an odd bet to make."

"I'd like to know who made it." His hands were shaking, and he looked around the room, as if he could discern by merely looking just who would write such a foul thing.

Dervish made a play of clapping him on the shoulder, drawing him toward the door. "Please God, not to call him out?" His voice was as low as he could make it.

Edward didn't answer. He would make some retribution, even if it wasn't an actual calling out. "I'll tell you when we're outside." He negotiated the stairs and the front entrance, tolerating the sideways looks and leers of men who usually minded their own business.

"Well?"

They were outside, but there were enough coaches coming and going for Edward to shake his head again and start walking toward St. James's Park. It was after midnight but there was enough moonlight for the walk to be an easy one, and the breeze was cool and welcome. "Last night we suspected they'd try to blackmail you again, but with Frethers dead, they can't do it as easily. They've found someone else, although I'm not sure where they got their information on her."

"Her?" Dervish had been keeping pace with him along the tree-lined street but now he stumbled to a halt.

"Charlotte Raven."

Dervish blew out a breath. "For a moment, I thought it was your sister."

"It being Miss Raven is as bad," Edward said, teeth gritted, and Dervish snapped his mouth closed with a look on his face that said things had just become clear.

Good. Edward wanted them crystal clear.

"What have they got on her?"

"That's part of the mystery. They've got a lot less on her than they could have. Their plan to blackmail her is their biggest mistake so far. She'd told me the secret they threatened her with revealing some time ago."

"They threatened to reveal her secrets to *you?*" Dervish asked, confused.

"To me, and then for good measure, to the rest of the ton." He shrugged. "They think she wants to become my wife. Which was their first mistake. And their second was thinking that she would never tell me the truth about herself."

"I don't understand."

"It is I who want her, not the other way around." Edward found saying it wasn't so hard as he thought it would be. "And she is not ashamed of her secret. She has kept it because she knows it will hurt Lady Howe if she is shunned by society, but I have known it for nearly a week."

"How did they approach her? Does she know who it was?" Dervish did not ask what the secret was, and Edward felt the first stirrings of real camaraderie for him.

"She knew him, all right. He approached her at the ball, in full view of everyone." Edward sent Dervish a slow, satisfied smile. "Lord Tavenam."

Dervish was speechless for a moment. "They must be desperate to be so brazen."

"Or too self-assured. Or both. We certainly never had Tavenam as a possibility, did we?"

"I certainly didn't." Dervish was rubbing his hands. Then he stopped again. "What did they want Miss Raven to do?"

Edward clamped his lips together and had to breathe through his nose as the rage flared in him again, replacing the smug satisfaction he'd had a moment earlier at knowing Tavenam had handed himself to them like a willing sacrifice. "They wanted her to report my conversations about the smuggling to them, to copy my notes, and generally give them as much information as she could find on the business from me."

"Do you talk to her about it?" Dervish asked, surprised.

"No, I don't. When she told Tavenam this, he told her if she couldn't do it another way, then she was to insinuate herself in my bed, and get the information from me that way."

"Ah." Dervish looked back at the club, although it was far behind them now. In fact, they were crossing the street into the park itself. "This is about the bet?"

"Yes." Edward wondered at the stupidity of it. Whoever made that bet was trying to profit from forcing a woman to another man's bed. His bed. Charlotte Raven's reputation was unimpeachable. It beggared belief that someone could have made that bet without knowing what Tavenam had instructed her to do. The timing was too perfect.

It made him sick, even as he was grateful for the man's greed. It would mean he was as good as caught, along with Tavenam.

"That is the coldest thing I've ever heard." Dervish's voice was weak with shock. "If you do want to call whoever made that bet out, I'll be your second."

Edward smiled bleakly. "I may take you up on that. Perhaps I could ask you to find out who it is? I don't trust myself not to throw myself at him if I do it."

Dervish nodded. "Of course, their thinking she is helping them could work in our favor."

"But ruin her reputation. If they believe she has made herself my mistress to get the information, that won't stay a secret for long. Not with idiots among them betting on that outcome."

"Then you have to follow all the proprieties with her. See her enough socially to make it believable that she's getting information, but nothing that would give even the slightest hint to the scandalmongers."

Edward made a noncommittal sound. "And give her false information to pass on, you mean?" They had stopped just short of a small copse of trees and he tipped his head to look up at the stars. "We would have to be very careful. One slip, one uncovered lie, and either they'll try to silence her, or they'll follow through on their threat and ruin her."

"We can be careful. And vague. They can't argue if she brings them a map of places where we've caught boats in the past, that sort of thing. That will hold them for a while—her giving them information they already know we know."

Dervish was right. But it was not something they could risk for long. "We need to end this quickly. Too much is at stake, and Charlotte Raven has too much to lose when her only crime was doing the right thing."

"I would love to ask you more about Miss Raven, and how she came to be involved in this." Dervish lifted his hands as Edward turned to him. "I said I would love to, but I won't. I hope one day you can share it with me. I won't ask it of you now."

Edward said nothing, and after a while they continued on their walk, taking the circular path that would put them back near St. James's Square.

"There is something I meant to tell you, before I spoke to Miss Raven and heard of blackmailing and bets. Geoffrey was involved in smuggling."

"What?" Dervish stumbled to a halt.

Edward gave a short, decisive nod. "My problem with Geoffrey's involvement was always that it was very uncertain odds I would renege on my duties and lie about my investigation to protect him. No one could say for certain I would help him—it's no secret how much I disliked him. Geoffrey being brought in just to catch me didn't make sense—especially as they put my name forward. I wouldn't be involved in this at all, but for their interfering. But Geoffrey being brought in so they could use his land to pick up and drop off their smuggled goods—now *that* I can believe. And when they heard from you that someone would be appointed full-time to investigate, well, they must have scrambled around for a list of likely candidates and looked at whose connection would be the strongest. Geoffrey was probably the best they could do on short notice."

Dervish started walking again. "Is your sister safe, up there on her own?"

Edward nodded. "She was never involved in it, and I can't believe any of the smugglers would approach her."

"I wondered where they were storing the guineas before they shipped them. On private land with the blessing of the lord of the manor would make sense. There could be some there right now."

Edward conceded the point. "You want to go up there?"

"Yes. I'll take a small team of men with me to search. It will be a victory to find a stash of guineas before they leave the country."

Edward thought Dervish looked better than he had before this affair became a sordid mix of blackmail and murder. Stronger, and far less melancholy. "I'll write a letter to my sister, and tell her to let you have the run of the place."

"Thank you." Dervish looked, for the first time, discomforted. Almost shy.

And if Edward wasn't in the same position of lovesick swain himself, he might have missed the yearning in Dervish's face.

# 27

Charlotte dressed in Betsy's clothes, making sure all her hair was under a cap, to fool Tavenam's watchers.

She didn't leave too early. Things started a little later on a Saturday morning in the rookeries. So much robbing and filching to do on a Friday night, a pickpocket had to get his or her sleep.

Of course, no matter how late they rose in Tothill Road, they were still up hours before the good gentlemen and ladies of the ton.

She took Gary with her, unwilling to expose Kit to more antagonism after his run-in with Sammy, but halfway there Kit swung into step with them anyway, whistling as if he'd been walking with them all along.

She touched his arm, and when he looked across at her, lifted her brows, but he just grinned at her. Gary was more relaxed with him since he'd helped her get Edward out. More friendly.

Kit was hers.

They were on either side of her, sentinels guarding a commander going into hostile territory.

The comparison stabbed at her. When had she started thinking of her old home as hostile? A place where she had to take two men to protect her, and where every face peering from a doorway, every sudden movement, had the potential for danger?

She walked up the stairs to the gin house and opened the door without knocking. They could complain to Luke if they didn't like it.

Down below, in the weak light that struggled into the pit through the filthy windows on the ground floor, a woman swept the debris of the night away, and another mopped behind her, the smell of carbolic and stale gin mixing together in a toxic perfume.

She didn't call to them, or even greet them, taking the stairs quickly as they stopped their work and stared at her and then at Gary and Kit coming behind her.

"Didn't recognize you in that maid's getup. He's no' here." Charlotte saw it was Jess Blackwell, Bill's wife, who spoke now that she was closer and her eyes were accustomed to the gloom.

"Hello, Jess." She'd always liked Jess, and the woman nodded her head at the greeting, her face showing nothing but calm interest.

"Will Luke be gone long?"

Jess shrugged, but there was no insolence or attitude in it.

"Bill and Sammy upstairs, then?"

"Now what'd you be wanting wit' them?" The woman with

the mop thrust out a hip and frowned, and Charlotte recognized her as Flo Jump, Sammy's woman.

"That'd be my business." It came out sharper than she intended, but Flo was everything Charlotte disliked about this place. Excess, and lack of self-control, and a crudeness that grated on her nerves.

And even as she thought that, she cringed inwardly, because she knew the kind of life Flo had had. And no Luke to help her. Not until life had thrown its worst at her.

She started forward to the office and Jess stepped out of her way. Flo made a sound of fury behind her, and she heard the women arguing with each other as Gary and Kit followed her in and closed the door.

"You're no friend to that one," Kit murmured, and didn't need to say which of the two women he meant.

"She's no friend to anyone," Gary said. "Especially if they wear a skirt."

They took the spiral staircase up to the living quarters and Bill met them at the top, relaxing when he saw who it was. He eyed her maid's clothes, confused but too polite to say anything. "Luke's not here. Jess should 'ave told yer."

"She did." Charlotte looked at Sammy, standing near the window, then at Kit. But they were ignoring each other, both trying desperately not to catch the other's eye. "I was hoping you could help me, as he's not here."

"What do you need?" Bill asked, but Sammy put his hands on his hips, in an unconscious mimicry of Flo's actions below.

"She don't get help from us just by askin'." The gaze he

turned her way was narrow-eyed, no doubt remembering the night she'd slipped past him and locked him out of the office. "You an' th' boss are having stormy times, way I see it. Not sure we should 'elp you at all, 'less it's at his say-so."

Gary made a movement, shifting his weight, and Sammy swung in his direction, fists half raised. They stared at each other.

She stepped between them, facing Sammy. "His deal with Frethers. To smuggle gold guineas out the country. I want to know the details."

For the first time, Sammy looked uncertain, lowering his fists. "He told you about the guineas?"

"How else would I know?" She did not feel the slightest remorse at her misdirection.

Bill spoke softly. "Thought it was to be absolutely secret."

She crossed her arms over her chest. "I'm not surprised by that. This has to be the biggest pie Luke ever stuck his finger into."

Sammy and Bill shared an uneasy glance.

"If he told you about the guineas, why'd you need more information from us?" Sammy asked.

"We had an argument before he finished telling me." She sat on the arm of a chair. "What is Luke about?"

"Revenge." Sammy sighed. "Just revenge. But I won't lie to yer. Bill and me, we're nervous o' this one. He's too focused on it. Won't see any o' the dangers, any o' the drawbacks. He's too determined this is what'll sink the nobs."

"We're makin' money like we're printing it in the back

room," Bill said. "It's too easy. We're being led somewhere, and when we get there, I don't think we'll find it's a party."

"You can't put the brakes on him?" Gary asked.

Sammy threw himself onto a delicate scarlet and gold chaise longue. "What would really put the brakes on is you coming back, where you belong." He pointed to Charlotte, bitterness lacing his words. "He's gotten like a rabid dog some days, since you threw his heart in the gutter and stamped on it."

She shook her head. "That's the pain of his injury, not me." And also, but she dare not mention it, the way his injury had stripped him of part of what it meant to be a man. She'd spoken to him about it only twice, but the acid of rage and bitterness leaped behind his eyes each time. She shook her head again, pushing the horror of what had been done to him away, and looked Sammy in the eye. "He's had years to get used to the idea—"

"Years to brood, you mean." Sammy's lips twisted. "And 'e never made a clean break. Neither of you did. He doesn't go a week without seeing you, with your knowledge or not. Followin' you about."

"Though why he should brood over a stuck-up bitch like you, when there's plenty o' lively lasses right here in the stews, I don't know." Flo had come up the stairs, silent even though she limped. She crossed to Sammy's side and slid a proprietary hand on his shoulder.

He shrugged her off. "Watch your mouth, Flo. You know what Luke has to say about bad-mouthing Charlie."

Flo's lips thinned, almost disappeared, and she turned

away, walked to a dresser and fussed with it, dusting and moving bowls around.

"Sammy's right; his temper is partly to do with you." Bill spoke quietly, but with absolute certainty. "If you were 'ere, he'd be better."

"I wish I could believe that—"

"You don't want to believe it, because you don't want to be here, back wi' the likes o' us." Flo shot a defiant look at Sammy while she spoke.

Kit caught Charlotte's eye and jerked his head to the stairs. He was right. It was time to go. They would get nothing out of Sammy and Bill with Luke gone. And nothing but the unpalatable truth from Flo.

Charlotte turned slowly, the weight of her guilt dragging her down. *Was* she so selfish?

"Wait." Bill hunched his massive shoulders, as if to defend against a blow. "We don't know much about it, neither. Just enough to be worried Luke's got in way too deep. Deeper than it's worth."

"Bill." Sammy's word was a warning and a threat in one.

But Bill rounded on him, suddenly dangerous—Luke's weapon rather than the gentle giant he was most of the time. "You don't command me, Sammy Bayton. Give Charlie anything she wants, Luke's told me often enough. And I'm going to do just that."

Charlotte looked between them, saw Gary and Kit held themselves a little more ready than usual.

"Go down to Billingsgate, to an inn called the Barking Ram. Ask for a sailor called John Norris. May be you can get 'im to talk. He's part of it all, did business with Luke sometimes. Organized things for Luke."

"Why would he help me, then?"

"He's out of it, as o' last month. Luke was upset when Norris said he wouldn't do it no more. They exchanged words. My guess, Norris wouldn't mind an injection o' cash now he's off the money boat. It may be he'll sing for 'is supper." Bill shuffled a little in place. "Take the boys with you; it's rough down there."

"Thank you, Bill." She went on tiptoe to kiss his cheek. She nodded to Sammy and Flo and let Gary lead the way down the stairs.

Jess gave them a nod as they passed through the pit and up, still sweeping away the rubbish from the night before.

Charlotte stepped into the street, her eyes taking in all of it. The mud and filth, the dilapidated houses, the woman curled around a gin bottle in the gutter. And over it all hung the stench of hopelessness.

"You're not to feel guilty." Gary spoke so angrily, she jerked.

"She's right, though." She lifted a helpless hand toward the houses on the other side of the street. "I don't want to be back here. Not for anything. Not even Luke."

"Luke's responsible for this." Gary started walking, so fast she had to skip to keep up, and even Kit had to lengthen his stride.

"You know he's not." She couldn't accept that. It had been like this since she could remember. Luke had nothing to do with it.

"Luke could pay some of the people in this street to clean it up. Make it decent. And give them a daily wage, besides. He could move his people and himself to a better area. But he won't. He likes living in the stews. It helps him get his hate on good an' proper when he needs it to justify whatever it is he's planning—looking at the poverty and the stink around him." Gary stopped suddenly. "He's suffered. No question. All of us 'ave. And we shouldn't forget it. But to wallow in the mire, just to remember it—that's wrong, Charlie. Wrong. When he's got more money than 'alf the nobs in the ton? It's evil, almost."

Charlotte looked back down the street and a hot breeze, like fetid dragon's breath, blew in her face.

"Best thing I ever did, takin' the job you offered me," Kit told her. "This place gets a grip on you, don't easily let go. It's all tied up with family, and friends, and loyalty. But holding yourself down ain't the same as helping others up. Like you've done, Charlie. How many from here 'ave you helped up? And how often do you see 'em down here now? Never, most like."

She'd known it, had thought it many times, but suddenly that knowledge freed her.

Luke was bitterly reliving the past, over and over. The pit in the gin house, with its echoes of the Hulks; the grim reality of the stews.

He'd fashioned a new jail for himself, all of his own making. He could escape whenever he wanted, and yet he chose to remain.

But she did not.

She turned her back on it and walked home to Catherine.

# 28

"Lord Durnham, good morning." There was the most minute censure in Lady Howe's greeting as she entered the withdrawing room where the elderly butler had left Edward to wait.

"I apologize for the early call." Edward sketched a bow to her, wondering how blunt, how honest, he could be. "I walked rather than take my carriage, and came by a backstreet. I entered the house through your kitchens so I wouldn't be seen." Betsy, Charlotte's maid, had let him in, and had led him through to the front of the house with speculation in her eyes, but none of the shock or rude curiosity he'd expect in the servants of other members of the ton.

"I agree this is early for a call, but why would you go to such lengths to not be seen? Most people will still be in bed, anyway." Catherine cocked her head to one side and gave him the hard, sharp stare of a thrush contemplating a worm.

"I seem to have caused a stir last night at Lady Crowder's ball. And my name is being linked to Miss Raven's—"

"That isn't *her* fault." Catherine drew herself up, as if ready for battle.

"It is mine, and mine alone." He spoke calmly, soothing the lioness. "But something was pointed out to me last night, something that affects Miss Raven very much, and I wanted to talk to you both about it without causing further harm."

"Harm to Charlotte?" Catherine indicated a chair with a sweep of her arm.

He didn't want to sit, but forced himself to after she had sunk down onto a small sofa.

"Is she here? Can you call her, and I can tell you both together?"

Catherine shook her head. "She is out with Gary and Kit—I suspect visiting Luke, and you're somehow to blame for that, as well, I think." She twisted her lips in a parody of a smile. "You've been nothing but trouble since you set foot into this house, Lord Durnham."

He didn't react to her statement, his mind still spinning over Charlotte visiting Luke the morning after he'd told her all about the guinea smuggling.

"How loyal is Charlotte to Luke? To her old friends in Tothill Road?" If the question was more blunt than he'd meant, he couldn't help it.

Lady Howe studied him, cool and unhurried. "Loyal enough."

"Would she betray . . ." He struggled to think what he

was to her. A friend? A potential lover? An acquaintance? He was torturing himself.

"Charlotte is loyal to all her friends, Lord Durnham. If she considers you as such, she will do nothing to betray you, everything to help you."

He could only hope that was so. And why should she consider him a friend, when it came down to it? What had he done but tear down all the defenses she'd put in place and expose her to the world?

"There is no man in this house," Catherine said into the silence. "So I'll ask you as Charlotte's guardian. What are your intentions, Lord Durnham?"

"My intentions are to remain in Miss Raven's company as much as possible for as long as she will tolerate me."

"That—" Lady Howe leaned back on her sofa. "That was an excellent reply. I think I see . . ."

"See what?" He was watching her for any hint of whether she was pleased or not.

She shook her head. "What is it that you think will harm Charlotte? You may as well tell it to me, and then to Charlotte later when she comes in. I have to go out in fifteen minutes, anyway."

"There is a bet. Entered into the book at my club shortly after last night's ball. It wagers whether I'll propose to Charlotte or take her for my mistress."

Lady Howe gasped, and stood, unable to contain her distress sitting down. "Are you in the habit of taking young unmarried women of the ton as your mistresses, sir?"

"No." His answer was short, as he stood, too. "And as far as I'm aware, Charlotte's reputation is impeccable."

Catherine gave a sweep of her head, as if that went without saying.

"I came to say that I will be extremely circumspect with Miss Raven from today. I will pay court to her, but only in the most proper way, and I think it best we are never alone."

"I don't know I want you near her at all." Lady Howe paced to the window, then turned back to him, fear in her eyes.

"That would only fuel the gossip more, surely? And do her reputation no good, either, if I suddenly gave her the cut, after spending every minute I was at Lady Crowder's ball in her company." What he said made sense, but he had the feeling he was fighting for his life in this conversation. He would not suffer a ban on Charlotte's company, no matter what Lady Howe decreed. And he was not sure which of them would win, if Charlotte had to choose between them. He had a sinking feeling it would not be him.

He would be relegated to the same hell as Luke.

Catherine lifted her hands to her cheeks and thought. Then gave a tiny nod. "You're right. But no more arriving at balls and sweeping my ward out into the garden."

He had to turn from her, had to clench his fists in front of his body where she would not see them, as her words evoked images that set his heart pounding and made his mouth dry. "No." He struggled to keep a guttural note from his voice. "I won't do that again."

"Do you know who made the bet?" Catherine stood straight again, composure back in place.

"No. But I intend to find out."

There must have been something in the way he said it that satisfied her, because she gave a nod and the warm smile she sent him held a hint of the fires of hell. "Good. Make sure you do. And I would like his name, myself."

He realized that whatever plans he'd had paled in comparison to hers. She looked like an avenging fury, and he thought he might like to be present when she meted out whatever revenge she was planning behind those pretty blue eyes.

---

Charlotte came into the breakfast room from the garden, lifting Betsy's cap off her head as she stepped through the open French doors, and came to a sudden stop.

Edward looked up from reading the paper, the movement slow and deliberate, and she noticed a half-drunk cup of tea near his elbow.

"Oh." Her eyes flicked round the room, looking for Catherine, and then settled on him again. "Good morning."

He stood, and she had an urge to touch him that was so strong, she clenched her hands, pulled herself up as tight as she could.

"Lady Howe." His voice came out like wheels over gravel and he cleared his throat. "Lady Howe invited me to wait for you. She had an appointment."

Charlotte nodded. "I'm sorry I wasn't here." She started

taking off her gloves, recalled he was watching her, and tugged them back on. "What has happened?"

"I don't think I've ever seen you without gloves," he said, his gaze on her.

What did it matter? He knew most of her secrets anyway. She pulled at the fingers and slid the thin cotton things off her hands, then draped them over the back of a spare chair with Betsy's cap.

He made no sound, gave no indication of shock. She looked at her hands herself and flexed her fingers. She was used to the hundreds of scars, but it would shock most high-born men or women, she knew. "You were going to tell me why you're here so early?"

He raised his eyes from her hands. "Yes, I was."

"Do you mind if I help myself to breakfast, I haven't had any yet, today? And will you join me?"

"Please go ahead. I've eaten already." He stood, waiting patiently for her to finish adding things to her plate, and only sat when she did.

"What is it?"

But he was looking at her hands again.

"Should I put the gloves back on?" Her words were like a whip crack, jerking him to himself.

"Who did that to you?"

"Not who, what." She began to smear butter on her toast, suddenly starving. "Chimneys, Lord Durnham. Lots and lots of chimneys. I used my hands to keep myself from falling down them, or to shimmy up them, and they were often rough, and sometimes very sharp. And because no one cleaned the wounds properly, or treated them in any way, they healed badly with a lot of scarring." She took a bite of toast and grimaced. She'd forgotten the bramble jelly. She glanced up at his face and with a sigh, held her hands out again. Wriggled her fingers. "They're a lot better for the years of idleness and creams I've had in Catherine's house. You wouldn't have believed how bad they looked when I first came here."

"Where were you? Earlier today?" It wasn't a demand, or harshly spoken, but intense all the same. He held himself stiff, not relaxed in her company at all.

"I was in Tothill Road." She took a sip of coffee and spooned on some bramble jelly.

He did not respond for a moment. "To tell Luke what I'd told you about the smuggling?"

She raised an eyebrow.

"Dammit, Charlotte. Did you go to talk to him about it?" The words burst from him in a hot, bitter rush, and she froze, her eyes meeting his.

It was not anger in his eyes, but pain.

"No. I went to ask him for information on his part in it, to give to you. But he wasn't there."

He did not relax. "Would he have told you?"

She shrugged. "Maybe he would. Maybe not. I thought to give it a go."

Edward seemed to struggle with himself. "Thank you for trying."

"I did more than try." She took a bite of toast again, and

made a sound of appreciation that brought his eyes to her mouth. "Some of Luke's men told me where to find a man who used to be involved until a month or so ago. He might be persuaded to talk if we offer him enough money."

He leaned back in his chair, arms folded in front of him, every inch the arrogant lord. "We?"

She stared back. "All right. Me."

He came out of his chair so explosively, she started and nearly overset her coffee cup.

"I don't want you mixed up in this."

She gave him a look of incredulity. "I *am* mixed up in it. And you won't get within sniffing distance of this character, your lordship. It's come with me, or let me go alone."

He hung his head, hunching his shoulders and rubbing his temples as if he had a headache. "I don't like it that you're involved. I blame myself and on top of it, if anyone catches wind of our going off together to some illicit place, after the bet . . ."

"Bet?"

"One of Tavenam's cronies made a bet in the book at my club last night. After the ball. It wagers how long it will take me to either propose marriage to you, or make you my mistress." His fingers curled around the back of the chair he'd been sitting in.

Her eyes widened. "But—"

"It can only be someone who knows what Tavenam ordered you to do. There is no other reason they would wager on your becoming my mistress—the idea is ludicrous unless they think that is what you will become, on Tavenam's orders."

"Well, that was a huge mistake on their part."

He frowned at her. "Do you understand? One of Tavenam's co-conspirators, perhaps Tavenam himself, has compromised you for gain in a wager. Your reputation has been called into question, and the consequences for you are far-reaching." He spoke sharply.

"I understand." She kept her tone slow and measured. "But it seems to me whoever has made this bet has made it that much more difficult for me to see you easily. Which would defeat what Tavenam is trying to achieve. If I point it out to him, we'll no doubt know who made the bet by waiting to see which member of the ton is murdered next."

He hadn't thought of that, she could tell by his quick intake of breath, and the way his eyes narrowed. "Will you tell him?"

She gave nod. "Without compunction."

She caught him staring at her. "You think me vicious to do it? Knowing a man might die?"

He shook his head. "I think they've underestimated you completely."

"We can go tonight to see this seaman. Wear your valet's outdoor clothes. And don't scare the man off. Let me do the talking."

He shot her a dry look but said nothing.

She couldn't help the grin that lifted her mouth at the corners. He utterly delighted her when he reacted to her like that. Like she was a real person, instead of a dull heiress or a thing to be possessed.

"What went through your mind, just then?" He moved the chair he'd been gripping aside, and she looked away from him, suddenly flustered.

"Just . . . I'd rather not say."

He reached out, leaning over the table to touch her face with his fingers. "Please."

"I . . . thought how much you delight me."

He drew in a sharp breath, and the pressure of his fingers increased. Then he stepped back, his eyes still on her. She could not say what he was thinking, but the fingers that had touched her skin curled a little, and at last he looked away.

He walked toward the open doors to the garden, stopped just short of them, in the pool of warm light that spilled over the gleaming wooden floors. "There is still the matter of your reputation until the bastard who made the wager is dead or the bet retracted. I've already spoken to Lady Howe. I will pay you court, but only under the most respectable conditions, so not a hint of scandal can attach itself to either of us."

"You will pay me court? Under respectable conditions?" She looked from him around the empty room, and he had the grace to flush.

"Obviously, from this meeting on. I walked, came the back way, and entered through your kitchens this morning, no one could have seen me."

She watched him, uneasy. "Then let us get back to 'pay me court.'" She suddenly needed to stand herself, even though he was on the other side of the room. "What does that mean, Lord Durnham?"

"It means what it says." His words were short.

"I need an explanation. Call me an ignorant girl from the gutters, and spell it out."

He was suddenly furious. She could see it in the way his jaw clenched and his eyes flashed. She couldn't understand how one question could have such an effect on him.

"I." He drew in a seething breath. "Pay. You. Court. I offer you gifts, engage you in conversation, take you on outings with a chaperone. And . . ."

"And?"

"And then ask you to marry me." He almost spat it out.

"Because of the bet?" she asked, trying frantically to work it out. "Because someone has wagered on my reputation, you must marry me to save me?" She looked up, startled. "Why? I'm either dead or ruined by the end of this anyway."

"You are not. I won't let that happen. They will not win." He was all but shouting, stalking toward her. He grabbed her arms and gave her a little shake. "This time, the bastards don't win. I win."

"What do you win?" she whispered.

He bent his head and crushed his lips to hers.

# 29

"I hope that shouting wasn't directed at Miss Raven." Lady Howe's dry voice from the doorway forced Edward to lift his head, but he did it in his own sweet time.

The woman was the most damnably efficient chaperone he'd ever encountered.

Charlotte's face was still lifted to his, eyes closed, her cheeks pink and her mouth soft and red from his kiss. He kept his hands on her waist a moment longer and breathed in the rose fragrance that always seemed to surround her.

"It was not," he said at last.

"Good." Catherine stepped into the room, and Charlotte seemed to collect herself, stepping away from him, her eyes widening as he let his fingers trail against her until he could no longer reach her. Taking everything he could.

"Perhaps it is high time you were off home. Before anyone suspects you are behaving with impropriety toward my ward." Lady Howe arched a perfectly shaped brow.

"Of course. You're right." He stepped forward and took Charlotte's hand, kissed it, and for the first time realized why the gesture had come into being. He could feel her fingers tremble beneath the brush of his lips.

"I will send you a note about tonight," she murmured to him, and he nodded.

He bowed to Lady Howe and retraced his steps through the kitchens and out into the narrow lane behind the house, biting into a bun rich in lemon peel and raisins the cook had given him on his way through her domain.

He nearly tripped over the man lying near the alley entrance, half curled up, his hair matted and the sour smell of unwashed body rising from him.

The man cringed as Edward towered over him, and Edward recalled Luke saying the watchers that had replaced Twigs were mostly wounded ex-soldiers. He expected Luke had his eye on them all, but he didn't trust Luke to pass along any information unless it suited him.

"You working for Tavenam and his lot?" he asked bluntly, crouching down.

The man eyed the bun, with one bite out of it, as if he couldn't hear Edward over the sight of it.

Edward held it out to him and he snatched it, his long, jagged nails scratching Edward's hand.

Edward looked away from him as he took the first bite. There was something animalistic about it, starvation reducing a man to the level of a beast.

"It doesn't look like they're paying you enough," he said eventually, when the bun was gone.

"Money goes to me boss. Rogers. He gives us our share, when he gets it. But they aren't good payers. Typical gentry." He spat.

"I'm a good payer." Edward sat back on his heels.

"I ain't no snitch on me friends, mister." The eyes that looked out of the filthy face were hard.

"I'm not interested in your friends, only the men paying you—or not paying you, as it goes." Edward pulled out a coin and the man eyed it.

"Go on."

"If you can get any information about who they are, I'd be very obliged." He handed the coin over. It was only a shilling, but it seemed to have an effect. "All I ask is that you try to find out who hired you and, if they are planning anything against the people in that house"—he pointed behind him—"that you let me know." He paused. "Do you know who I am?"

The man grinned, revealing surprisingly good teeth. "Aye. Lord Durnham. I've been on watch duty at your place, too, a time or two."

"I'll tell my staff to expect you, and I'll leave a shilling a day here in this lane." He looked around. "Under that rock?"

The man gave a nod. "Name's Harkness, your lordship." He moved, getting himself more comfortable, and Edward saw with shock he had lost most of his right arm.

"You were injured in the war?"

Harkness looked up abruptly and then away, hunching over what was left of his arm as if to protect it. "In Portugal, my lord."

"And your friends, your boss Rogers, the ones helping you in watching the house? They served in Portugal as well?"

He gave a reluctant nod.

"I'm willing to offer them the same terms as I've given you."

Harkness scratched his cheek. "I'll tell 'em."

There was something very alive about him, intelligence bright in his eyes, now he had a bun inside him. He would be a good man to have, even with one arm. But he was lying in the gutter, struggling to make a living any way he could, and even that wasn't going well. Edward gave a nod of farewell, rising from his haunches.

Harkness touched the fingers of his left hand to his bare head in salute, and curled up again as Edward walked out of the lane.

Edward looked back, but Harkness lay curled up, facing away from him, looking like a heap of rags—like so much rubbish in the gutter.

———

"I'm sorry, Lady Callaghan, I see Lord Tavenam over there in the corner, and I need a quick word with him." Charlotte smiled at her hostess and made her way to Tavenam at an oblique angle, so he would not easily see her until the last moment.

She'd noticed a change in the general atmosphere around

her tonight. Instead of blending in, as she'd tried so hard to do since she gained entry to this elite circle, she was being watched.

Not by everyone.

News of the bet had surely not spread quite so fast as that, and most of the men would not have told their wives. But it was only a matter of time.

There was a gleam in some of the younger men's eyes. A speculation as to whether they might have any luck with her if Edward failed.

"Lord Tavenam, just the man I was looking for." Charlotte placed a hand on Tavenam's arm, taking him completely by surprise as he stood with his wife and two daughters.

"Miss Raven, ah . . ." Tavenam's affected surprise did not reach his eyes.

Charlotte gave Lady Tavenam a genuine smile. "So lovely to see you again, my lady. Your husband is being very kind to a young woman with no father to turn to, and giving me advice on certain legal matters."

Lady Tavenam sent her husband a sharp look. "So that was what all that gesturing was about last night?" She turned to Charlotte. "Honestly, when I tried to find out what he was saying to you at Lady Crowder's, he wouldn't be drawn."

"How very discreet of him." Charlotte kept her smile sweet.

"Of course." Lady Tavenam stepped back. "Well, we'll let Oscar help you in relative privacy, m'dear."

Tavenam had no choice but to take her arm and walk with

her toward the door out to the balcony. Charlotte stopped short of it, though. They were well away from the crowds here, but still in full sight of everyone.

She would go nowhere alone with him.

She smiled prettily at him and prepared to lie.

"What are you about?" Tavenam hissed through his whiskers.

"Either you, or one of your little gang, has made it even more difficult for me to get information from Lord Durnham. I want the damage reversed. Or at least minimized. I doubt you could completely erase it." Charlotte spoke coldly, the Ice Queen to the tips of her pretty, embroidered rose slippers. Throughout it all, she kept a friendly expression on her face. The look you gave a mark before you picked his pocket.

Tavenam gaped at her. "What are you talking about?"

"There is a wager in the betting book at a certain club in St. James's Square that says I will become Durnham's mistress or his future wife by next week."

Tavenam froze. "What did you say?"

"If you were trying to make it impossible for me to do as you asked, you couldn't have gone about it better. I cannot see Durnham now without a great deal of attention being paid to me, and if he gets wind of this bet, he may think to get as far from me as possible, either because he has no wish for a wife or a mistress, or because he is trying to save my reputation." She crossed her arms in front of her chest. "Either way, it does not help me get anything useful from him. Were you serious when you said you wanted information, or is this all a cruel trick?"

Tavenam stood still, and she realized he was shaking. "How do you know about the wager?"

"One of Lady Howe's old friends is a member of the same club. He informed us, deeply worried about it, and its impact on my reputation." It was an all-too-possible scenario. One that Tavenam would accept. "And you only need to watch some of the men here tonight to see that it is already having an effect."

Tavenam clenched his jaw. "I will deal with this. Make no move toward Durnham for a day, maybe two, and I will make sure this is passed off as a prank in poor taste. Pretend you know nothing about it."

She said nothing, raising her brows.

"It's a mistake. Someone thinking to profit . . ."

"Profit from my being forced into intimacy with Lord Durnham, no matter my thoughts on the matter, or my own sensibilities." She kept her voice even.

Tavenam went red. It started below his collar and crept up his neck, to stain his cheeks. He looked away from her. "This was not on my orders. It is someone not thinking clearly."

"And you will make him see the light?"

Tavenam looked at her at last, and the expression in his pale, almost opaque eyes forced her to suppress a shiver. "He'll understand his error before I'm done with him. I can assure you of that."

# 30

The note arrived for him at his club just after ten in the evening. Edward took the envelope off the silver salver presented to him by the club's butler and slit it open with the letter opener provided.

It was from Charlotte, giving the location to meet her, Kit, and Gary this evening. He studied her handwriting, the loops and flourishes of it, which spoke of a joy in putting pen to paper. A celebration of the skill of writing.

She must only have learned how when she came to Catherine.

He folded the paper and slipped it into his top pocket.

"Good news?" Lord Aldridge asked, and with a start Edward noticed he was sitting very close by, in the same dark corner of the room. He leaned forward and increased the light on the small lamp beside him, beating back the gloom a little.

"Why do you say that?"

"You looked . . ." Aldridge looked suddenly uncomfortable. ". . . well, happy."

Edward damped down his surprise. "Yes. In a way, I am."

"Well, good luck to you." Aldridge stood. He was a few years younger than Edward, and almost too good-looking. Edward had known his older brother quite well, but Gerald had died six months before of appendicitis, and he knew Aldridge had come off the Peninsula Campaign to take up the title and the running of his family estate. He looked too thin, and careworn.

"Aldridge, if you need help or anything—" Edward stopped. He had no time or inclination for diplomacy, but even he could see that asking outright if the Aldridge finances were in a mess would be rude.

But Aldridge was smiling ruefully. "Nothing like that. Gerald was a paragon of virtue and economy, as was my father before him. No, we're sickeningly well-off. It's just very final, taking the title. I was always grateful to have dodged being the heir, but there's no running from it now. And if only I could get some decent food—" He stopped and laughed.

"Food?" Edward knew his mouth was open in astonishment.

"I find France and Spain have ruined me for life. I can't eat boiled beef or overdone fish anymore." He sighed. "At least, not a lot of it."

Edward gave a sympathetic twist of his lips. "Get a French cook then."

"Hmm. Hard to come by. I've already tried." He tugged

down his sleeves and pulled his jacket straight. "Well, I best be off."

"Wait." Edward looked up at him. "Were you in Portugal?"

Aldridge gave a nod. His eyes had narrowed slightly.

"Ever have someone under you by the name of Harkness?"

Aldridge's eyes flew wide. "I did. Excellent chap. Outstanding bravery. If there was a medal I could have recommended him for, I would have. Terrible waste, his death."

Edward hesitated. He suddenly realized Aldridge could be one of the men he was looking for. The watchers outside his and Charlotte's houses were ex-soldiers from the Peninsula Campaign. Men Aldridge would have known. By his own admission, Aldridge had been in France and Spain enough to have lost his taste for English food. Certainly long enough to work out some smuggling routes.

And yet, he seemed genuinely respectful of Harkness, and genuinely thought him dead.

"May I ask, how do you know Ted Harkness?"

"His family lives near my country estate." Edward felt the lie stumble and trip off his tongue, unwilling and surly.

"That would explain it." Aldridge gave a nod and walked out, and if Edward hadn't been watching him, he would have missed Tavenam entering the room.

He was looking for someone, and Edward wondered if it was him. Tavenam's fingers twitched as he stood in the doorway, eyes moving from group to group.

Then he walked over to the betting book and began to look through it, and Edward went very still.

Charlotte.

Charlotte had cornered Tavenam this evening. Either that or someone else had mentioned the wager to him. And he was coming to see if he could work out who had entered it.

Edward leaned back in his chair, grateful for the lack of light in this corner of the room. The only lamp was the one Aldridge had turned up, forming a small pool of light over his chair and a side table with a book on it. Edward leaned forward and turned it down again until it winked out with a tiny pop.

Tavenam turned to the card room, and then stood, head to one side in a strange, birdlike motion for his ample frame, as a group of four men walked out of it.

One of them, Blackley, stiffened slightly at the sight of him. "Uncle." He tried to find a smile. "Didn't know you were a member here."

"Just came to have a word, dear boy." Tavenam smiled genially. "Take a walk with me, will you?"

Blackley nodded, the movement uncertain and almost fearful.

Edward felt a rage rise up in him just looking at Blackley, strong as a deep winter storm at sea. He hadn't felt like this since the days he'd had to deal with his stepfather as a young man, and every smirk, every small, needling insult had taken real control to ignore.

He rose and watched Tavenam and Blackley as they left, and had the sense of a sharp movement just behind him. He turned and saw Blackley's friends watching him, their eyes wary.

He stared at them a moment, and then dismissed them, heading for the door and stairway.

He took the stairs two at a time and reached the doorway just as Tavenam and Blackley were walking down the street. Tavenam's carriage stood at the corner, and Tavenam was making use of every moment between the club and his rig to impress something upon his nephew.

He came to a halt, as if to make a particularly important point, at the opening of a narrow alleyway thirty feet from his carriage.

Hands came out of the darkness and pulled Blackley into the narrow gap. Edward watched, saw Tavenam tug a little at his cravat in discomfort, and then step into the alley after his nephew.

Well, well. Perhaps Tavenam hadn't realized it was his own family member who had made things so difficult, Edward thought, but that would not stop him administering a reprimand. Perhaps the reprimand would be stronger, so that Tavenam was clearly shown not to be favoring the idiot.

He wanted to hear what was said. Very badly.

He walked forward, so intent on keeping quiet, and trying so hard to hear any sounds from the alley that he was taken completely by surprise by the hand on his shoulder.

He only just prevented himself from crying out, spinning to look straight into Aldridge's eyes.

"I was walking home," Aldridge said quietly, his eyes flickering over Edward's shoulder to Tavenam's waiting coach, and then back, "and then I recalled your estates are in Devon.

Gerald stayed with you there once. I remember receiving a letter from him. But Ted Harkness was from Portsmouth—"

"Shh." Edward turned back to face the alley, his hand lifted to silence Aldridge. He could hear babbling and a calm, measured response from the darkness. A muffled cry of pain. He moved closer, aware of Aldridge behind him.

"What in hell is going on, Durnham?" He spoke at such a low whisper, Edward could barely hear him, and his respect for the man rose.

"There was a wager in the betting book—"

"Ah. Saw that." Aldridge said nothing more. He did not leave, though, and Edward cast a quick look over his shoulder.

Aldridge did not drop his gaze, his look even and curious, and with a shrug, Edward turned back. Pressed himself up against the wall at the opening to the alley.

". . . make an apology." Tavenam's voice was shaking with some deep emotion. Then Edward heard him walking out and stepped back deeper into the shadows. He could not see where Aldridge had gone.

Tavenam passed just by him, his steps jerky, followed by two men. One swung up into the driver's seat of Tavenam's coach; the other opened the door for Tavenam, saw him settled inside, and climbed to sit next to the driver. The coach rolled off.

Edward stepped into the alley, wishing for better light, but there was a little, spilling from a high window at the back of the house on the corner.

Blackley stood slumped against a wall. His face was unmarked, but he stood half hunched over. Ribs, maybe. Or kidneys. Perhaps just a quick blow to the stomach.

Certainly no more than he deserved. In fact, if Edward were the judge, substantially less than he deserved.

As he watched, Blackley straightened, pulled his cravat and coat to rights, and stared toward the street with an expression of growing defiance.

Someone still hadn't learned their lesson.

He moved. Fast and hard.

He had a hand just below Blackley's throat, and the other resting just by Blackley's ear before the insolent bastard could so much as react.

Blackley gasped, and then his eyes moved over Edward's shoulder.

Aldridge.

"You can ask me about Harkness later," Edward said, and even he could hear the anticipation in his voice.

Blackley began to shake. "I would like to accompany Lord Aldridge to the club," he said, his words tripping over each other.

"Oh, I don't think so." Edward did not loosen his grip. "You and I have matters of honor to discuss. The value of a woman's reputation, and other related subjects."

Aldridge sauntered over, coming up to Blackley's other side and leaning against the wall with one shoulder.

"Those are important subjects, Blackley. Ones a man should never, ever forget. Perhaps they don't seem important to you now. But give it time. One day, you'll have a wife. A daughter. In fact, you have a younger sister, don't you?"

Blackley went very still. "Don't you . . . *don't.*"

"What?" Edward looked him directly in the eye. "Don't what, Blackley?"

"I was mistaken. Very, very mistaken in that bet. I thought it a joke, but I see now there was nothing funny about it. Nothing at all. And I plan to retract it, and pay out the wager, and you can take this as my apology, Durnham."

Edward gave him a long, slow smile. "I didn't hear an 'I'm sorry.'"

"You don't need me here, I assume?" Aldridge straightened up.

Edward shook his head. "I don't really want to share, but thank you for the offer."

As he turned his full attention back to Blackley, he heard Aldridge chuckle as he walked away.

---

Edward had made the effort to blend in.

Charlotte studied the rough trousers and coarse cotton shirt, over which he wore an ill-fitting jacket too heavy for the current weather, and admitted to herself he knew how to don a disguise.

He even sported a bruise on his cheek, and a tiny cut on his lip that had bled a little and then dried. The perfect Billingsgate thug. He wouldn't be drawn on how he'd come by his small injuries.

His private coach had dropped them near enough to Billingsgate that they would not have far to walk, but far enough away that no one would see them arrive. They'd driven a fast and twisted route to their destination, and she decided Edward was taking no chance they would be followed.

She'd sat next to him, with Gary and Kit on the opposite bench, feeling the heat and the press of his body against her.

After the kiss he had given her that morning, it was a pleasant torture to be so close and sit with her hands primly on her knees.

Edward had said very little, but she thought he crowded her on the bench more than necessary, letting his leg rest against hers in a manner that would shock most of the well-bred ladies of the ton.

Gary and Kit said nothing to him at all, but the nod Gary gave Edward was friendly enough.

She was in Betsy's clothes again, a full money bag hanging from her belt, and covered by an apron. As they approached Billingsgate, she had to walk carefully so it didn't clink too much.

The men surrounded her, Edward and Gary on either side, Kit behind her, and she was glad to have them. The alleys they walked along were narrow and dark, and more than once a stranger had loomed out of the shadows, seen the three men, and thought better of his plans.

The stink of fish guts littering the docks hit her full force as they stepped into the open area where the daily trading was done.

The cobbles were slimy with scales and guts, and she walked carefully so as not to slip.

They found the Barking Ram right beside the docks, light spilling from the open doors and windows. There was a low murmur of voices, but no loud shouting or even much talking. A place where men came to drink seriously.

She wondered suddenly if they would allow her in—she had imagined a place full of women, singing, and laughter, not this grim, serious den. "Perhaps Gary should go in and get him, bring him out here? My presence may cause us to be noticed."

Gary gave a nod and went inside, leaving them to wait in uncomfortable silence.

"Let's 'ope this chap ain't lapping the gutter," Kit muttered, as the minutes stretched on. "No use to us if he can't see a hole in a ladder."

Charlotte had not thought of what she would do if Norris were blind drunk, but looked at Edward's face, set and serious, and so different to how he'd looked this morning, and decided they would come away with something tonight. He would find a way to make it so.

When Gary came at last, it was with a steady-footed man in tow, and she relaxed.

"What's this, then?" He looked from Gary to the three of them, standing in the shadows just outside the door.

When he saw her face, he tried to move back into the tavern, but his way was blocked by Gary. "I never seen 'er in me life. I swear. And I'm not responsible for any trouble she's gotten herself into—"

Edward cut him off by grabbing him by the back of the collar and pulling him deeper into the shadows, away from the pub.

"She's never seen you before, either, so you can relax. We aren't her family, come to force you to marry her, or anything of the sort." Edward's voice was cold and hard.

Norris went limp in Edward's hold, and Charlotte couldn't help wondering if there was a woman he knew had a claim on him, somewhere.

"What do you want, then?" He drew a filthy sleeve under his nose and sniffed.

"We hear you were involved in a bit of smuggling for Luke Bracken. We'd like to hear about it." Charlotte kept her voice low.

There was silence, and Charlotte shuffled her feet, trying not to breathe in the air too deeply. She'd forgotten how terrible Billingsgate stank. It used to be one of her favorite places to come on the rare occasion she had time off when she was young. She never noticed the smell in those days.

"You'll pay?" He sniffed again, a gurgling, phlegmy sound that turned her stomach.

"We'll pay," Edward said. He spoke as he usually did, his vowels perfect and as polished as the silverware that graced his table, and Charlotte saw Norris eye him with suspicion. But perhaps he figured a nob dressed up as a dockworker might be good for a bit of cash, because he gave a quick nod.

"Not 'ere, though."

"We could go to St.-Mary's-at-Hill?" Kit whispered, and

Charlotte became aware that two men stood in the doorway of the pub, looking out into the dark.

"Aye." Norris agreed, his eyes on the men.

Kit led the way, melting into the darkness, and as Charlotte made to follow, she was almost startled into a cry as Edward took her hand.

She looked up at him, but his gaze was ahead, on Norris.

"He seemed ready enough to talk," he murmured.

"You think too ready?"

He shrugged. "We'll see what he has to say."

It took them less than five minutes to get to the church, and Kit motioned them around the back into the small grave-yard.

Despite the eerie light of the moon on the gravestones, and the strangers that surrounded him, Charlotte noticed that Norris was more relaxed here, away from the watchful eyes on the dock.

"Let's see the money first," he said.

Before Charlotte could reach for the bag of money at her belt, Edward raised a small pouch of his own, handed it over to Norris to feel the weight of, and then took it back. "Only if you have something useful to tell us."

Norris gave a smile. "And how much trouble would I be in, say, if one of you worked for the Crown?"

"None at all." Edward's answer was immediate.

Norris looked at him for a long minute. "I'm down on my luck, as it 'appens. Came to London to cry off with Mr. Bracken nice an' formal, like. So there was no misunderstandings. But I came on very sick, with fever and coughing. When I was halfway meself again, all me money'd been taken, no one could tell me when or how, and I'm stuck here, so to speak. Stuck and wanting a way 'ome. So you might say I'm in the right frame o' mind to spill the beans." He looked the rest of them over, but his gaze kept going back to Edward, and when at last he spoke, it was as if the rest of them weren't there.

"It weren't that I was opposed to the smuggling in this job. Done it all me life. But my boy . . ." Norris shrugged. "Idiot signed up for the army. Fell for a girl down Deale way, daughter of a customs officer, and couldn't find a good job. Not as good as owling, anyway."

He sniffed again. "So, while I'm happy to make money, even with the French, even while we're at war, I had to draw the line somewhere, see? It's all right if it's private enterprise. That's normal. But when it's government enterprise—I was helping the men trying to kill my son, way I saw it. An' no matter the blighter was daft to sign up, the fact is, he did. I couldn't to be in any scheme that would 'elp the enemy. No matter Mr. Bracken shoutin' at me that there is a greater plan, and me son will be better off in the long run. If he's dead, the long run's not much help, is it?"

"Are you telling me," Edward said slowly, "that the shipping of guineas out of England is being arranged by the French government?" He was all but shouting by the last two words.

Norris drew a sharp, whistling breath through his nose. "I am."

"What evidence do you have of that?" Edward looked like

some dangerous beast, ready to spring, but Norris didn't seem intimidated. Instead he started to laugh, slapping his thigh, and then suddenly began to cough and hack.

When he at last had his breath, he was still smiling. "Perhaps it's the small harbor where we take the guineas that was the clue." He chuckled wickedly. "Gravelines, it's called. Enough accommodation set up to take three hundred smugglers at a time, there is. They don't like us to leave the harbor, scared someone might sneak spies in by posing as an owler, I s'pose, so we're not allowed beyond the wall. And then out bustle the little French officers, with their papers and quills, counting the guineas, working out a rate for us, and letting us have the brandy and gin and silks, and whatever else they're exchanging for the gold."

"Do you bring anything else to exchange with them other than gold?" Edward asked.

Norris shook his head. "I speak a little French. Been owling since I was ten, and helped me father. Been to France more times than most, I'd say. I heard two of the officers talking in French, once, when a lad from my part o' the coast asked if they'd accept wool, too. Said they had strict orders from the emperor himself to only take gold. Nothing else."

"And this is all quite organized? Government run?"

Norris looked annoyed. "That's what I'm telling you. Organized in every way. Housing, accounting, receipt and exchange of goods. They're all business." He broke off, and looked away, into the small graveyard behind the church. "Too businesslike, seemed to me. Too slick. They were rubbing their hands when we came in, and a few times I heard . . ." He rubbed his cheeks with his palms and sighed. "I 'eard them say that England's economy must surely be close to collapse, given the number of guineas coming over."

"They want to bleed us of our gold," Edward said, and there was stunned wonder, absolute awe in his voice, "and they've gotten us to hold out our arms and slit our own wrists for them."

Norris winced. "Aye. But don't look to the owlers. We just do the dirty work. Get what comes to us an' we takes it over. It's the ones getting the guineas in th' first place, they're the ones you want. The ones Bracken wants, too, by the looks o' things. But while he tries to catch 'em all in his net, more and more gold is leaving, and each time we help Napoleon, I'm betraying my boy a little more." He hacked another cough and spat. Charlotte tried not to wince.

"Me wife was taken ten years back, an' I raised my boy. All I got left, he is. I told Mr. Bracken. I can't be having truck with this no mor'. 'Specially since once or twice—not me, mind—but some o' the others on the run, they didn't just take guineas over. Escaped prisoners, they said, or French spies going back to report. Some get a little extra for bringing English newspapers over, too, for old Boney to read, and learn what our boys are doing. I can't be havin' truck."

There was silence as Edward weighed his small bag of guineas in his hands. He seemed to be coming to grips with what Norris had told him, his face tight and closed off as he dealt with information that surely must tip his world a little on its axis. "Did you ever hear any names mentioned that might be significant? On the French side, or the English side?"

Norris shook his head. "Not on the English side. Only ever dealt with Mr. Bracken. On the French side," he shrugged, "a few, but clerks, is all. No one who looked more important. They made sure to stay out o' our sight."

Edward handed him the bag and he weighed it with satisfaction.

"Think I'll go back 'ome now. Wait for me son. Do me no 'arm to get out o' London Town." He spat again, lifted his hand to his cap, and, without waiting for a farewell, walked around the back of the church, slipping into the darkness as smooth and quiet as the smuggler he was.

# 31

Edward was still reeling at the notion of Napoleon's plan, so he didn't notice Luke Bracken was waiting for them at the carriage until they were almost upon him.

Luke leaned against the door with one shoulder, and Edward's driver sat very still, as if afraid to move.

"Good thinking." Luke straightened up as they got closer. "Leaving the carriage a little way from the docks. Took me 'n' Sammy thirty minutes of circling to find it." He tugged at his too-big jacket. "And *we* knew you were here."

Since the moment she'd seen Luke, Charlotte tried to pull her hand from his, but Edward held on tighter, and after a brief resistance, she gave in. She made a tiny sound, as if in defeat, but Edward would not let her think he would hide anything from Bracken.

"Why are you here, Luke?" Charlotte asked.

"To stop you meeting Norris. I thought there was a danger you'd tell some of his story to your nob." Luke jerked his head toward Edward. "I never thought you'd actually bring him along."

Luke seemed to throw the mantle of calm he'd been wearing off with a flourish, and he went from lazy insolence to stuttering rage so fast, Edward felt Charlotte shrink back.

"Jesus, Charlie, how could you? You might not have known much about what's been going on, but I told you the other night I had a specific plan. You knew Lord Nob here could ruin it. And what do you do? Bugger me if you don't find a way to give him all the details. What do you think you're bloody doing?" He jabbed his finger as he spoke, moving closer, his face red and his eyes wild.

Edward shifted, blocking Charlotte from Luke, at least partially, and dropping her hand at last so that both of his were free.

Luke looked at him, at the way he was standing, and drove his hands into his hair and tugged it straight up, spun away from them both. "Damn it to *hell*, Charlie."

Charlotte closed her eyes and bowed her head, her hands clasped together before her. Then she moved a little to the side so she could see Luke again. She waited for him to turn. "I need to stop these men, Luke. And it seems the longer you look for your evidence, the bigger the hole you dig for England, and the wealthier these thieves get. Edward wants them stopped as badly as I do, so yes, I've shared my information."

"I need more time, Charlie, before I can close 'em down."

"But you're betraying your country, same as them, while

you try to trap them in, what? A hope that evidence of their betrayal will lead to the collapse of the whole system of government?" Edward ground his right fist into his left palm in frustration. It was a ludicrous plan.

"Betrayal? You want to talk to me of betrayal?" Luke reared back. "You want to talk about the thousands starving in the stews, while nobs like you ride past them in carriages that cost enough to keep them for life? You want to talk about the Hulks, and Old Bailey, where they lock up children as young as six years old, punishing them as if they were adults, all for taking a scrap or two to feed themselves or their families? You want to stand there and tell me I betrayed England? No, Lord Nob. England has betrayed *me*."

There was silence for a moment. Edward looked at Kit and Gary, at Charlotte, and could see that in this they sided with Luke.

He thought of Harkness, lying in the gutter, and wondered if they didn't have the right of it.

"So," he said, slowly, "you can commit treason if you like? Because you aren't considered a true citizen of the country?"

"Well put." Luke smiled. "Until I am considered a true citizen, I'm at liberty to sell my country out, except, I never have. I only got involved with this to show as many as I could that even with their full citizenship, their full bellies, and their full bank accounts, the nobs are the ones selling England out, not us."

Edward had no quick answer this time. "But it isn't as simple as that, is it?"

"No." Charlotte's voice was hesitant, as if she were trying to think it through. "Edward, you ride that fancy carriage, and have more money than most will ever see, but I know you work for the good of England, you're no layabout; and Luke, you can't say you don't profit as much from poverty as most of the nobs. And you give as little back to the community as the nobs do. I know—" She held out her hand when Luke tried to interrupt. "I know you're giving the profits from this scheme back into Tothill Road, but that's guilt money, because you know you're doing them down, eroding the whole system while you prove your point, and things will be worse for them before they get better, if they ever do get better." She wrapped her arms around her waist and looked down at the cobbles before raising her head again. "And then there's me, caught in the middle." She quirked her lips in a twisted smile.

Luke stared at her, as if seeing in her something he'd never seen before. Then he shook his head. "Charlie, stop queering my pitch for another week or so. I need more time, as I said. They keep it all so close to the chest. They're so scared of being found out."

"So I discovered." Charlotte's words were dry. "In a very personal sense."

"What do you mean?" Luke focused on her like a hound on the scent. He rubbed his hands along his arms, as if he were cold.

"They approached me. They're trying to blackmail me into reporting what Edward knows about them."

"Blackmail you?" Luke's voice was very soft.

"They threatened to out me to the ton. To tell everyone I'm the bastard daughter of a whore."

Gary and Kit had spread out a little when they'd seen Luke, readying themselves, Edward thought, for a fight. But at Charlotte's words they drew closer, horror on their faces.

As servants of the upper class, they would know only too well the impact carrying out that threat would have on Charlotte's life in the ton.

It would end it.

"Who was it threatened you? Exactly what did they say?" Luke moved forward, and Edward thought better of blocking Charlotte from him again, but he held himself loose and ready.

Charlotte looked away from them, and for that alone, Edward wanted to kill Tavenam all over again. "They said I was to tell them everything, copy his notes, report what he said. But Lord Durnham hasn't told me anything. Neither of you told me anything." The last sentence was spoken quietly, and Edward flinched at the guilt it laid on him.

Luke drew in a breath through clenched teeth, the whistle of it sinister in the dark silence. "How were you to get it then?"

"I told them I couldn't do it, that Lord Durnham didn't confide in me, and they said I would have to become his lover, then. Some of them even made a bet on how long it would take me in the wager book in Lord Durnham's club—"

Luke howled. An animal sound that grabbed Edward by the back of his neck. "I'll kill him."

"You know Lord Tavenam?" Charlotte asked him, and her voice shook.

"Tavenam? Never 'eard of him. But I know who sent him." Luke turned his gaze, hard and cold as a dead fish, on Edward. "What did your nob here say to all this, Charlie? I presume you told him?"

"I told him about the blackmail. He's the one who told me about the bet." Charlotte still hugged herself at the hips, and at last she looked up again. "He came to warn Catherine and me about it, and arrange things so there could be no gossip about us."

Luke carried on staring, and Edward felt his fists curl again. "You got something to say, Bracken?"

Luke looked away, dismissing Edward suddenly, and turned his attention to Charlotte. "Don't trust him. He's a nob and he'll hush it up and hide the guilty away quicker'n you can blink. No nob will go down for this crime. If they can get me, or the owlers, so much the better. But when they find the nobs at the top, well, it'll be a slap on the wrist, and 'don't be a naughty boy, and let's not see you do this again.'"

"You're wrong there." Edward tried to relax, to speak to Luke civilly, even though, knowing what he was to Charlotte, what he had been, all Edward wanted to do was go for the throat.

"I won't cover it up. If you've got information, give it to me, and I'll make sure they take their rightful punishment."

Luke threw him a look so laden with contempt, it hit Edward like a blow. "You? You'll have no choice. You'll cover it up. If you aren't already doing just that, following all the

trails, hoodwinking Charlie into leading you to the witnesses
so you can bump 'em off."

"I don't understand." He didn't dare take his eyes off Luke.
"Why would I have no choice?"

"You must know." Luke sneered, but there was something
in the way he looked at him that made Edward think he
wasn't so certain of himself anymore.

"If you know something, then spit it out!" He lost all patience. "What do you think these men have on me? Why
would you think I'd be in league with them?"

Luke took a step back and almost ran into the carriage
behind him. "You really don't know." He spoke slowly, and
with a twisted sense of satisfaction.

Edward said nothing. He stood waiting, and was surprised at
the dread he felt. Whatever came next would not be pleasant.

"The man behind this is your stepfather, Lord Nob. Hawthorne is the kingpin of this little operation."

Edward felt the earth shift a little beneath his feet, a shuddering resettling of the world into a slightly different configu-
ration. He sucked in a deep breath, needing air. "And how do
you know that?"

Luke's eyes flashed in what little light came from the lamp
on the corner. "He approached me, as I was the only criminal
he knew, to set this little lark up for him. That's how I got involved. He thinks I'm a moneygrubbing little bludger. But
even so, he's been right tight about what information he gives
me. The going's been slower than I thought to catch 'is little
lot out."

"How did he know to come to you to start? Why are you the only criminal he knows?" Edward bluffed it out with disbelief, but he knew Bracken must be right. It made a twisted sense.

"'Cause I found him, years ago it was now. Went lookin' for Charlie's father. Just to make sure 'e was totally out o' the picture. Didn't want some cove turnin' up out of the blue to claim her." He turned to Charlotte. "I'd asked around, back when you first came to work with us—with that bastard Ashcroft. I tried to find out 'bout your mum, and what happened to 'er. I wanted to be prepared, see. And I found out quite a bit—your ma told a neighbor everything, that your father was a nob an' all. She asked the neighbor to go to him an' ask for help for you if she didn't make it. Course, the cow decided it would be more of a sure thing to sell you to the brothels than try to squeeze money from a lord. But she gave me 'is name, for a price."

There was something in the way he said this that made Edward shiver. He wondered if the woman had lived very long after she told Luke that tale. He doubted it, and yet he could not find any sympathy for her, either.

"I didn't tell you, Charlie. There was nothin' to say. No way 'e would be a problem, given who 'e was. I let him know I knew all about it. Just in case. And I've kept in touch, you might say. Just to keep 'im off balance, keep him running a little scared. And don't he deserve it? The way he forced you an' your mum into the life you 'ad."

It was the most Edward had ever heard Luke speak, and through it all, Luke kept his eyes on Charlotte, and stood, open and arms a little out, as if he were some kind of angel, delivering a tiding.

Edward took a quick look at Charlotte's face. It was white, and she looked smaller somehow, as if the shock of Luke's revelation had diminished her. He took a step toward her, but she lifted her hands and shrunk back from all of them, as if they were all about to do her harm. Her eyes were shadowed and impossible to see.

"What has this to do with my stepfather?" Edward asked, his gaze still locked on Charlotte, the sense that he was losing her, that she was slipping through his fingers like fine gold dust, growing stronger by the moment. And he was sure what was coming next would not help him.

"Surely that's obvious? He's Charlie's father," Luke spoke quietly, and with a tremble to his voice, as if at last he regretted his impulse to speak but realized he'd gone too far, that he had to finish now. Perhaps he felt her pulling from him, just as surely as Edward did. "He raped his chambermaid, and when she fell pregnant, he kicked her out into the street."

It was the final hammer's blow. Edward watched Charlotte flinch, and it seemed to him the chains that bound her were at last severed.

# 32

Charlotte was almost crouching back, waiting for the blow of Luke's revelation, and when it came, it wasn't so bad. She'd had worse. Much worse.

The thought steadied her. And made her realize what she was doing.

Hadn't she promised herself never to cower again?

She straightened, suddenly lighter. She'd never thought much about her father. She'd relegated him to one of the men her mother prostituted herself to. To find out her father was the cause of her mother's hardship skewed her view of her old life, twisting it like the toffee confections in the bakers' windows.

She'd never had the sense of being a burden, in the few flashes of memory she had of her mother. And tears pricked and welled in her eyes at the thought of how much she'd been loved. Despite everything, her mother had sacrificed so much to keep her.

"Ah, Jesus, Charlie, I'm sorry. Don't cry." Luke looked in agony.

She didn't know what to say to him, did not want to comfort him, even though she was not crying for the reasons he thought. She looked to the side, into the darkness, and jerked with surprise as she caught sight of Sammy. He was lurking just out of the light, watching Luke's back, but there could be no doubt Luke's revelation was as much news to him as it was to everyone else. He was gaping, dumbstruck.

And then Charlotte remembered Lord Hawthorne's face that day in Edward's breakfast room and jerked her gaze to Edward, wondering if he was thinking the same.

She hadn't known she'd been so like her mother in looks. But that surely must be who Hawthorne thought she was for one moment, until common sense intervened. And then he'd immediately used what he knew about her and sent Tavenam after her that same night. Using his newfound daughter, and trying to prostitute her for information almost the moment he realized she was right in front of him.

Just like he had forced her mother to prostitute herself to keep her child alive.

A tiny, hard seed of hate sprang to life in her chest, but before she could focus on it, the thought occurred to her again that she must look very like her mother.

It comforted her, more than she could have believed.

She brushed the tears that slipped down her cheeks away with the backs of her hands and saw all five men staring at her.

"I met Hawthorne at Edward's the other day. You might

have warned me before, Luke. You must have known there was a chance we would meet."

"I didn't want to tell you about Hawthorne, not if I didn't have to." Luke would not look her in the eyes. "He doesn't attend balls. He's got such bad gout he barely goes anywhere but his club. That's how I know he can only draw his co-conspirators from high society. I never knew you'd be going to Lord Nob's house and even if you did, I've never known Hawthorne to visit there. Or that he'd somehow recognize you if he did."

She looked properly at Edward. He held himself more tightly bound than ever. As shocked as her.

She wanted to slip her hand into his again, and give him some comfort, but something in the way he held himself prevented her. "Edward . . ."

He turned to look at her, and his anger gave him a lean, hungry look. "I need to go." He moved to the carriage door, and it was only then that Charlotte remembered the coachman. She looked up and caught him staring. He turned away hastily and she had to hope Edward had discreet, trustworthy staff.

"Wait." She reached out and finally touched him, taking hold of his arm as she turned to Gary and Kit. "Go home without me. I'll be accompanying Lord Durnham."

"What, to confront Hawthorne?" Luke spoke incredulously from the shadows. "There's no telling what he'll do. He's behind Frethers's death, for certain. I forbid you to go."

Edward had gone still under her hand the moment she

touched him. "I hate to agree with Mr. Bracken, but I would not like you there, either."

"But that's where *you're* going." She dropped her hand, stepped away from him, then turned to Luke. "You've never had the right to forbid me anything, and you certainly don't now. You need to put a stop to this guinea smuggling, Luke. The end doesn't justify the means. You need to finish it." She turned away without waiting for him to respond. "Lord Durnham," she gave a tiny bow. "Would you be so good as to give me the address of your stepfather?"

He jerked as if she'd slapped him. "You wouldn't—"

"I'll take Kit and Gary with me, of course. Perhaps Sammy will come along, too?"

Sammy nodded from the shadows, and something tight in her chest eased a fraction. "In fact, if Sammy's been watching Lord Hawthorne for Luke, I could get the address from him." She smiled brightly. "No need to trouble you further. I'll be on my way."

Edward stared at her, his face sharp and exquisitely controlled. Then he pulled open the door of the carriage and held out a hand. "You are, of course, welcome to accompany me. After you." He spoke with an exaggerated politeness that spoke of anger and frustration held in close control.

She looked at his hand for one long beat.

"Please," he said.

She put her hand into his and he helped her in.

She looked back at Luke as she sat on the bench seat of

the coach, but he made no move to stop her. He stood quite still, as if lost in thought.

Kit closed the door, and she caught a glimpse of his face as they began rolling down the street. He was afraid.

She peered out the window, then across to Edward. "Better ask the coachman to hurry."

"Why is that?"

She winced at the honed edge of his words. "Because Luke would like to kill Hawthorne before we get to him. I can promise you that."

---

Edward liked control. And there was no doubt, with Charlotte Raven, he had none.

"You are very angry with me," she said. But she did not look sorry. She looked annoyed with him.

He wanted to laugh, suddenly. She was completely uncowed.

"I'm more angry than I can ever remember being. I stopped myself feeling anger, and hurt, and unhappiness, when I was a child. Hawthorne liked to make me cry, and so I refused to do it. I refused to be upset, or miserable, or anything too strong. And I never am."

She leaned back and studied him. "Is happiness on the list, too?"

He shrugged. "If you are happy, you can be made to feel otherwise."

She nodded. "I know only too well what you mean. But I think you know you still feel all those things. You just bury them." She kept her gaze steady. "Why don't you hide them with me?"

He couldn't look away. His heart stopped beating and then came to life again like a hard, painful punch. "I can't seem to help myself where you're concerned. It goes against everything I've done for most of my life." His voice was rough, the air in the coach close and suffocating.

She closed her eyes slowly, then opened them again. "You make me wish for things I thought I could never have. Want things I never thought I would want." She stopped and clenched her hands in her lap.

The coach rolled to a stop, and Edward glanced out, saw they were at his stepfather's.

He considered driving on, calling to the driver to keep going until all of this was left far behind them.

But his stepfather would be between them, no matter what. Luke had seen to that.

"I'm not looking forward to this. It has to be done, but I would rather be anywhere else." Charlotte looked out the window, leaning close to him, and he could feel the warmth of her body, smell the faint scent of some light floral powder.

He took her hand and slowly, deliberately, stripped off the thin cotton glove she had borrowed from her maid for this evening's work.

He lifted her palm and kissed it, then kissed the web of thin white scars on her inner wrist. He could feel her pulse beneath his lips, and raised his eyes.

She was sitting with her eyes closed, her face perfectly still, facing out the window in profile.

He cupped her cheeks, turned her toward him, and leaned into her, brushing his lips with hers and then deepening the kiss, coaxing her mouth open and tasting her.

She breathed in, a quick, sharp movement, and he felt the brush of her breasts against his chest, the tremble of her body.

He was so tempted to slide his hands over her, to cup her breasts, follow her rib cage to her waist, and lift her up to straddle his lap. He threw himself back—away from her.

"Please." His voice was a whisper, an octave lower than usual. "Please, whatever you hear in there, remember I am nothing to do with my stepfather. I've spent my life trying to avoid him, cursing the day he came into it."

She blinked—a long, lazy, sensuous sweep of her eyelids that did something to the blood in his head, making him feel quite dizzy.

She gathered her cloak about her to take the steps, and he saw a shudder pass through her, caught the faintest scent of arousal, and cursed his stepfather and Luke to the lowest levels of hell.

"Of anyone, I know better than most we are what we make ourselves." Like his, her voice was husky. Deeper. "I won't hold your stepfather against you." She gave him a tentative smile. "If you don't hold him against me."

# 33

Hawthorne's butler was under a great deal of stress.

Charlotte noticed his hand shook as he opened the door, and his face held the stiff mien of someone who has recently been slapped or sworn at and is still dealing with the shock of it.

He went down the hall to inform Hawthorne of Edward's presence like a schoolboy walking to the schoolmaster's office for a hiding.

Hawthorne had lost his temper with his staff today. There could be no doubt.

The butler came back with a slightly lighter step. Hawthorne was glad Edward was here, it seemed. Edward hadn't given her name and perhaps the butler had not even mentioned her presence.

So much the better, if so.

"One moment, Clavers." Edward pulled the man aside and murmured very low in his ear. Clavers went white, and then flushed very red, looking down at the toes of his highly polished shoes. When Edward stepped back, he gave a short, decisive nod, then turned to lead them down the passage.

He did not look her way once.

Edward followed, taking her with him, his hand on her arm, his thumb brushing the cotton of her glove in a light, circular movement.

She thought it was unconscious, and even more sensual for that. It revealed his mind more clearly than anything he could say or do deliberately.

They stepped into a large library, the warm leather of books lending the large space a cozy air. Most of the furniture was leather, too, burnished and gleaming.

Hawthorne sat with his back to the door, facing a small fire even though the evening was still very warm.

As Clavers murmured Edward's name and closed the door, she expected Hawthorne to turn, but he did not.

"Took your time to come. You didn't let me know what the magistrate had to say about Geoffrey's death."

Edward slanted her a look, then fixed his gaze on the back of Hawthorne's chair. "I've brought you a visitor. A lady."

At last Hawthorne turned, stiffly and with difficulty, and she saw he had one foot bandaged and up on a footstool. She'd noticed nothing about him the first time she'd met him; his behavior had taken all her attention. But now she could see the blunt, hard lines of his face, the bags under his eyes, and the tiny broken veins under his skin. His nose had the bulbous red look of a drunk's.

His eyes flickered at the sight of her. He said nothing.

"Good evening, Lord Hawthorne. I understand from Luke Bracken you are my father."

At that, his foot slipped from its footstool and he let out a cry of agony, and then began to swear; dirty, vicious words that most would consider more commonplace at Billingsgate or in the stews than in this fine library.

She knew better.

Edward ignored the vitriol and kept his hand on her arm, gently stroking, as if soothing a wild animal.

"So tell me, did you rape Miss Raven's mother before or after you decided to marry mine?" he asked Hawthorne.

Hawthorne's temper tantrum cut off abruptly. "What does it matter?" His eyes glittered in the firelight. "What does the timing matter?"

"It doesn't, I suppose," Edward agreed easily. "The fact that it was done, rather than the timing, is more important."

"Important to what?" Hawthorne snapped out, half bravado, half contempt.

Edward did not answer that, and Charlotte wondered what was racing through his mind. He had let her go, his arms dropped to his sides, and his hands fisted.

"What is the purpose of this?" Hawthorne said, slowly lifting his foot back onto its footstool, his attention on it, his body turned away from them, a dismissive, disrespectful movement.

For a moment, anger spiked through her deliberate calm, making her want to knock his leg off its stool again, or strike out at him, and she forced herself still—wrestled with herself. The whole reason she'd come here tonight was to find out about her mother, speak to Hawthorne about her, but she realized how foolish that had been. She would get nothing from him. He never knew her mother, anyway. He'd just used her.

Edward gave her a quick look, and she turned away a little, so he would not see her battle for control.

She needed to find Charlie the sweep, or Miss Raven, the be-gloved wallflower, not the Charlotte that had been close to abandoning herself to a man's kiss not twenty minutes ago.

"The purpose is for you to understand it is all over. You will tell me who else is involved with you in smuggling guineas out of the country; you will tell me who you sent to kill Frethers, and Geoffrey, too," Edward said, and his voice was thick. Harsh.

Hawthorne looked at him over his shoulder. "Geoffrey? Geoffrey was an idiot. I can only assume he killed himself, because his death has been most inconvenient to me. When I got a letter from him, telling me what Frethers had proposed to him in order to clear his debts, I was furious. But it was too late. You came the next day to say he was dead. I realized how Frethers had maneuvered him, making him think debtors' prison was in his future, that he had no choice but to hand over his children, when all along we'd planned to pay his debts for him. We wanted to keep him on edge and then make him very grateful to us for saving him, keep the use of his estate for the smuggling. I was very angry that day. Frethers couldn't be allowed to continue. Not when his appetites were exceeding his sense. He should have left Geoffrey and his family alone. You *never* foul your own nest." Hawthorne chopped a hand sharply downward. "But as for names? I won't tell you anything." He was breathing heavily. "I'm in control here, Edward, not you. You think I haven't been crafting evidence against you from the beginning? I bribed someone to appoint you to investigate this mess, and since then, I haven't heard a word mentioned about your involvement from anyone in my circle. They're keeping it quiet, which shows just how little confidence they have in you.

"If you try to move against me, or any of my group, you will be in disgrace. You may eventually work your way free, but there will always be whispers attached to your name, and because of the indiscretions Geoffrey committed, your nephews and your sister will be dogged by his mistakes for the rest of their lives." He glanced at Charlotte, and his lip curled. "As for her"—he tossed his head—"she will be exposed for the gutter scum she is. Tell me, my dear, how have you managed to survive all these years?"

She was at last Charlie Raven again. Nothing could touch her. "My own wits, and Luke Bracken."

She saw surprise flash in his eyes. He tilted his head back a little to see her better. "So Bracken did actually use some of the money he extorted from me to keep you, eh? Although you'd have been on the streets for some time before the black-mailing little bastard came to me."

She was quite simply dumbstruck. She opened her mouth to speak, and then stood, jaw agape, with no sound coming out. Perhaps the veneer of Charlie Raven was becoming a little thin.

"Bracken extorted money from you?" Edward asked, his voice cool.

"Didn't tell you that, eh? While he was telling all manner of other things he shouldn't have been." Hawthorne slid a sly look her way. "Took me for as much as he could get. Said he'd expose me, at a time when that would have been . . . inconvenient. Kept popping up again, like a bad smell for the last twelve years, just hovering in the shadows, making sure I knew he was there. Thought I might finally put him to some use with this scheme."

"Twelve years ago." Edward sat suddenly on the arm of a chair. Perched there like a hawk readying itself to swoop. "That's when my mother fell so ill. When she begged me to look after you financially when I was able to, when I had full control of my own money and you were no longer in charge of my trust. If either of us had known about Charlotte, about what you'd done to Charlotte, I'd have cut you off without a cent."

Hawthorne shrugged in agreement. "It would have been difficult for me to explain. And Bracken had some proof I had forgotten about. If it had come to light, it would have been cause for some unpleasant questions." He steepled his fingers. "Funny to think I did end up supporting you, in the end."

"You misunderstand." Charlotte at last found her voice, although it was rusty, as if it had been unused for days. "Luke Bracken took care of me and helped me for no reason other than genuine affection when I was very young. He kept me safe and unharmed for no money at all. The sum he extorted from you was done at a time when I was financially secure already, and had no need of your money."

"He used it to rise up," Edward said, quiet and sure. "He thought if he grew powerful and wealthy enough, he could win you back."

She looked across at him. "Yes." She was glad Luke had gotten money from Hawthorne, glad it was him running Tothill Road and not some other thug. But he'd never told her. Even though he must know she would have approved.

Edward laughed, and the sound was tinged with despair. "You don't blame him, do you? I can see it in your face. The only problem you have with what he did was that he kept it from you."

She didn't answer. This was not the place or time for this conversation.

"You've already forgiven him." Edward spun away, and then seemed to take himself back under control.

He turned to Hawthorne. "Whatever evidence you think you've engineered against me, my accusations will be just as difficult for you. At the very least, it will be the end of your treachery."

"I don't think you'll out me." Hawthorne chuckled as he shot a look at Edward. "You're too proud. The thought of the men you respect thinking you a traitor on my word will prevent you from acting against me. You won't be welcome at your club, or anywhere else." He massaged his raised leg, a half smile on his face. "Just like when you were younger, Edward, you're my puppet, now."

## 34

Edward laughed. He realized as the sound burst out of him and filled the room that he didn't laugh nearly enough.

Then he caught sight of Hawthorne, and the laughter died.

"I am not your puppet, and while you've been scheming and profiteering, I've been working for the Crown. Have done so since I took my seat in the House of Lords." The surprise on Hawthorne's face was worth a hundred of the lashes he'd been given as a child. "I was involved in other, equally important work, and my superiors moved me across reluctantly, and only because Dervish pushed for it, because you were blackmailing him. As for your not hearing about it, my role has always been kept quiet. I've been involved behind the scenes for ten years, and I not only have friends, Hawthorne, I have powerful friends. Men who know me well. Who work with me every day and respect me. I've proved my loyalty, my dedication, a thousand times over. They won't believe a word you say."

He walked to the fireplace, lifted one of the exquisite Chinese figures on the mantel. "I've paid for your lifestyle since my mother died, but I won't do it anymore. You will move out of this house tomorrow. And I'm sure with some digging, we can find where you've stashed away the profits you've made from your betrayal." He set the jade carving down. "As for Miss Raven. One word from you to besmirch her reputation, and you'll find an interesting assortment of men lining up to teach you your manners. I'd think long and hard before taking a step like that, if I were you."

Hawthorne looked like a frog, mouth agape. "I think you overestimate yourself, Durnham. You always have. You used to look at me with that same supercilious expression when you were young. The little lord of the manor."

Edward ignored him and turned to Charlotte. "I have some things I must still see to this evening, and you don't need to stand here and listen to my stepfather spew his venom. I would send you home in my carriage, if that suits?" Edward held out his arm to her, and she took it with a nod.

He didn't want her here when things got ugly. And they would.

He walked her out of the room; behind him he heard Hawthorne slam his stick down on the wooden floorboards in fury. "Come back here, Durnham, damn you."

Clavers stepped out of Hawthorne's study, and Edward gave him a nod as they passed. He disappeared back into the room.

"What was that about?" Charlotte asked as Edward opened the front door for them.

"I've got Clavers boxing up every document and piece of paper to be found in Hawthorne's study. When my carriage comes back from dropping you off, I'll transport them back to my house. It should make interesting reading."

She smiled. And then she laughed. "Something so simple. And yet, I don't think he would have thought you'd do that."

"Well, it's not gentlemanly to go through another man's papers." Edward grinned back. His coach was still waiting outside the door, and he handed her in, gave the driver instructions to return.

He stepped down onto the pavement to close the door, and she reached out a hand and gripped his sleeve.

"About Luke." She looked down to her lap, then up to his face again. "I don't understand why you were so angry in the library. Of course I would forgive him for taking money from Hawthorne. After everything he did for me when I lived on the street? He probably got less than he deserved."

Edward stepped back up onto the running board and braced his hands in the doorway. "I don't care how much Bracken got from my stepfather. I hope Hawthorne paid through his nose. What sparked my temper was your immediate forgiveness. You're always on his side. You always will be, won't you?"

She stared at him, her eyes wide, and he would have given everything he had to know what she was thinking. "I will always love him. He is my family and we saved each other."

He couldn't endure any more of this. He started to push back, but she cried out and lunged forward, grabbing him by the lapels of his coat. "Wait! I love him, but I'm not *in* love with him. I've just told you, he's my family. My brother. Yes, I was his lover, but that was at his insistence at a time I felt too indebted to him to refuse. But since then, when he was taken to the Hulks, I have never felt any wish to lie with another man. Not once. I thought I was too cold inside. Dead there, because I was too young before and while I pretended I was happy to sleep with him, it felt wrong to me. And I dreaded it. I dreaded it so much that for a time I was relieved when he went to the Hulks. Relieved! While he was suffering unspeakable agony, I was happy I didn't have to pretend to enjoy what he did to me."

Her eyes were focused on his, as if all that was keeping her upright was what she saw in his face.

"And you've lived with the guilt ever since." He spoke quietly, afraid to make any movement that would end this.

"I lived with the guilt, but I didn't put him in the Hulks—that would have happened no matter how I felt about our sleeping arrangements, and I got him out. I've forgiven myself for my feelings of relief. As much as anyone can." She kept her eyes on his still, and he could not look away now, even if he wanted to. "It wasn't that, it was how he was when he came out—what was wrong with him after the Hulks—that's stopped my thinking about anyone else."

"His injuries?" Edward frowned. "Because his hips were crushed?"

"That injury didn't just make it hard for him to walk without pain." Charlotte's words were so soft, he could barely hear them. "It left him unable to . . ." At last she looked away, and there was more pain and sorrow in her eyes than he thought a person could hold. "He can't lie with a woman anymore."

"He's impotent?" Edward breathed just as quietly.

She nodded. "And while he could not, and wanted me so much, and accused me of not coming back because of that, because we could no longer live together as lovers, I could not give myself to anyone else." She drew in a shaking breath. "No matter how often I told him I did not love him that way, that the reason I didn't return was because of Catherine, and the life I would live with him, not his abilities as a lover, he never believed me. Or chose not to."

"And you've cut yourself off from every man who's ever shown any interest in you because of it." Edward's grip on the doorway tightened.

"Yes." She released her hold on his coat and settled herself onto her bench. "Until now."

The air seemed to leave his lungs, and his legs lost some of their strength. Edward stepped back, staggering a little as he landed on the cobbles. The coachman must have thought him ready, because he flicked the reins, and Edward was just able to slam the door before the coach rolled off.

He stood, dazed, and watched it rumble away.

"My lord?" Clavers spoke behind him. "Lord Hawthorne is trying to summon me. Shall I go to him?"

Edward forced himself into the present. Shook his head. "No. How is the packing going?"

"Very quickly, my lord. I have six boxes ready, and in another three, I should be done."

"Good. Then carry on. I'll deal with Hawthorne." He looked down the street one last time. "When my carriage returns from taking Miss Raven home, please get the footmen to start loading the boxes in it."

Clavers nodded and withdrew into the house. From the library, Edward heard the sound of a bell being rung as if by a messenger with news of war. He was sure he didn't imagine the satisfied smirk on Clavers's face as he deliberately ignored it.

Edward stepped back into the house again and steeled himself for another round with Hawthorne. His chances of getting a confession were almost none; he realized that now.

Hawthorne had been lying and dissembling for so long, he would not break. He'd keep up his lies until the bitter end. Go to the hangman's noose still claiming his innocence.

The ringing bell was quite maddeningly irritating.

"Even though you must have amassed a fortune with your smuggling, you've been happy for me to foot your bills. And that's working against you, now. Clavers works for me. And I have told him to ignore your summons. So keep ringing that bell if you wish, but you're wasting your time." Edward propped himself up with a shoulder and stood in the doorway, looking into the library.

Hawthorne had managed to turn his chair and his footrest so that it faced the door more, and he was panting with exertion, wiping his forehead with a kerchief with one hand while ringing the bell with the other.

"You would deny me my own servant? And all for a piece of fluff, a light-skirt from the gutter, and a little private enterprise on the side?" Hawthorne lowered the infernal bell, and Edward realized his shoulders had tensed with the incessant ringing, and he forced them to relax.

"Charlotte Raven is worth ten of you, Hawthorne. And I know all about Gravelines, and the official welcome your guinea smugglers get there from the French government. Please don't insult Miss Raven again, or my intelligence, or I'm afraid I won't be as reasonable as I am now."

He saw Hawthorne absorb that, saw him droop a little.

"My lord?" Clavers's call was soft, and Edward looked over his shoulder, saw Clavers standing with two footmen and a pile of boxes in the entrance hall.

Edward pushed away from the door, leaving Hawthorne without another word, and went into the study. It was empty of papers, but if Edward knew Hawthorne at all, there would be at least one hiding place. "Clavers? Go and see his lordship. Tell me what he wants you to bring him so urgently."

Clavers nodded, and Edward could see the gleam of understanding in his eyes. He came back two minutes later. "He wanted to know where you were, and I said outside with your carriage. Then he asked me to bring him a box of French brandy from a shelf in here."

Edward did a slow sweep of the room and saw the wooden box sitting on a shelf. It was a beautifully made thing, two different woods grafted together, with a small lock with no key in it. He picked it up, and it felt heavy enough to contain a full bottle of French brandy.

"I'll take it to his lordship. You supervise the loading of my carriage." Edward hefted the box, but there was no movement inside. No clue as to what was within.

Clavers allowed himself the luxury of a small smile. "Certainly, sir."

Edward walked back down the passage, and he could hear Hawthorne slamming down his cane over and over on the floor. "Clavers! Clavers!"

"Clavers has a little job to do for me. Is this what you were looking for?" Edward stepped into the room and held the box up with one hand.

One look at Hawthorne's face, and he knew this would contain something to damn his stepfather.

"Give it to me."

"I'm sorry, I'm taking it with me. That and all the papers from your study I had Clavers pack up for me. He's helping the footmen load them now in my carriage."

Hawthorne's face twisted, and Edward took a step back at the sight of the hate in his eyes. He wondered if Hawthorne could live much longer. He was sure to give himself an apoplexy.

"Damn you, Durnham. Give me my property!" Hawthorne's voice was guttural.

Edward turned and walked away, and even when he reached the front door, he could still hear his stepfather's stick, beating the floor in frustration.

# 35

When Charlotte stepped into the house, it was quiet. Greenfelt let her in and told her Lady Catherine had returned from her evening out, and was now in bed.

She heard the censure in his tone. Not for the late hour, or that she had been off somewhere by herself, but because Catherine would be worried about her.

She took the criticism with a bow of her head. "I'll go up myself, but don't call Betsy. I can manage on my own." She was wearing Betsy's own clothes, after all.

Greenfelt hesitated, as if he wanted to say something. She waited him out, but he merely drew himself straight and gave a nod before melting back into the gloom that led to the kitchens.

She was halfway up the stairs when the knocker sounded. Loud. Almost defiant.

She ran down and hauled at the heavy door with one hand, the candle Greenfelt had given her held high in the other.

Luke stood on the doorstep, the angles of his face sharp in the flickering light. He'd always been lean, but Charlotte realized now he was thin. Almost as thin as he'd been when they'd lived by their wits on the street.

"Going to let me in?"

She yielded wordlessly, drawing back so he could enter.

"You've never come before."

"Things have changed, haven't they?" He stood in the entryway and looked around. At the sweeping staircase, the black and white tiles on the floor. The rich cream walls.

"Come this way." She indicated to the withdrawing room, her tone oddly formal, even to her own ear, and he gave her a look, and a slight smile, as he entered the room.

Even in his ill-fitting clothes, with his hair too long and his face slightly stubbled, he owned the room in a way that would have made many noblemen of the ton jealous. He had presence.

"No wonder you never wanted to come back. I could never compete with this, could I, Charlie?" Luke took it all in, the blue silk and the velvet drapes, and she raised her head to look him in the eye.

"Don't play that game with me, Luke." She would not rise to his taunts. Especially ones like these. "You could have competed with this any time you liked in the last five years. You know it was never about the money." She crossed her arms. "And when were you planning to tell me about the blunt you managed to ramp out of Hawthorne?"

He sucked in a breath. "So he told you about that?"

She gave a tight nod. "And you should have known I'd wish you all the best with it. There was no need for secrets. Why make it one?"

He gave a shrug, but it was not so nonchalant as he'd like it to appear. She saw his fingers were stiff against his thighs, and he looked away. "It was just after I got out o' the Hulks, and you were living here with Lady La Di Da." He turned to Charlotte, then, almost pleading. "I had to get you back, Charlie. An' I couldn't compete with what you had 'ere. I didn't have the strength then, nor the money.

"So I went to him. And he was at a tricky stage, round that time. Didn't want anything bad comin' out 'bout what he'd gotten up to way back when.

"There were some letters. Your ma's old neighbor told me about 'em. Begging letters your ma sent to him, asking for help. I told Hawthorne I had 'em. I knew he'd sent 'em back without an answer, but they were long gone. The neighbor probably burned them herself. Not that he knew that. And he gave me some money to make me go away. Gave me my start, so to speak. A leg up.

"I never ramped him again, but I kept him in my sights, and he knew it. Felt good, you know? Keeping him a little scared." He turned away, walked toward the window. "God, I hate him. I hate the lot of 'em."

There was nothing to say to that. She'd always known it. Tried to soften it. But it shaped his life, and kept him shackled worse than Ashcroft or the Old Bailey or even the Hulks had ever done.

"How different are things now, Charlie? Tell me straight."
He spun around to face her from across the room, and she felt
her mouth go dry at what she saw in his eyes. "Will things ever
go back the way they were?"

She shook her head, and a lump of charcoal seemed to
lodge itself in her throat, making speech almost impossible.
"I've seen things—patterns I've been caught in, that weren't
helping anyone, least of all you and me. We can't go back to
you terrorizing every man who looks at me, and my pretending
I don't really exist."

He narrowed his eyes. "And this is Lord Nob's doing?"

"No." She choked it out on a cry. "It's my doing. Me. I
have come to this. I've been stumbling along so long with my
eyes on the ground, Edward simply jolted me, made me look
up and see where I was. And I didn't like the place at all."

He stared at her for a long time, tapping his fingernails
against the desk just to the right of him. "And what was that
place?"

"Nowhere. I wasn't with you, and I wasn't truly in the
world Catherine made for me. Limping along trying to please
everyone, and pleasing no one."

"And you've chosen what? To finally throw yourself into
afternoon calls and the season?" His voice dripped with contempt.

"No. I've chosen to be myself. To follow my own heart for
a change. I don't think I ever have."

"And that's a path straight to Lord Nob, am I right?"

She hesitated, saw him spin away from her again. "Luke! I

cannot help loving you, but I will never love you the way you want. I don't know what will happen with Edward and me. But I want to be free to see what *can* happen. I haven't been free, and I've just realized it."

He stood with his back to her, leaning against the desk with one hand. "I'm not blind. Lord Nob is going to snatch you up as soon as he can. He can barely keep his eyes away from you."

"I don't know about that." Her response was soft. "But it makes me glad to hear you say it. I hope it's true."

He turned slowly. "You mean that. You really mean it."

She nodded.

"Then my hate is all I have left, Charlie. The only bit o' me that loved was the bit you held."

"I still hold it. I've never let it go!" She dashed tears away that sat, fat and hot, on her lower eyelashes. "Don't you understand, I love you in a way that doesn't change with who you are, what you do? I love you like I would a brother. You're my family, Luke, you and Catherine. I'm sorry if you can't accept that, but I'll say it to you as many times as you like."

He ran a hand down his face, then rubbed his cheeks with both palms. He stood still, eyes closed, hands on his cheeks, his head down, then suddenly reared up, as if coming to a decision. "I don't know if I *can* accept it. I just don't know." The small clock on the mantel softly chimed the hour, one o'clock, and he stared at it. "I didn't realize it was that late. I've got to be going."

He reached into the inner pocket of his coat and pulled

out a sheaf of papers. "Mind how you use this, Charlie. It was my undoing, seems to me. Make me proud with it." He walked toward her and gave her the neat bundle, his step only slightly off, just the hint of a limp. He lifted his hand and curled it around the back of her head, pulled her toward him, and kissed her forehead.

She stood still in his embrace. Breathed in the familiar, the oh-so-familiar scent of him. Wool, the faintest hint of brandy, and something that was pure Luke. Then he stepped away and she watched him walk out of the drawing room, heard the front door open and close.

She looked down at the bundle in her hand and a thought crept up on her. She began to fight with the cord that tied the papers together, then finally went to the desk and cut it with a pair of scissors. She lifted the first sheet with shaking hands and scanned the page.

It was Luke's proof. His hard-won evidence. A bill of exchange, some signed by Frethers, others by Hawthorne. She had no doubt the bundle contained everything he'd managed to get so far. Hawthorne would never be able to snake his way out of what she had in her hands.

And then she saw it.

There were two people who would be damned by this evidence: Hawthorne, but there in the corner, smaller, but most definitely there, was Luke's name, too. He couldn't bring down Hawthorne with what he'd given her, unless he also brought down himself.

He'd be a hunted man, if the Crown got this evidence. He

must have known it. That's why he'd kept going, looking, always looking, for something that would damn the nobs and not point to him. But he hadn't had the time.

Because of her.

Which meant only one thing. If he'd given this to her, he planned to take Hawthorne himself. Not lead the newspapers to him, and make a point. Luke would take his revenge personally.

And he thought there was a chance he wouldn't be coming back.

# 36

Edward set another box aside with a sigh. The little wooden box had contained the evidence his stepfather had manufactured against him, but the papers he'd taken from Hawthorne's office were not damning enough.

He pulled the next box closer and then frowned at the sound of a knock at the door. It was past one in the morning. He got to his feet and walked through, but his butler had beaten him to it.

"Lord Dervish, my lord." Jasper's hair was standing on end on one side, and he wore slippers rather than his day shoes, but he stepped back and presented Dervish with a flourish.

"My thanks, Jasper. That will be all for this evening." He eyed Dervish with surprise. "Thought you'd still be in Kent."

"I've come straight from there. Brought the carriage here directly." Dervish followed him into the library, stripping off his gloves. "We got them, Durnham! We got them dead to rights. Five thousand guineas and barrels of brandy and silks, all hidden in the caves on Geoffrey's lands." Excitement and the thrill of success came off him in waves. He smiled, and Edward realized it was the widest smile he'd ever seen on Dervish. "It's a serious blow to the whole operation. Whoever we didn't arrest will have to find a new hiding place. We're winning. I never thought we would." He stopped in the center of the room and frowned at the boxes piled around Edward's desk.

"There have been some advances in the case from this side, as well." Edward waved a weary hand to the boxes, then sat down on the edge of an armchair. "It appears the man behind this plot is my stepfather, Lord Hawthorne."

Dervish sat himself. Heavily. He opened his mouth, and closed it again, at a loss.

Edward lifted the brandy decanter to Dervish inquiringly, but he shook his head. Edward considered having a small glass himself but set the crystal bottle on its silver tray, unopened. He leaned back, massaging his neck. "Of course, Hawthorne's involvement explains Geoffrey being mixed up in this like nothing else can. It also explains why they originally thought I would be easily bribed. But Hawthorne won't confess to anything. He won't so much as speak a name. So I confiscated his papers and I'm going through them."

"And?" Dervish eyed the pile with more enthusiasm.

"Nothing." Edward rubbed a hand down the bridge of his nose. "Yet." But he'd seen Hawthorne's face when he'd realized Edward had his papers. There would be something useful here.

"Your sister sends her regards." Dervish spoke suddenly, with a suppressed nervousness.

"She well?" Edward watched Dervish through half-closed eyes. The man was utterly smitten with Emma. There was no doubt about it.

"She's well. Finding it hard to cope with the neighbors, I think. But she'll be back down in a few days. She wanted to arrange for some repairs to some of the workers' homes before autumn and winter arrive, now that you've put some money into the place."

Edward gave a nod and left it at that. Emma knew her own mind. She would encourage Dervish or not, as she decided, but he rather thought, if anyone could understand Dervish's past, it would be Em. Her sons had nearly suffered the same fate. She would not hold it against him.

"How many smugglers did you arrest?"

Dervish pursed his lips with frustration. "Only four. Even with those, we never caught them actually loading boats. They were simply checking on the merchandise. Claimed they'd heard there was treasure in the caves, and came to see for themselves. They may get off."

"Forget them. We need the planners." He suddenly realized Dervish didn't know about Gravelines. He could hardly believe, himself, how much had been revealed in the last day. "There is a small port called Gravelines on the French coast. That's where the smugglers go with the guineas. They have an area fenced off there, and buildings with accommodation for three hundred English smugglers at a time. The boats come in and

French government clerks meet them, count the guineas, and then give the smugglers the silk, gin, and brandy for the trade. That's why they aren't afraid of the French government stealing the guineas before they can exchange them. They are delivering the guineas straight to the French government itself. In a place set up to make the smuggling as efficient as possible."

"How did you discover this?" Dervish gripped his knees, his knuckles turning white.

"I managed to find a smuggler involved in this business. He decided to get out of it, because he didn't want to betray England. He said the emperor has decreed that only guineas are to be accepted for their trade items, with the intention of denuding England of all her gold."

"Napoleon is trying to bring down the economy?" Dervish gave a slow nod of his head. "Because we went off the gold standard, he may be hoping if there's no gold in England, the economy will collapse."

"Could that happen?" Edward leaned forward.

Dervish shrugged. "I don't know. Do you really want to find out? I can't believe this, it's . . ."

Edward nodded. "I know. When I first heard it, I was struck by the scale. The daring of it. It's diabolical, and yet, I cannot help admire Napoleon for it. And if he succeeds, if our economy is in tatters, we won't have the money to support our troops on the Continent. We won't be able to support our allies."

"We'll be at Napoleon's mercy." Dervish rocked a little on his seat. "Did this smuggler also tell you about your stepfather?"

Edward hesitated. There was no need to bring Luke into this. To do that would bring Charlotte in, too, and he could not guarantee that her secrets would be safe with everyone who worked for the Crown. He gave a slow nod. "He gave me my stepfather's name."

"My God." Dervish stood, his movements jerky, as if he didn't know what to do with himself. "If Hawthorne is involved, who else? This could be the straw that broke the camel's back. Forget having no gold, and a tumbling economy. The riots are bad enough as it is; what will they be like if the man in the street learns they're being betrayed to the enemy by the House of Lords? For profit! Napoleon won't have to bring us down. We'll collapse from within."

"We don't know how many are involved. Tavenam, Hawthorne, Tavenam's nephew, Blackley." Edward stood himself. "Those are the only names I have, other than Frethers and Geoffrey, who are dead."

"If only that was it. That would be containable. A few bad eggs. We wouldn't even need to say anything. Just the concept of this is dangerous. It could cause a run on the banks, and total panic."

Edward thought of Luke, of what he was trying to engineer, and realized his idea had not been so far-fetched at all. With proof of a few more noblemen involved in the plot, he could have stirred up a great deal of trouble. Trouble that would be justified, even as it tore England apart. "Perhaps we'll be lucky—"

The hammering on his door cut him off. There was a panic

imbued in the staccato rapping that made him run to the hall. This time he beat Jasper to it.

It was Clavers. "My lord." Clavers was wild-eyed, and there was the pungent odor of smoke about him.

"A man. A man broke into the library through the window. Calm as you please. And he . . ." Clavers raised a shaking hand to his eyes, and then straightened. "He and Lord Hawthorne argued, and then he killed Lord Hawthorne with a knife. Quick, with no fuss, like he was having his Sunday dinner. Cool as that."

Luke.

Edward stepped back to let Clavers in.

"No. No!" Clavers stepped back, strain and urgency in every line of him. "The house is on fire, sir. Hawthorne threw his lamp at the man. Just laughed, the killer did. Just laughed as the fire caught the sofa, then the tablecloth. Said it was fitting his lordship bled out slowly in a living hell."

"What happened then?" Edward was already out on the street with him.

"Didn't see. I ran here fast as I could."

Edward started running himself. And he was not sure, other than to rescue his house, what he was running for.

## 37

Charlotte ran.

There had to be another way. A way they could all win. She turned over what that way could be as she sprinted full tilt, her skirts held up and to the side with one hand.

She didn't notice the man until she ran into him. He took the hit with an oomph, grabbing her with one arm and swinging her around to prevent them both going down.

"In a hurry?"

She reached out to steady herself on his forearms, and jerked back with shock when she realized he only had one arm.

"Yes. My apologies." She pulled away to run on, and he tightened the grip he had around her.

"Not so fast."

He was thin. Too thin. But he had height on her, and a strength she couldn't match.

She looked up at him. "What do you want?"

"To know if you're the servant girl you're dressed as, or the lady of the house, trying to pretend to be a maid?"

She narrowed her eyes. "What's it to you?"

"My job." He shrugged. "It's my job to know."

She tried to tug herself free, but before she could say anything more, he gave a yelp and was yanked to the side.

Bill stood behind him. "Been watchin' you." He took a firm grip on the man's shoulders, and Charlotte saw her attacker's face pale. "You all right, Charlie?"

She nodded. Dodged around both men and kept running. She heard a thump behind her, and then Bill was running with her.

Up ahead, somewhere in the direction of Hawthorne's house, a plume of smoke blackened the moonlit sky and the smell of burning seeped into the air.

She ran faster but Bill overtook her and she could do nothing but follow him, grateful he knew the way better than she.

She took the last corner and stumbled to a stop, panting.

Bill was gone, as if he'd been a figment of her imagination.

The fire was around the side of the house, she would guess in Hawthorne's library, and the insurance firemen were busy dousing the flames.

As she stood and stared, the red glow of the fire was extinguished.

"It wasn't much of a fire, anyway." Luke's voice came from the left, from the dark shadows at the corner of an empty town house. "Not near hot enough for my liking. I'd have preferred that he burn." There was a wistfulness about his words.

"I didn't understand, Luke. Until I saw the papers, I didn't understand." She tried to see him, but he had chosen his hiding place well. "How can we get the proof you want without throwing you to the wolves as well?"

"Ah, we can't." She could almost see him shake his head. "I got the pig to squeal a little before I cut his throat. There are only five of them. Five nobs. The rest of their little army are all merchants." He gave a bitter laugh. "I should have realized. Who else has access to guineas? Who rakes it in, day in and day out, but the merchants and bankers of the city? So there goes my big plan to bring the nobs down. All that work, all that gold gone out . . . for nothing."

He stepped out at last. "Maybe you'll use those papers I gave you, maybe you won't. But Lord Nob will no doubt find this interesting." He held something out to her, and she took hold of it, felt the smooth, cool touch of a brass cylinder beneath her fingertips. He kept his hold on it, too, and it linked them, the brass gleaming in the moonlight.

"What is it?"

"Hawthorne's list of co-conspirators. The paperwork that came before those papers I gave you. Who they are, how many guineas they gave him, how much he paid them in return. It was hidden underneath that footstool of his. He was fishing it out when I first got there. I was interested enough to wait until he'd taken it out before I let him know I was there."

"Why? Why are you giving it to me?"

"Because I don't care no more—whether they cop it or not for what they done. Maybe it's time I took a holiday. I don't think I ever took a holiday, Charlie. Ever. Bill and Sammy can look after the patch for me while I'm gone. Do me good."

"Yes." She let the tears that suddenly welled in her eyes fall. She saw there was blood on his collar and on his sleeve. Hawthorne's blood. "It will do you the world of good."

"Well, 'bye. See you when I get back?" He kept his voice casual, bright.

She nodded, and he kissed her again as he had done in the withdrawing room, gently on the brow. Then he let go of the cylinder and stepped back into the shadows.

She never heard him walk away, but after a moment, she realized he was gone.

There was a shout from an intersecting street a little way down from where she stood and three men ran toward the house.

One of them was Edward. She would never be able to mistake him.

He disappeared into the house, walking now that he could see the fire was out, and after a moment's indecision, she turned away from him.

Started back home.

It wasn't the time to give him the cylinder she had in her hand, and she would have to think about whether she would give him the first set of papers that damned Luke.

She thought not.

She would not put a barrier to Luke's return to London when he wanted. He wouldn't try to box her in any longer. Not anymore.

A cool breeze had risen, and it tugged and twirled the hair that had fallen loose from her pins during her run. She lifted her face to it and enjoyed the play of air over her cheeks.

And was happy.

# AUTHOR'S NOTE

The plot by Napoleon to cause an economic collapse in England by smuggling out all of its gold was true. There are several letters by him to his brother and his officials, outlining the plan, and Gravelines did exist—a small port set up by the French for accepting the smuggled guineas.

For those readers interested in learning more about the economics of Napoleon's plan you can read Eli F. Heckscher's *The Continental System: An Economic Interpretation*, which was published in 1918. For more details on the actual smuggling, and information on Gravelines, I found a lot of useful information in *The Historical Journal* 50, 2 (2007) article "Napoleon and the 'City of Smugglers,' 1810–1814" by Gavin Daly. To learn more about the darker side of Regency London, I highly recommend *The Regency Underworld* by Donald A. Low.

Regards,
Michelle Diener

# THE EMPEROR'S CONSPIRACY

### MICHELLE DIENER

# INTRODUCTION

Charlotte Raven hasn't always been a proper lady. Beneath her prim and proper gloves lie the scars of her former life: Charlotte used to be "Charlie," a girl of the streets who dressed as a boy to work as a chimney sweep. After Lady Catherine Howe took her in, Charlotte gained access to the cream of the crop of London society. But Charlotte keeps a foot in her old world—she still visits the "rookeries," London's seamy side, to see her childhood friend Luke, who has worked his way to the top of London's organized crime system.

With her unique access to the rookeries, Charlotte is indispensable to a top-secret investigation: England's gold is slowly disappearing, and the Crown is desperate to stop the smugglers. A handsome secret agent, Edward Durnham, needs Charlotte's help to untangle this vast conspiracy of society lords and crime lords. But when Charlotte finds herself falling for Edward, Luke's jealousy threatens to boil over. Charlotte soon discovers that Luke is a linchpin in the gold conspiracy, which is Napoleon's scheme to ruin England's economy.

In the end, Charlotte realizes that as much as she longs to begin a new life with Edward, she will always be faithful to herself, from chimney sweep to proper lady.

# TOPICS & QUESTIONS
# FOR DISCUSSION

1. *The Emperor's Conspiracy* opens in 1799, with a frightened child stuck in Lady Catherine Howe's chimney. What is the effect of this brief flashback, before the novel switches to Charlotte's adventures in 1811? What do we learn about Charlotte and Catherine's bond through their unusual first meeting?

2. Discuss the risk that Charlotte takes in warning Emma Holliday about Lord Frethers. Why does Charlotte choose to trust Emma with the secrets of her past? How does Emma react to Charlotte's unusual tale?

3. Recall your first impression of Lord Edward Durnham. What kind of welcome does he give Emma when she and her sons show up at his door? What does Charlotte observe about Edward on their first meeting? How do her impressions of him change throughout the rest of the novel?

4. When Charlotte considers her dual life, "She smiled at the idea of being a captive princess in the rookeries, or a restrained mouse in the glitter of the ton" (page 144). In what ways is this image of Charlotte's life an exaggeration? What kernel of truth does the statement

contain—what kind of "captive" or "mouse" is Charlotte within these two worlds?

5. By living in the gin house on Tothill Road, Luke has made "a new jail for himself, all of his own making. He could escape whenever he wanted, and yet he chose to remain" (page 227). Discuss how the gin house resembles the Hulks, the jail where Luke was confined as a youth. Why has Luke recreated the horrors of the Hulks on Tothill Road?

6. Peter, an informant from the rookeries, calls Charlotte "a hope-killer. . . . But kindness? Luck like that—it's a million-to-one chance, and you already took the one chance going" (page 90). Explain what Peter means by a "hope-killer." Why does he believe that Charlotte's fate is unique? Is her success due to luck, effort, or a combination? Explain your answer.

7. Discuss the smuggling operation that Edward and Charlotte discover in *The Emperor's Conspiracy*. Which part of their investigation did you find the most surprising? At which point do Edward and Charlotte begin to understand the enormity of this conspiracy?

8. Consider the two villains in *The Emperor's Conspiracy*: Lord Frethers and Lord Hawthorne. What kinds of

harm did each inflict on Charlotte or Edward in the past? What scars do Charlotte and Edward still bear? Which villain did you find more menacing in the end, and why?

9. Discuss the levels of surveillance on Charlotte and Edward. Why are they followed by "watchers" at every turn? How does the threat of gossip affect their budding relationship?

10. At Lady Crowder's ball, Charlotte wonders about Edward, "Could she both want to see him, and wish she never saw him again, at the same time?" (page 191). Discuss Charlotte's conflicted feelings for Edward. Why does she have trouble pinpointing how she feels about him? How does Lady Crowder's ball serve as a turning point in their relationship?

11. Consider which characters in *The Emperor's Conspiracy* are the most loyal and disloyal to England. Which lords of the ton and crooks of the rookeries seem most willing to betray their country? Which high-class and low-class characters try to defend the Crown, and why?

12. According to Charlotte, "we are what we make ourselves" (page 281). Discuss how this statement applies to each of the main characters of the novel: Charlotte,

Edward, Luke, and Emma. How have they made their own fates? What forces are beyond their control, and how do they attempt to remake themselves within those limitations?

13. Discuss Charlotte's relationship with members of her staff: Gary, Kit, and Betsy. Why has Charlotte brought them to Lady Catherine's house? How does she earn their loyalty? Why does Kit agree to stop spying on Charlotte for Luke?

14. Discuss the novel's ending, when Charlotte wonders if she will share evidence that implicates Luke in the smuggling conspiracy. Why would Charlotte choose to hide the proof from Edward? Do you think this represents a rift between Charlotte and Edward? Explain your answer.

## ENHANCE YOUR BOOK CLUB

1. Learn all about London's dynamic street language by tuning in to an NPR radio program about "Cockney rhyming slang." Listen here: http://www.npr .org/2012/03/14/148574426/olympics-letter-from-london.

2. It's not just in the "stews" of old London that people are homeless and hungry. Visit www.volunteermatch

.org to find a nonprofit organization that helps the homeless in your area. Consider volunteering or donating to a local shelter.

3. Come to your book club meeting dressed in the styles of Regency England! Whether you choose to be a chimney sweep of the rookeries or a lady of the ton, wear some accessories that represent early-nineteenth-century England. For some inspiration on the fashions of the era, visit http://www.fashion-era.com/regency_fashion.htm.

4. *The Emperor's Conspiracy* is inspired by a true story: France's secret smuggling operation during the Napoleonic Wars! Read about England's struggle to suppress smuggling before, during, and after the wars at this informative site: http://www.smuggling.co.uk/history_expansion.html.

5. Learn about the Hulks and other jails in British history through this illustrated BBC News timeline: http://news.bbc.co.uk/2/hi/uk_news/4887704.stm.